Praise for
Spill Simmer Falter Wither

Winner of the Rooney Prize for Irish Literature for 2015
Winner of the *Sunday Independent* Newcomer of the Year Award
Short-listed for the Costa First Novel Award 2015
Long-listed for the *Guardian* First Book Award, Readers' Choice
Long-listed for the Warwick Prize for Writing 2015
Long-listed for the 2015 Edinburgh First Book Award

"A tour de force . . . No writer since J. M. Coetzee or Cormac Mc-
Carthy has written about an animal with such intensity. This is a
novel bursting with brio, braggadocio and bite. Again and again
it wows you with its ambition . . . At its heart is a touching and inspiriting sense of empathy, that rarest but most human of traits.
Boundaries melt, other hearts become knowable . . . This book is a
stunning and wonderful achievement by a writer touched by great-
ness."   — Joseph O'Connor, for *The Irish Times*

"Extraordinary . . . *Spill Simmer Falter Wither* is a heartbreaking
read, and heralds Baume as a major new talent."
                                             — *Independent on Sunday*

"A deft and moving debut . . . It's not easy to tell such a sparse
tale, to be so economic with story, but the book hums with its own
distinctiveness, presenting in singing prose an unforgettable landscape peopled by two unlikely Beckettian wanderers, where hope is
not yet lost."   — *Guardian*

"Ambitious and impressive . . . Baume's engaging, intriguing and brightly original first novel may mark a comparably significant debut."

— *Times Literary Supplement*

"One of the most quietly devastating books of the year . . . With *Spill Simmer Falter Wither* [Baume] has created a dark, tender portrait of what it's like to live life on the margins."

— *Sydney Morning Herald*

"Every so often a book comes along that is so perfect it takes your breath away, and leaves your heart hammering with the beauty of the writing and the sadness of the story. Sara Baume's debut, *Spill Simmer Falter Wither*, is such a book . . . Baume's prose is full of wonder—inventive, poetic and dazzling, concerned with the smallest details of the natural landscape and the terrains of human emotion. Absolutely astounding."

— *Psychologies*, "Book of the Month"

"An important and quite brilliant new Irish writing talent."

— *Irish Independent*

"An ambitious stylist with an astonishing eye for detail and a clear passion for language. But it is the beautifully measured control of plot and the authenticity of the narrative voice that most impresses."

— *Irish Examiner*

"In a relentlessly inventive language that, it seems, can maneuver anywhere and describe anything, Baume's story of a man and his dog examines and elegizes the myriad strange, ramshackle, and ephemeral worlds locked deep inside the world. An exceptional, startling, and original book."

— Colin Barrett, author of *Young Skins*

"Powerful, heartbreaking, told with great control. The writing is superb . . . I had an image of all language standing to attention, eager to serve this writer."

— Mary Costello, author of *Academy Street*

"Touching and weird and sometimes comical and sometimes heart-breaking . . . Sad, solid, fragile, witty."

— Kjersti Skomsvold, author of *The Faster I Walk, the Smaller I Am*

"Unbearably poignant and beautifully told."

— Eimear McBride, author of *A Girl is a Half-Formed Thing*

"This book is like a flame in daylight: beautiful and unexpected. It packs a big effect for something that seems so slight, and almost hard to see."

— Anne Enright

spill
simmer
falter
wither

SARA BAUME

Houghton Mifflin Harcourt
Boston   New York
2016

First U.S. edition

First published in the Republic of Ireland by Tramp Press in 2015
First published by William Heinemann in 2015
First published in Great Britain by Windmill Books in 2015

For information about permission to reproduce selections from this book,
write to trade.permissions@hmhco.com or to Permissions,
Houghton Mifflin Harcourt Publishing Company, 3 Park Avenue,
19th Floor, New York, New York 10016.

www.hmhco.com

Library of Congress Cataloging-in-Publication Data
Names: Baume, Sara, author.
Title: Spill simmer falter wither / Sara Baume.
Description: First U.S. edition. | Boston : Houghton Mifflin Harcourt, 2016.
"2015 Identifiers: LCCN 2015037012 | ISBN 9780544716193 (hardcover)
ISBN 9780544716223 (ebook)
Subjects: LCSH: Human-animal relationships — Fiction.
Dog owners — Fiction.
BISAC: FICTION / Literary. | FICTION / General.
Classification: LCC PR6102.A86 S65 2016 | DDC 823/.92 — dc23
LC record available at http://lccn.loc.gov/2015037012

Printed in the United States of America
DOC 10 9 8 7 6 5 4 3 2 1

For Mum, of course

spill
simmer
falter
wither

PROLOGUE

He is running, running, running.

And it's like no kind of running he's ever run before. He's the surge that burst the dam and he's pouring down the hillslope, channelling through the grass to the width of his widest part. He's tripping into hoof-rucks. He's slapping groundsel stems down dead. Dandelions and chickweed, nettles and dock.

This time, there's no chance for sniff and scavenge and scoff. There are no steel bars to end his lap, no chain to jerk at the limit of its extension, no bellowing to trick and bully him back. This time, he's further than he's ever seen before, past every marker along the horizon line, every hump and spork he learned by heart.

It's the season of digging out. It's a day of soft rain. There's wind enough to tilt the slimmer trunks off kilter and drizzle enough to twist the long hairs on his back to a mop of damp curls. There's blood enough to gush into his beard and spatter his front paws as they rise and plunge. And there's a hot, wet thing bouncing against his neck. It's the size of a snailshell and it makes a dim squelch each time it strikes. It's attached to some gristly tether dangling from some leaked part of himself, but he cannot make out the what nor the where of it.

Were he to stop, were he to examine the hillslope and hoof-rucks and groundsel and dandelions and chickweed and nettles and dock, he'd see how the breadth of his sight span has been reduced by half and shunted to his right side, how the left is pitch black until he swivels his head. But he doesn't stop, and notices only the cumbersome blades, the spears of rain, the upheaval of tiny insects and the blood spilling down the wrong side of his coat, the outer when it ought to be the inner.

He is running, running, running. And there's no course or current to deter him. There's no impulse from the root of his brain to the roof of his skull which says other than RUN.

He is One Eye now.

He is on his way.

spill

You find me on a Tuesday, on my Tuesday trip to town.

You're Sellotaped to the inside pane of the jumble shop window. A photograph of your mangled face and underneath an appeal for a COMPASSIONATE & TOLERANT OWNER. A PERSON WITHOUT OTHER PETS & WITHOUT CHILDREN UNDER FOUR. The notice shares street-facing space with a sheepskin overcoat, a rubberwood tambourine, a stuffed wigeon and a calligraphy set. The overcoat's sagged and the tambourine's punctured. The wigeon's trickling sawdust and the calligraphy set's likely to be missing inks or nibs or paper, almost certainly the instruction leaflet. There's something sad about the jumble shop, but I like it. I like how it's a tiny refuge of imperfection. I always stop to gawp at the window display and it always makes me feel a little less horrible, less strange. But I've never noticed the notices before. There are

SARA BAUME

several, each with a few lines of text beneath a hazy photograph. Altogether they form a hotchpotch of pleading eyes,
foreheads worried into furry folds, tails frozen to a hopeful
wag. The sentences underneath use words like NEUTERED,
VACCINATED, MICROCHIPPED, CRATE-TRAINED. Every wet
nose in the window is alleged to be searching for its FOREVER
HOME.

I'm on my way to purchase a box-load of incandescent bulbs because I can't bear the dimness of the energy
savers, how they hesitate at first and then build to a para-
sitic humming so soft it hoaxes me into thinking some part of
my inner ear has cracked, or some vital vessel of my frontal
lobe. I stop and fold my hands and examine the fire-spitting
dragon painted onto the tambourine's stretched skin and the
wigeon's bright feet bolted to a hunk of ornamental cedar, its
wings pinioned to a flightless expansion. And I wonder if the
calligraphy set *is* missing its instruction leaflet.

You're Sellotaped to the bottommost corner. Your photograph is the least distinct and your face is the most grisly. I
have to bend down to inspect you and as I move, the shadows
shift with my bending body and blank out the glass of the
jumble shop window, and I see myself instead. I see my head
sticking out of your back like a bizarre excrescence. I see my
own mangled face peering dolefully from the black.

—

4

The shelter is a forty-minute drive and three short, fat cigarettes from home. It occupies a strip of land along the invisible line at which factories and housing estates give way to forests and fields. There are rooftops on one side, treetops on the other. Concrete underfoot and chainlink fencing all around, its PVC-coated diamonds rattling with the anxious quivers of creatures MISTREATED, ABANDONED, ABUSED. Adjacent to the diamonds, there's a flat-headed building with unsound walls and a cavity block wedged under each corner. A signpost rises from the cement. RECEPTION, it says, REPORT ON ARRIVAL.

I'm not the kind of person who is able to do things. I don't feel very good about climbing the steps and pushing the door, but I don't feel very good about disobeying instructions either. My right hand finds my left hand and they hold each other. Now I step up and they knock as one. The door falls open. Inside there's a woman sitting behind a large screen between two filing cabinets. There's something brittle about her. She seems small in proportion to the screen, but it isn't that. It's in the way the veins of each temple rise through her skin; it's in the way her eyelids are the colour of a climaxing bruise.

'Which one?' she says and shows me a sheet of miniature photographs. As I place the tip of my index finger against the tip of your miniaturised nose, she ever-so-slightly smiles. I sign a form and pay a donation. The brittle woman speaks into a walkie-talkie and now there's a kennel keeper waiting outside the flat-headed office. I hadn't imagined it might be so uncomplicated as this.

He's a triangular man. Loafy shoulders tapering into flag-pole legs, the silhouette of a root vegetable. He's carrying a collar and leash. He swings them at his side and talks loudly as he guides me through the shelter. 'That cur's for the injection I said, soon's I saw him, and wouldn'cha know, straight off he sinks his chompers into a friendly fella's cheek and won't let go. That fella, there.'

The kennel keeper points to a copper-coated cocker spaniel in a cage with a baby blanket and a burger-shaped squeak toy. The spaniel looks up as we pass and I see a pair of pink punctures in the droop of his muzzle. 'Vicious little bugger. Had to prise his jaws loose and got myself bit in the process. Won't be learning his way out of a nature like that. Another day, y'know, and he'd a been put down.'

I nod, even though the kennel keeper isn't looking at me. I picture him at home in a house where all of the pot plants belong to his wife and the front garden's been tarmacked into an enormous driveway. His walls are magnolia and his kitchen cupboards are stocked with special toasting bread and he uses the bread not only for toasting, but for everything.

'Any good for ratting?' I say.

'Good little ratter alright,' the kennel keeper says, 'there he is, there,' and now I see he is pointing at you.

You're all on your own in a solitary confinement kennel beside the recycling bins. There's a stench of old meat, of hundreds and hundreds of desiccated globules stuck to the inside of carelessly rinsed cans. There's dust and sweet wrappers and cardboard cups whirling in from the whoomph of traffic passing on the road. There's the sound of yipping and whinging from around the corner and out of sight. It's a sad place, and you are smaller than I expected.

You growl as the kennel keeper grabs you by the scruff and buckles the collar, but you don't snap. And when you walk, there's no violence, no malice in the way you move. There's nothing of the pariah I expected. You are leaning low, nearly dragging your body along the ground, as though carrying a great lump of fear.

'Easy now,' the kennel keeper tells you. 'Easy.'

—

What must I look like through your lonely peephole? You're only the height of my calf and I'm a boulder of a man. Shabbily dressed and sketchily bearded. Steamrolled features and iron-filing stubble. When I stand still, I stoop, weighted down by my own lump of fear. When I move, my clodhopper feet and mismeasured legs make me pitch and clump. My callused kneecaps pop in and out of my shredded jeans and my hands flail gracelessly, stupidly. I've always struggled with my hands. I've never known exactly what to do with them when they're not being flailed. I've a fiendish habit of picking the hard skin encircling each fingernail, drawing it slowly down into a bloodless hangnail. When I'm out in the world and moving, I stop myself picking by flailing, and when I stand still I fold my hands fast over my stomach. I knit my fingers in restraint. When I'm alone inside and unmoving, I stop myself picking by smoking instead.

In certain lights at certain angles, reflecting certain surfaces, I am an old man. I'm an old man in the windshield of the car and the backside of my soup spoon. I'm an old man in the living room window after dark and the narrow mirrors at either side of the tall fridge in the grocer's. Whenever I go to close the curtains or lean in to reach for milk or margarine or forest fruit yoghurt, I'm an old man. My brow curls down to tickle my eyeballs, my teeth are stained ochre, my frown lines are so well gouged they never disappear, not even when I smile. Although I'm impervious to my own smell, I'm certain I smell old. More must and porridge and piss, I suspect, than sugar and apples and soap.

I'm fifty-seven. Too old for starting over, too young for giving up. And my name is the same word as for sun beams, as for winged and boneless sharks. But I'm far too solemn and inelegant to be named for either, and besides, my name is just another strange sound sent from the mouths of men to confuse you, to distract from your vocabulary of commands. There's a book on one of my bookshelves, now its pages are crinkled by damp, but it's about how birds and fish and animals communicate, and somewhere it says that animals like you are capable of learning to understand as many as one hundred and sixty-five human words, roughly the same as a two-year-old child. I'm not so sure, but that's what the book with crinkled pages says.

There was a time when my hair was black as a rook with flashes of electric blue in certain lights at certain angles, now it's splotched with grey like a dishevelled jackdaw. I wear it fastened into a plait and flung down the stoop of my boulderish back, and sometimes I think that if I had people I bantered about with, they'd nickname me CHIEF for the wideness of my face and the way I wear my womanly hair, for the watery longing in my wonkety eyes. Only I don't have anybody I banter about with. My confinement has walls and windows and doors instead of PVC-coated diamonds, but still it's solitary. Still I'm all on my own, like you.

Everywhere I go it's as though I'm wearing a spacesuit which buffers me from other people. A big, shiny one-piece which obscures how small and dull I feel inside. I know that you can't see it; I can't see it either, but when I pitch and clump and flail down the street, grown men step into the drain gully to avoid brushing against my invisible spacesuit. When I queue to pay at a supermarket checkout, the cashier presses the backup bell and takes her toilet break. When I drive past a children's playground, some au-pair nearly always makes a mental note of my registration number. 93-OY-5731.

They all think I don't notice. But I do.

—

'In!' The kennel keeper tells you.

We are three of us standing on the compound's concrete, and you are refusing to climb into the car. The triangular man is beginning to bristle. It must be almost lunchtime and so his mind's already sitting in the canteen, already eating fat sandwiches on his mouth's behalf. He hoists you from the ground and plonks you onto the back seat.

'Right you are now,' he says, his voice is toneless, insincere. 'Best of luck.'

You try to resist the slam of the door, spinning your head around to check for other ways out. What does my old car smell like? Like salt and oil and dust mites, stale popcorn and wizened peel? The back seat is covered by a red blanket and the fibres of the blanket are embedded with sand. Have you ever seen sand before? I don't expect so. You bow your head as though contemplating all of these most minuscule and pearliest of stones. In the driver's seat, I'm fastening my belt, slotting key into ignition. As the engine begins to putter, you lift your head to the rear windscreen. You watch as the flat-headed cabin shrinks to the size of a photograph on a postcard, a picture on a stamp, and now gone.

Now we are driving from the city and into the suburbs. There are cherry trees lining the roadway in full flower, spitting tiny pink pinches of themselves into the traffic. See the rhododendron and laburnum getting ready to rupture, the forsythia and the willow, weeping. There's enough laurel to hedge a stadium arena, and every time we speed up, everything is transformed to a mulch of earthy colours and overstretched shapes. But you back away from the mulch and stretch. You clamber into the front of the car, over the handbrake and the passenger seat. You crouch beneath the dashboard with the heat of the bonnet pressed to your back and the gush of tarmac just a fine layer of steel beneath. Now the suburbs become dual carriageway, the cherry blossoms subside to central embankments of overgrown lawn. The shorter grass is frothed with daisies. And it's a handsome little piece of wilderness, a tiny refuge of imperfection.

But you won't come out to look. You stay beneath the dash with only your nose protruding. The particular way it moves reminds me of a maggot squirming. What are you whiffing through the air vents? Pollen and petrol and painted plaster? Now we are passing houses with people inside and shops with goods inside and churches with chalky gods inside, now we are rounding a roundabout and pulling off onto the back road for home. Brace yourself for the potholes and corners, the bump and slide. You hit your head against the glove compartment and grunt, a perfectly hog-like grunt. Now if your lost eye was inside your maggot nose you'd see a field of rape at its yellow zenith against a backdrop of velvet grey, which is the sky. You'd see the rape caving into never-ending blue, which is the sea. Has your maggot nose ever seen the sea before? I don't expect so. We're following the curve of the bay, we're parking with two wheels abutting the footpath outside a salmon pink house, which is my father's salmon pink house and my solitary confinement, which is home.

Sometimes I think if I took the handbrake off, anywhere in the world, the car would roll itself back here, to the footpath outside the terrace beside the bay, grudgingly yet irresistibly. But I've never been anywhere in the world. I wouldn't know how to get there in the first place.

Now you're refusing to climb from the car. I squat on the ground and you glower from your crawl space. I push the door wide to let the salt air in. It's rich and giddying, cloying with rot and fish and tang and wet. Your maggot nose catches the cloy and wriggles to life. Now it tugs your front paws forward and your front paws drag the rest of you after them. You grunt, but this time it has a different pitch; this time it's an inquisitive grunt. Grudgingly yet irresistibly, you step out of shelter, and onto the sea front.

Welcome home, One Eye, my good little ratter.

—

I don't know exactly where I was born. A hospital, I suppose. Surrounded by spotlights and freshly laundered bed-sheets and a trolley of sterilised birthing tools. I find it hard to picture some scrubbed-up stranger wielding my naked, squawking self about as though I were a broiled ham. Instead I like to pretend I was born all alone without any fuss, without any gore. And right here, in my father's house. I like to believe the house itself gave birth to me, that I slithered down the chimney, fell ignobly into the fire grate and inhaled my first breath of cold, swirling ash.

My father's house is one of the oldest in the village. It's two storeys tall and capped by slanting slate. Some slates are broken and some slates displaced and each is dusted with green down and rimmed by tiny hedgehogs of moss. The facade is garishly salmon and the roof is a manmade hillside all shaved and pressed out of shape from the creep of soil beneath its surface. Most of the ground floor is taken up by shop space, that's the reason for the signboard between hanging baskets. It's a hairdressing salon, which means the sounds that push through the floorboards are rushing water and hood dryers, pop music and high heels, the slicing laugh of the Polish hairdresser as she fakes friendly with whomever has just walked in.

When I was a boy, the ground floor of my father's house was a ladies' boutique. The lady who ran the boutique always stood two decapitated mannequins in the display window, and I couldn't understand why she dressed them so fashionably yet never bothered to fix on their heads. I used to be afraid that the mannequins' forgotten faces would chew their way out of a cupboard by night to rove between the sleeping clothes rails. I'd swear I could hear them, gnashing and dragging themselves across the carpet by their eyebrows. After the boutique shut down, the estate agent used the window as a billboard for advertising his properties. For several years I got to snoop inside every house for sale or rent within a three-village radius without ever travelling beyond the front footpath. As a boy, I imagined I lived in every last one. And in every last newly renovated semi-detached with off-white walls and a fitted kitchen, I imagined I was a different boy, a new boy, a better boy.

Apart from the salon, there's a Chinese takeaway, a grocer's, a chip shop and two pubs. It's a village of twitchers and silly-walkers, of old folk and alcoholics and men dressed in high-visibility overalls. There's a hummock of fat tanks at one end, that's the oil refinery. There's a chimney painted in red and white stripes like a barber's pole at the other end, that's the power station. In the middle, it's a nature reserve. Mallards and grebes paddle cheerfully through the drizzle. Herons stand stock-still and knee-high in tidal mud, pretending to be statues. Because of the oil refinery and the power station, the village murmurs. Sandwiched by the tunelessness of industry, the birds shriek and sing, defiantly.

—

Follow me past the steel gate and down a laneway to the front door. Here's the hall, which looks like the inside of a clothes recycling unit. Wool and tweed and oilcloth spilling off coat hooks onto my wellingtons and the radiator, the banister. Almost none of the coats are mine, or at least they weren't mine to begin with.

Now here's the kitchen, dark and poky with chipped tiles

on the walls and unidentifiable stains on the lino. It smells
of garlic and coffee and cigarette smoke and bins, and the
bins smell of garlic skins and spent coffee grounds and cigarette butts. Leave the bins alone, okay? You're not allowed
to pilfer tin cans and chicken bones, tissues hardened into
abstract shapes by snot. Here's my mug with its indelible
coating of black sludge. If I was a gypsy I'd read you my
sludge like tea leaves, and if I was a visionary I'd show you
the shape of a Jesus face on the base. Can you see it; can you
see the Jesus face?

Now follow me up the stairwell past the salon's partition
into the upstairs hall. See my ornamental plates covering the
decomposed plasterwork. They come from every snicket of
the globe. This one with a picture of St George is Bermuda.
The kookaburra is Australia and these two moustachioed men
bartering their cockerels hail from Puerto Rico. Now Andorra
has a cable car and Mallorca has almond trees and Hawaii has
HAWAII embossed in gold letters, but Djibouti is my favourite.
I've no idea where that is.

This room with the carpet concealed by rugs is my
bedroom. Each rug is made from the ripped and re-bound
rags of strangers from foreign lands. The rug strangers have
bigger families but fewer belongings, brighter clothes but
dimmer prospects and I feel somehow closer to them than I
do the people deflected by my spacesuit in the street. Here's
the bed, the rocking chair, the wardrobe and the fireplace, the
grate into which the house delivered me. The buckets either

side are one for coal and one for the logs I axe up on an ash stump out the back. Ash is the solidest of all wood; the log against which all other logs will inexorably split. What does my bedroom smell of? Damp spores, fluffed dirt and dead sap? See the black mould on the end wall, how it's mush-roomed into a reverse constellation: the night sky a white wall and the white stars black and wet and furry.

This curtain of wooden beads hides the bathroom, and when they get stirred up they make a noise like a landslide of Tic Tacs, like a leak in a button factory. You're not allowed in the bathroom, okay? You're not allowed to lick splashes from the enamel. From every other lintel, multicoloured ribbons dangle from a thin strip of pine. It wasn't until after my father was gone that I nailed the rainbows up. Sometimes I tread on the ends and they snap back like a tiny riding crop. Sometimes they get tangled around my limbs as I pass and I rip them clean down, without meaning to. They are annoying. I know they're annoying. And yet, I nail them up again, every time. The bowerbird within me insists.

Now for the living room, which lives up to its title and is the room where most of life takes place. I heard on the radio once that animals like you see in the same way as a colour-blind human, that your world is yellower and bluer and greyer than mine. If this is true then my living room walls will sear your lonely peephole, I'm sorry. They're painted the colour of purest egg yolk. Now the front window faces south and touches the roof beams. Here's the sofa and the coffee table and the television set which is mostly switched off with its screen turned to a dark mirror instead, to a tiny replica room all drained of its vibrancy. I look old in the switched-off television screen. It's one of the places I am an old man. Here are the curtains and indoor hanging plants and pictures in picture frames. I always forget to water the houseplants until their compost is so dry that the water trickles straight through and drips into the carpet. Or sometimes the plant's famished and gulps too much, drinks until its leaves go limp and pale and spongy, drinks until it drowns itself. Here's my aloe vera, see the bubbles through its translucent skin. See the picture frame. These smiling strangers inside, I don't know who they are. I just buy the frames and accept whoever comes inside them. They're just models chosen by the frame company, told to pose.

Bowerbirds are the artists of the creature kingdom; impossibly susceptible to prettiness, they deck their nests like vortex-shaped Christmas trees. There's a picture in one of these books on one of these bookshelves laden with spines of all different heights and colours and states of decay. Here are spines and spines and spines, raised to towers on the coffee table, queued into rows along the skirting boards. What do they smell like? Paper-worms and crackled glue, stale toast and aged Sellotape.

Now here, at the furthest end of the corridor, is the final room, the room with the trapladder reaching up through the trapdoor and into the roof where the spate of rats took place.

See the well-worn knob and the keyless keyhole. See the draught snake laid across the threshold with its pink felted tongue sticking out from its untidy stitches in a menacing fork. You don't go in here, do you understand? I don't go in here either.

—

I see how you watch me closely, startle at the slightest of sudden shifts. I see you're still frightened, even though I haven't even raised my voice. Are you waiting for me to whip out a choke chain? For a backhanded nose slap, the butt of my boot? Now I have to put you out the kitchen door and shut you in the backyard, just for a moment. I have to go and buy groceries and I'm not sure about leaving you in the house alone just yet. Spaghetti hoops and gingernuts, a carton of milk and some tinned sardines.

The backyard is a misshapen square with a stone fence the whole way round and a timber gate into next door's garden. It's floored by cracked cement and limestone chippings with weeds in places. Here's herb-robert, spurge, fumitory, a few other species less beautiful. Most of the green or brown or barely leafing plants in the pots lining the perimeter wall are the skeletons of last summer. Here's some purple sprouting broccoli, the stems already gone to bolt, the heads to seed. Windmills spin furiously amongst the skeletons. Elsewhere wind-broken blades lie twitching on the gravel. Beneath the sheet of marred tarpaulin is the axing stump, the log pile, the garden hose. Here's the rotary washing line, the glass-topped table, the plastic patio chairs, and these are tens of bashed and fractured buoys in bleached shades of orange and yellow, and tens more shards of broken buoy, some still sharp but mostly sanded harmless by the sea. These are a collection, my collection. Please don't piss on them while I'm gone.

As I leave, you're sitting on the mat. You're sitting with your whole body tensed as though in preparation for a blow. You look so mournful and helpless as I leave. You raise your head and watch as the kitchen door closes.

Out the front and into the village, there's a blast of salt wind off the bay, an empty crisp packet gusting down the footpath, a string of bunting flapping from a telegraph pole. The grocer's girl, April, talks loudly on the telephone as she scans my goods, forgetting to proffer a paper bag. I've always imagined April was born in April and has three sisters called May, June and July, perhaps an only brother called December because if the summer is a woman, so the winter must be a man.

I'm back at the gate and fumbling with the door key, milk and biscuits in one armpit, fish in the other, when I see you, when I see that you've escaped. You're on your way out of next door's laneway. Now you make a break across the road to the wall which follows the curve of the shore and you race alongside it past the street lamps and flowerbeds.

How could you summon the will to jump so high? Five foot at least to scale the wooden gate. As you landed in next door's identical backyard, were you disappointed to find it was no more than the same cement and spurge and rotary line, another stone wall and five-foot gate?

Now you're running, running, running, as though by running, you might understand. And I am watching, helpless. You arrive at the end of the village and seem to slow. Now you stop and turn around and look back over the length of where you've just run. Can you see me on the footpath? I've dropped the carton and stumbled to my knees. A rivulet of spilled milk catches the crisp packet, sails it to the gutter. Suddenly I don't care whether people can see me and hear me and know who I am; I don't care what they're thinking. My arms are outstretched and I'm calling your name over and over, louder and louder, wailing into the bay and sending all the oystercatchers soaring.

'ONEEYE ONEEYE ONEEYE ONEEYE!'

Why do you stop so suddenly? Is it that you can't remember where you're going any more, that you can't think of a place that's home or see anything more familiar than what's now behind you? The man of must and porridge and boulder and plait, the car, the salmon house, the village that murmurs. Now you sit down in the ditch. Now you stay until I reach you. I slip my fingers under your collar, and you don't resist as I lead you back.

We have sardines and spaghetti hoops for our supper,

with stacks and stacks of buttered brown toast. We have a tin apiece, except for the crumbly little spines, which I extract from the flesh and skin and sauce about my plate and toss to your waiting jaws. Gossamer ribbons swing from your beard and when they hit the kitchen tiles they form a viscous puddle of drool. There's something resplendent about the way you sit in your viscous drool, and it suits you. Resplendence suits you.

—

You hover in the living room doorway as I haul out the old armchair.

With my sewing scissors and staple gun, a ball of twine and heap of frayed fleece blankets, I'm going to fix you a bed. The old chair is unusually low-sized and broad-bottomed, like something that belonged to a child and sat in a nursery in the days when children could still be sent to such rooms and instructed to be quiet. It's so familiar I can't remember where it came from, only that it's always been here. I suspect my father was the child who sat quietly in it, and once he'd outgrown the low chair, still he brought it with him, to this house. Looking closely, the wood of its arched arms are stippled with the tracks of tiny fingernails.

Everything is filled with stories, an old woman neighbour told me once, the same old woman neighbour, as it happens, who taught me to sew. This is when I was extremely little, too little to understand that most things don't mean exactly what they seem, that meaning is a flighty thing. Because of what she said, I split the seam down the back of my favourite teddy, Mr Buddy, with a serrated kitchen knife. I was searching for stories, commanding words to tumble out and configure into horizontal lines like the ones inside my story books. Instead I found Mr Buddy was all stuffed with minute clouds. I shoved the clouds in again and punched him down the back of the washing machine so that my father wouldn't see what I'd done. And even though he never did, for years and years I could hear Mr Buddy's button nose clacking against the wall whenever the washing machine went into a spin. The machine doesn't work any more, but it sits in the same spot in the kitchen, and I suppose Mr Buddy is back there still.

The upright part of the old armchair is a mesh of mucky wicker. There's a lattice cut of thin ply filling the gap beneath the arch of the handle on the left side, while on the right, the lattice is missing. The original cushion is missing too, but with a ragged fleece and a bundle of shredded fabrics, now I fold and fashion and stitch a replacement. Over the grimy wicker, I drape a tasselled throw-blanket in a chequerboard pattern of pinks and blues. See how it's soft and bright now, how nice and comfortable it will be.

I carry your new bed down to the kitchen. I've never had a pet bigger than a kiwi fruit before, yet I have the impression from somewhere that the kitchen is the proper place in a house for an animal to sleep. I settle it into the nook beneath the apron hooks. 'In your bed,' I tell you, 'good boy.' Now I switch the light out and close the kitchen door. You on one side, me on the other.

You don't like being left behind. I should have expected this. I suppose you've never been alone in a kitchen before, where the floor is cold and slippery and the walls are built from lofty appliances which sigh and shudder and bleep. Can you hear the drippling faucet? Now the pipes expanding and contracting as though the walls are cricking out their bones, now the scribble-scrabble of claws behind the skirting boards, a rat or two left over from the spate. Can you hear me bumbling overhead? Water running down the bathroom plughole, slippers moving from lino to carpet, the squeak of the wardrobe door opening, the thud as it swings itself shut again. Now silence as I smoke. These are the sounds of my bedtime ablutions and I perform them each night, trance-like, at the same time in the same sequence. Teeth, face, slippers, pyjamas, smoke. Finally I trip the bedside lamp switch and kill the last incandescent bulb for the night.

Now I'm listening too. I hear you rise from your cushion and walk to the kitchen door. I hear you stop there and begin to whimper. It's a sound somewhere between cooing and keening, from an organ some place between belly and lung. Plaintive and elegiac, cavernous and craven. I listen for thirteen minutes exactly. I watch the luminescent numbers morphing into one another on my digital alarm clock.

For thirteen minutes exactly, I lie rigid on my old springs, entranced.

I get up, descend the stairs, push the door into the kitchen. You're sitting on the cold lino, eye wide. I touch you between the ears, I mean it in consolation and yet you wince. I lift the low chair and heft it back upstairs, and in the bedroom, I wedge it into a hollow between the wardrobe and the bed. When I turn around, you're standing cautiously at the threshold. I can see your nose trembling over the moths and kindling and coal dust. I squat down and pat the tasselled blanket.

'Come here,' I tell you, 'here.'

You tippy-toe over the rug, clamber onto the chair. You're watching as I switch the bedside lamp out, still watching as I nestle beneath the duvet. Now I can see the small reflection of your lonely peephole. It catches the green light from my digital clock and glints though the dark. I wonder can you hear all the things I can't any more, all the things rendered soundless by familiarity, in the same way I could never smell my father's smell even though I know he must have smelled. The hum of the generator in the grocer's yard, the echo of feathers in the chimney pot where the jackdaws nest, my shilly-shally breaths and the rasping of my tarry lungs. I wonder can you see through the open curtains to the outline of continents on the moon. The moon oceans and moon mountains and lakes full of moon water. Now I watch as your glint flickers and snuffs. Now I listen to your soft snores and grunts, the gruff lullaby of a strange animal who ought properly to be kept in the kitchen.

Sleep sound, One Eye.

—

Tonight, I dream a strange dream. I dream it's dungeon dark and I'm belting through forests and over fields. Demented, directionless. I dream the grass blades thwacking my legs and a whirlpool of flies dizzying about my ears. I dream the crackle and pop of invisible rain. I dream chickweed, hawkweed, knotweed, knapweed, bindweed. Now I come to the last stretch of hillslope before a roadway, and here I stop, exhausted. Below the field, there's a road. Down on the road, there's a house with a glowing window. The curtains are hooked open and I can see a vase of wilted daffodils outlined above the sill, a mirror hung on the wall behind, and in the mirror, the black through the window with a wisp of angry cloud. My legs give way and I crumple. Now there's a gap, a tunnel of black. It's a thousand miles long in dream time, and it ends in a perfect circle of blazing light, as though the sun's been plucked and fixed into a grill, mounted onto a metal stalk and propped, just to warm me. Up close, the smell is of slightly singed fur and smouldering newsprint. Further away but all around, the smell is of faeces, disinfectant, the secreting fear glands of petrified animals. In the dream, smell is everything to me, smell is my native language. I hear voices and pivot my head around to the right, but there's only a blank wall with its white paint scuffed. I see I'm behind a locked door; the locked door of a cage which is high up. My head is all doddery and my face is stinging, throbbing. Now I realise that when I pivot my head around to the left, there is nothing.

It is spring in my dream. At first I think I know this innately, but of the things I think I innately know, I rarely do, I've only forgotten where they came from. And so I remember, it was the cut daffodils which showed me that it is spring.

—

I'd say you're about the size of a badger, just differently proportioned. I've seen tens of them over the years, bludgeoned to the hard shoulder, dead as the dirt they've been splattered by. I read an article in the paper about how the Roads Authority is obliged to install a special underpass every time a motorway intersects a badger's territory. Nonetheless nine hundred and ninety-six get killed trying to cross the road every year, so the newspaper said. Every year, nine hundred and ninety-six badgers ignore the special underpass and go the way they've always gone. I think that's immense, appalling.

What size was your badger? Was she a thickset mother sow, angry as a thwacked wasp because of the litter of newly-borns squashed into the dark behind her? Is that why she turned on you with her curved claws slashing? You don't seem to realise, but you're skinny as a mink. Your presence may be ten foot tall, even so, you're squirty as a tomcat. Your ribcage caves into stomach. Your rump tapers to a quarter-docked tail and your weight's tipped to the front like a dinky wheelbarrow. Your legs are all bone, your shoulders all brawn. Your neck's too thick for your body, your mouth's too wide for your head, your ears are just about long enough to kink back in on themselves. Now that your face is healed, you have a hollow and a gaudy scar in the place where your left eye used to be. A gouge of your lower lip is missing, and it draws your mouth down to an immoveable grimace. Save for a feathery white beard from underside muzzle to uppermost nipples, you are solid black, dark as a hole in space.

—

A week has passed. It is Tuesday again, my Tuesday trip to town.

The post office first. The bell on the door sounds my arrival. I approach the counter and slide my card beneath the indoor window. Always, it's the old postmaster. Although he's been old for as long as I can remember, the postmaster never appears to have grown any older. Even sitting in his office chair, he seems sprightly, as though the air on the opposite side of the indoor window is somehow purer than the air out here, somehow life-preserving. As he counts my notes and coins he usually says something about the weather, about how the day is 'fierce' or 'soft' or 'desperate' or 'close', and every Tuesday I say the same thing in reply. I say *Sure you'd never know from one minute to the next what's coming,* and the postmaster always agrees. I scoop up my money. I thank him. And the bell on the door chimes again, as though it doesn't understand that I am leaving.

Today, I bypass the jumble and head for the pet shop instead. I've never been inside the pet shop before. It smells like chipped wood, bird poo, meat-flavoured biscuits. You'd like it. You'd especially like the lop-eared rabbit in a box on the floor, methodically chewing its cardboard walls down. It's made a hole almost big enough to squeeze its head through and I wonder if I should alert one of the shop assistants. But I don't want to insult the rabbit's efforts, so I hurry on past. I find the collar and leash section and as I browse I listen to the background lull of scrabbles and gurgles and flaps. The only noise which singles itself out is a curiously rhythmic stamping, as if of tiny feet and as evenly spaced as a human heartbeat.

I want you to have a new collar for your new life. A collar I chose for you. I pick out a red one with small metal studs and a tag in the shape of a bone. What kind of bone is it supposed to be: a femur, a clavicle, a rib? At the counter, the shop assistant makes me write down the letters of your name and the digits of my telephone number. Now she punches my scribbles into a machine and feeds the tag into a slot. An invisible needle engraves the bone and the machine spits it back again. The assistant's forehead is high and mealy. I stare at it to avoid her eyes. Somehow I manage to make myself ask about the stamping sound.

'That'll be the gerbil,' she says, 'he'll be warning the other gerbils.' She hands me my change and moves on to the next customer.

Let me see you in your new collar. Let me fix your inside-out ear. You look resplendent, even more resplendent. I know you can't see for yourself, but that jingling sound is the tag batting the collar's buckle every time you move, everywhere you go. I know you can't read either, but on the back it says 0214645207, and on the front it says ONEEYE, capitalised and spelled as though all one word like something in African, like you are some kind of African prince.

—

What did I use to do all day without you? Already I can't remember.

You sit, spine against the wicker mesh in front of the living room window. Here I've angled the low chair so you can see through the glass, over the road, across the bay, and all that goes on there. Beside you in the potbellied armchair, I sit and see too.

We see cargo vessels coasting in and out of harbour, containers heaped like toy building bricks. We see wading birds at falling tide, gouging the mud with their sporky beaks, pillaging a subterranean civilisation of salted organisms. And at high tide, we see pairs of ducks, always pairs. Ducks are like socks. If you've only got one, then something's wrong. We see the cars which park in the street, the people who cross to the grocer's and cross back again juggling armfuls of bags, boxes, bottles, sachets, tin cans. 'LOOK,' I say, and point. See the fat man's stockpile of fridge ornaments. They're for staunching some great hunger in some small part of himself which isn't his stomach. 'LOOK,' I say again, and again, I point. Now I wait for you to find the tattered cat who is prowling the shore wall, stalking a scrumpled tissue. You make a noise in your throat like a tiny propeller and this is how I know you see the cat too.

Sometimes a delivery van parks on the footpath in front of the house and all we can see is the dirt on its canopy, the skid marks of a low bridge on its rooftop. You tilt your head to the left. I know now this is the thing you do when you're trying to understand, as if the world somehow makes more sense at an angle, with your sighted side slightly higher than the side the badger blinded. Sometimes the vans collide with my hanging baskets as they leave. We watch as they carry the scarlet heads of my geraniums to their next delivery. Now even the geranium heads are better travelled than I.

The low-sized and broad-bottomed chair is your safe space, now it's where you always go to hide. You contract to an orb in the middle or unfurl to full stretch and kick your paws through the gap where the lattice is lost. Cloaked within the tasselled throw blanket, you are protected, and nothing bad can touch you. I hadn't expected there'd be so many commonplace, inanimate things in my father's house, my safe space, for you to be frightened of. Is it that they mean something else to you? Have you seen the ways they can be transformed into instruments of torture? Plastic bags with their rustle and squeeze, aluminium foil with its twinkle and gash, dishcloths with their thrash and wallop. And even though I've never tried to whip or choke or strangle you, still you scamper away to your safe space whenever I open a drawer or start drying the dishes.

I kneel on the cold tiles of the kitchen floor. I roll out a length of foil. I place down a chocolate button and hold it out in offering to you. I know you're disconcerted, but I do it because you have to learn to fathom your way through a world of which you are frightened, as I have learned.

—

Most of my boyhood fears dwindled as I grew in size and sense. I figured out the footsteps I heard by night were only the cricking pipes, that the man who skulked up the laneway in the morning to force leaflets through my door was only the postman. I started going into town and buying groceries in the big supermarkets, and there I learned how to face a shop assistant over a checkout and exchange meaningless pleasantries without whispering or muddling my words.

But it's okay to be frightened sometimes. I'm still afraid of almost every single form of social situation. I still steer clear of uniformed officials. I've always had a guilty face, an incriminating nerviness, even when I was innocent. Sirens overwhelm me; only in the face of flashing bulbs do I long for the draining dimness of the energy savers. I'm afraid of swallowing spiders in my sleep, of a moth crawling into my ear drum, of toppling a display in the chemist's, of my car breaking down and blocking the dual carriageway at rush hour. I'm afraid of the tiny screens that everybody carries in their pockets, of the irate way they shiver and growl. And I'm afraid of children; I'm especially afraid of children.

—

I roll the aluminium foil away and drop the button to your bowl.

Now the food bowl is the epicentre of your existence, to which the house is attached and everything beyond radiates from, like sun beams, like the stingers of winged and boneless sharks. I collected tokens from boxes of breakfast cereal and sent them away for that bowl. The day it arrived the postman rang my doorbell and I signed my name in his ledger. Now it lives on the kitchen floor in the cubby hole beneath the apron hooks, and you check it constantly, countless times every day.

It's a cubby hole as grubby as a seedy city alley. There's a layer of filth sunk into the grooves of the skirting board, buttered across the lino. Bugs creep out of the wall at night to gnaw the filth and its stickiness gathers tiny tumbleweeds of passing hair in spite of how thoroughly you clean after each meal. I see you licking every bit of surface some fugitive morsel might have touched down on, sucking up fluff and dust and sand and bugs as you go. Your food bowl is restocked three times a day, but you never take this for granted. You gobble every meal hardly using your teeth, nor your tongue, nor your swallowing muscles.

'Please chew this time,' I say, every time. 'Please chew.'

I read somewhere, or maybe heard on the radio, that an animal starved in youth will devote the remainder of its life to the pursuit of eating. There's nothing here in my father's house to contest you for your scraps, not the apron tails which tease the back of your neck as you guzzle nor the appliances that sigh and shudder and bleep. Still you eat every bowlful at the speed of light, and afterwards you sit in the kitchen cubby and regurgitate the undigested lumps of kibble, catch them in your mouth for mashing and swallowing all over again. And once you're finished for a second time, again you check your food bowl.

Now you know the slightest of sights and sounds which indicate I'm preparing to eat. You know the curt compression of air which signals the opening of the fridge, the click of the cupboard's magnet, the whirr of the springloaded drawer.

You know the screech of spatula against the base of a margarine carton, and you know this means it's ready for you to slather out. You know, when I eat an apple with a paring knife, the exact angle my hand takes when I pare a piece especially to toss to you.

A full stomach is a kind of sanctuary, I understand that. I'm a scoffer too. Even though I'm never hungry, I remember hunger and so sometimes I scoff desperately, mindlessly, as though I can eat now every proper meal I missed in childhood. It took me many years to face the shop assistants, to fathom my way into town alone, and until then I was dependent on my father who could barely cook and kept the cupboards only erratically stocked. Now when I feel the food heat oozing from my belly, bulging through my blood, it makes me feel better. Can you feel the heat, the ooze? I know the reason you check your bowl compulsively is because I'm always dropping titbits into it. A splash of milk here, a spaghetti hoop there. Wherever you happen to be in the house or yard, you hear it and bolt to the kitchen, crash into the cubby hole, your head already dropped to bowl-level. I have inadvertently trained you, but you have trained me too. Now I let you slather everything out, every mixing bowl and plate and lid. With the herculean strength of your tongue, skilfully you propel my crockery around and around the kitchen floor, until it gets stuck beneath a stool, wedged into the fractured kickboard.

—

Tonight, again I dream as you.

I dream I'm inside a pen with a water dish but no food bowl. I dream a man who comes once a day with a basin and trowel and he slaps scraps onto the ground with a noise like a colossal bird plop. The scraps come from all colours but blend together into brown and taste like yeast and grease and soured milk. I dream the seasons passing, real seasons, like when I was a boy. In sun times, the scraps arrive congealed. In rain times, they come puddled, diluted by drizzle to a grizzly grey gruel.

Tonight, I dream of the place where you came from, the place where you were starved.

—

I'm going to teach you to walk nicely, and we're going to practise along the bird walk, to the very end and back again, every day.

The bird walk is a belt of concrete skirting the sea front from the main street of the village to the gates of the power station. Running alongside the concrete there's a squat wall and a row of street lamps. There are flowerbeds and picnic benches and a couple of ornamental ponds. As we cross the road, you're trotting steady with the planky soles of my shoes, keeping stride with the swoosh of my trouser legs. Here's the signpost that says BIRD WALK and here's the information board. See behind the cracked Perspex, each wader's portrait in peeling and discoloured paint. But you're distracted by the tumult of smells rushing from the banks of the path to meet you. You launch into the weed-beds, nose first.

The ponds are filmed by gunk too thick on the surface for skeeters and too stagnant underneath for frogspawn. What once were blooms are now mostly weeds, and even the weeds are smothered by the gloop of leaves still festering from last autumn. What are not weeds are the descendants of seeds sown by the resident's committee, years and years ago. Even though nobody tends them any more, some still manage to flower in spring and summer. See here, these buds will become marigolds, I think. And these leaves belong to the sweet-william. I know the names of most trees and flowers, but I learned them very slowly. With no one to guide me, everything I know is learned slow and fraught with mistakes. Now I know the wildflowers only by finding them, one by one, and searching in my nature book for a name, and then finding them over again and naming them for myself, until I've got them all right, and remembered.

At high tide, the sea rises to lap against the bird walk's wall and gulls bob at beak-level with the concrete. At low tide, the water falls back to expose a no man's land of stinking mud. It's at low tide that the wading birds come. Oystercatchers with their startled eyes, redshanks scurrying tetchily on strawberry legs, little egrets freshly laundered, whiter than white. The path ends in a copse of pines which curtain the security fencing and boxy buildings of the power station, but the trees are far too short to hide the chimney and its flossy smoke. In winter, the wind shakes their cones into the sea, and I find them washed up on the beaches. On every beach all around the bay, I recognise these pinecones.

As I turn back, you're still hustling amongst the greenery. I call but you don't seem to hear, you're hypnotised by smell. Now you zig-zag the concrete, hop onto the wall and shout at the gulls, bust into a frenzied run. Now you freeze beside a tuft of primroses and plug your claws into the ground and won't budge for all the chocolate buttons in my trouser pocket. How can you be so unremittingly interested? How can every stone be worthy of tenderly sniffing, every clump of grass a source of fascination? How can this blade possibly smell new and different from that blade, and why is it that some require to be pissed upon, and others simply don't? I wish I'd been born with your capacity for wonder. I wouldn't mind living a shorter life if my short life could be as vivid as yours.

You aren't exactly obedient. I want to believe your intentions are good, but I doubt they stand a chance against your maggot nose. I watch it working as we walk, drawing you into everything most vile, all the drippings and droppings left in the weeds by creatures gone before. The spraint of an otter, the spray of a tom, a bobbin of sweet shit which you try to wolf while I'm not looking. I haul you up, prise your jaws open, shake the shit out.

'BOLD!' I holler. 'BOLD BOLD BOLD!' But I know it's wrong of me to scold what's natural to you. I'm sorry, I shouldn't holler.

Another walker's coming toward us. A man in a fleece with a boxer, I think it is. Tanned fur and face ironed flat like a primate. The closer they come, the more you're tugging, tugging, tugging. I stop and draw aside from the path and bind my wrist into the leash's loop. Now you're barking and thrusting with all your strength and wrath, and I'm holding on so hard the blood drains from my knuckles. The man nods as they pass but the boxer just stares as though you're a lunatic, as though we are a pair of lunatics.

'Bold!' I whisper. 'Bold bold bold!'

I don't understand why you aren't throttled. I heave us on toward the information board. It takes until they've disappeared for you to calm down and walk forward again. Still for some distance, you glance behind. You whimper as though wounded, bereft.

Back inside my father's house, you rest beside my planky feet on the living room rug and I ruffle the red roots of your scalp as I smoke. Now you're yourself again. The self who doesn't sit or stay or halt or heel on command, who doesn't come back when I call, who doesn't walk very nicely, not nicely at all. Still I must admire the way you suit yourself. I don't want to turn you into one of those battery-powered toys that yap and flip when you slide their switch. I was wrong to tell you you're bold. I was wrong to try and impose something of my humanness upon you, when being human never did me any good.

—

See how sluggish the spring is this year. Almost May and still no sign of swallows. Look here, see this lump of flaky mud wedged into the roof cranny? It's a nest and has hatched ten generations at least. They fly all the way from South Africa, across the Sahara and the Pyrenees, just to lay their dappled eggs in my cranny. Every year they remember me, and come back. But sometimes swallows go hungry and sometimes storms knock them down and sometimes they just can't bear the slog, and stop.

When I was a boy, the seasons seemed to exist more than they seem to exist now. For the past ten years at least, all year round, the meteorologist who reads the weather forecast has always said the same thing, and the picture at the end has always showed the same symbol. A raining cloud with a very small sun shying behind it. There haven't been any intensities of hot and cold or light and dark; instead it's been the same glum, tepid day over and over, and it's made me feel similarly seasonless. Apathetic when I should have been elated, drowsy when I should have been upset. Then, out of the blue, last winter grew tremendously cold. The meteorologist said they were the lowest temperatures for half a century. It put paid to my theory of seasonlessness, but not in exactly the way I wished for. Unless I succumb to one of those brain-eating illnesses of very old age, I don't expect I'll forget last winter. Now it's spring again, see how the cold has delayed all the seedlings from sprouting, stripped the hedgerows to a tangle of naked brown, worn the country roads into scree. So many bulbs remain scrunched in their shallow graves. The hibernating animals oversleep. Where were you last winter? I find it hard to picture a time when we were simultaneously alive, yet separate. Now you are like a bonus limb. Now you are my third leg, an unlimping leg, and I am the eye you lost.

Do you think my swallows somehow sense how cold our winter was? If they know the way here from Africa, they must know other impossible things as well. Do you think they're breaking their flight on the continent, gorging themselves on sun-warmed flies? It's not too late, they might still be coming. Maybe, like the spring, my swallows are just overdue.

———

It's Tuesday, my Tuesday trip to town. The postmaster remarks how nippy it is and I say *Sure you'd never know one minute from the next what's coming.* The jumble shop has a set of Russian dolls and a brocade bag tied to the blade of a Samurai sword in the window, and I wonder what's inside the bag, I wonder is it an amulet. But I must pass by and stop again at the pet shop. I fish about in the collar and leash section for a muzzle that looks like it will fit. I don't hear the gerbil. Today, the gerbil is calm; the gerbil is safe.

At home, I tell you SIT. This is the first of your one hundred and sixty-five words and so you sit and I begin to fasten the straps and buckles around your head and neck. I promise it's not for always and everywhere, okay? Just certain places and situations to protect you, to protect us both. I promise.

You trust me enough to let me fix it on without a fidget of protest. I see how you trust me and I feel terrible that I use this trust to constrict you. Once the muzzle is on, the weight of the moulded plastic grill draws your neck down and you drop your nose, more sad than angry. At first you just sit motionless with your head hung. Gradually, you begin to panic. Now you thrash and claw at the muzzle, now you growl as though it were an enemy creature. And I feel immediately terrible terrible terrible, and free you. I hang the muzzle on the apron hook in the kitchen.

It's gone now, see? We will not speak of it again.

—

There's only one road in the village where nobody lives. It runs up the hill and past the oil refinery. About a hundred yards along there's an enormous signboard. It stands supported by two steel legs and wears a red bulb like a miner's helmet atop its litany of instructions. DO NOT PASS THIS POINT WHEN

LIGHT IS FLASHING, the signboard says, PROCEED TO
NEAREST SHELTER & WAIT FOR REFINERY PERSONNEL
TO ASSIST YOU. This is the road where we'll walk now, the
dimmest and most deserted, the best chance we have of being
left alone.

The ditches give way to forest either side. The oak and
ash and hazel and birch form an unwieldy guard of honour.
They're so tall their heads incline toward one another and
meet in the middle, leaving only a thin, jagged opening into
sky. The forest floor is knotted by briars and ferns. On one
side it gives way to the refinery compound. On the other
it casts off into a small expanse of cliff face, and now sea.
Listen to the blackbird bug-hunting beneath the celandine, to
the tap of the mussel dropped by a hooded crow against the
tarmac. Now he swoops down for his seashell and lifts and
drops it again, and so on until it's cracked enough to sup out
the soupy innards.

Step aside for the contract builder's van. Now the refinery
mini-digger, its bucket of sandbags. Sometimes there'll be
cargo lorries on their way to the refinery with gas cylinders for refilling, and sometimes they're on their way from
the refinery with gas cylinders freshly filled. Listen to them
clinking against one another with the bumps in the tarmac,
the sway of the axles. The road ends at the staff car park, at
an intercom beside a traffic barrier. But we don't stop here,
this is just the point at which we go off-road. Follow me over
the hedge and through the mud prints of tractor tyres to the

brow of the barley field, the top of the hill. Here we stop and here we look back across the space we've just trampled. The chimneys are sputtering sparky smoke into the morning, the refinery wind sock is jimmying about, and beyond again, see the whole of the bay all at once like a blue puddle, the village like a group of dollhouses, and my father's house in the middle, a bold pink speck amongst the beige. See the green sprouts in the gutters? I love the way the grass grows like that, high up on buildings, as though it's lost. And on the other side, see Tawny Bay sprawling below.

Now follow me downslope, through the ferns and furze, to the beach. Here at sea level, the grass turns sharp and straggly. It gives way first to an uneven row of hefty pebbles, desiccated bladderwrack, drift junk, and now sand. Have you ever seen a beach before? I don't expect so. What do you make of it? The sea's a kind of river but instead of flowing sideways against an opposite piece of land, it rushes on and bleeds into sky. Here's the sand you've already found dispersed about the car blanket, now it's truly everywhere, spread into bumps like the crunchy kind of peanut butter. In some places it's freckled with heavy stones, in others it collapses beneath your paws. Smell the rot and fish and tang and wet. Feel the air zinging your eyeball. Taste the salted spray of cresting waves on the buds of your lolling tongue.

There's no one else on the strand. It's too early. So I'm going to take a chance. I'm going to unclip your leash, unshackle your harness. I'm going to let you chase and rove

and zig-zag feverishly, to be your own unhuman and unpro-
grammable self, free as a fart.

'FREE!' I yell. And you run amok between the pebbles
and shallows and cliffs and caves, over the lug's extruded
trails and the seagull's beak punctures. You're chasing the
oystercatchers, licking beached jellyfish, guzzling crab legs
and pissing in the dunes. You're moving in a way I've never
seen you move before. Slack-limbed, almost jaunty. You wag
your tail. This is the first time I've seen you wag your tail.

'GOOD BOY!' I yell.

Now you wade in and lie down, just for a second. And
a tiny wave breaks across your shoulders, and you skitter
sheepishly back to shore.

We'll go this way every day now, I promise. Past the rat
holes and broken branches and litter. Past the lolly wrapper
lying in the verge at the base of the YIELD sign. Past the
banana skin by the refinery gates below the intercom, stealthily
perishing. And every day I'll wonder about the engineer or
security guard or whoever it was who ate that banana and
tossed it to precisely such a spot, without thinking.

We'll go when the wind is high and the seas are storming,
when the mud is fluid and deep and the rain so constant that
the trees afford no shelter as they should, but instead send an
onslaught of accumulated droplets down on our heads. Still
we'll go this way, I promise.

—

The mobile library comes every two weeks on a Thursday, and it smells like furniture polish and sticky-fingered children.

Today, I find a book about blood sports. I flick to the chapter on badger baiting and stand with my back as a bent shield to the librarian. The driver's out on the sea front, smoking, and there's nobody else in the bus. *Spring*, the book says, *is the season of digging out.* I think I knew this already, but I can't remember why. *Spring is when the sows give birth and become especially aggressive.* I skip down a few lines. *Badger cubs are pulled from the earth as trophies and given to the diggers to rag about amongst themselves, to finish off. It's the adult badgers captured in the woods that are kept for the baiting den, those still fighting or trying to fight.* I skip down another few lines, until I reach the part I know I'm looking for. *The diggers often end up with their bottom jaw clean off and a bleeding too great to be stemmed, at which point they're clubbed to death with a shovel and rammed back into the ransacked sett.*

Now an old woman who is one of my neighbours totters up the steps of the bus. At the top, she straightens her blazer and makes for the shelf of romance novels in enormous print. I snap my book shut and fumble it back. I check out one about Zen gardens instead, a collection of Indian folk tales and *Silas Marner*, again. As the librarian stamps my card, I wonder what a baby badger's called. A calf, a cub, a kitten? Already I can't remember.

—

I begin to nod off in the potbellied armchair with *Silas* lying across my chest, but I wake myself up to finish my cigarette. Now I smash the butt into the ashtray. As I begin to nod again, I see the silhouette of your head at the window. I see you staring past the shore wall, past the bay, past the opposite side of the harbour.

I dream myself inside a pen at the edge of a scrapyard. I dream the scrapyard has a view of the woods and the view's divided into a hundred tiny compartments with each surrounded by a frame of galvanised steel. I dream I'm gazing through the grating, keeping watch on the woods. I see rabbits at dawn, leaves at all different stages of falling, power-lines bending in the wind, rookeries against the moon. Now I dream myself into the woods and I'm running, running, running. I've forgotten every part of myself and all the parts of my surroundings except for my maggot nose. I've forgotten the cheeps and chitters overhead, the braying of my fellow diggers. I've forgotten the details of the forest floor, the splintered twigs and smithered bark streaming beneath my feet, clinging to the fur of my ankles. Now I'm so far from the scrapyard pen I've forgotten the rabbits and leaves and power-lines and rookeries; they melt behind me as I run. In the woods, in my dream, I'm strong as a boar and quick as a buzzard. I'm ten foot tall yet scarcely as high as the shrubbery.

Before I fumbled the library book back, I glanced at the glossy middle pages, at the photographs. There were three.

The first showed a badger yanked between two different pairs of teeth with blood trickling through the lesions in its pelt. The second showed a sett which had subsided with the digger still inside. One of his back legs was sticking up from the earth like a tiny totem. And the third showed a photograph of you, only a you with both of its eyes. *A breed calculated into existence*, the caption said, *for its exceptional obduracy.*

I wake up again. I switch on the television. It's still cold enough to warrant the nightly lighting of the Superseyer, and so I light it. You get up from the window and settle yourself directly in front of the glowing bars. You lean in to stare at them, you hardly move. What are you thinking? Now you sigh so hard from the pit of your lungs that it triggers an attack of the hiccups.

Sometimes I see the sadness in you, the same sadness that's in me. It's in the way you sigh and stare and hang your head. It's in the way you never wholly let your guard down and take the world I've given you for granted. My sadness isn't a way I feel but a thing trapped inside the walls of my flesh, like a smog. It takes the sheen off everything. It rolls the world in soot. It saps the power from my limbs and presses my back into a stoop.

———

In the evenings, we watch television. You like the nature documentaries, the ones that feature high-pitched bird noises in particular. I like the reality shows. I like how, without scripts, people don't know what to say or say the wrong thing. I like how, without onions, people cry anyway; people cry better.

I haven't lived like the characters on television. I haven't fought in any wars or fallen in love. I've never even punched a man or held a woman's hand. I haven't lived high or full, still I want to believe I've lived intensely, that I've questioned and contemplated my squat, vacant life, and sometimes even understood. I've always noticed the smallest, quietest things. A chewing-gum blob in the perfect shape of a pterodactyl. A two-headed sandeel coiled inside a cockle shell. The sliver of tungsten in every incandescent. I've read a lot of newspapers. They stack up on the coffee table for weeks before I get around to recycling them. I know how the system of society ought to work. It doesn't make sense to me, but I've come to believe this is because it doesn't make sense.

I'm not the kind of person who is able to do things, have I told you this already? I lie down and let life leave its footprints on me.

All the books I've read, they stack up too. The lines and passages bleed together. Sometimes I remember characters and think, just for a second, they were people I once knew. Sometimes I remember places and think, just for a second, that it's somewhere I once was. I never remember the titles or the author's name, but I remember the covers, I always remember the covers. A gigantic valley, a tiny horse galloping. A stack of polished silver spoons. A tall man and a small man both in cowboy hats walking a red road toward a blue mountain between a tall tree and a small tree. A great fish with a pointed nose, a loose line skipping. A profile, half-man half-wolf, a single eye in the very centre. And a man rising from a pen's nib in a suit jacket to drift amongst the skyscrapers.

But as for the words, the messages: I forget. And if I've been changed, so I change back again.

—

See the signs of summer, of the tepid seasons starting their handover with subtle ceremony. Now the forest floor is swamped by bluebells, the celandine squeezed from sight. See how the bells hover above the ground, like an earth-hugging lilac mist. Now the oak, ash, hazel and birch are bulked with newly born leaves, still moist and creased from the crush of their buds. The barley is up to my kneecaps and already it's outgrown you. As we crest the brow of the hill each day, you are shrouded by green blades.

In the village, a damaged rowboat appears. Somebody's hauled it into position between the signpost and information board at the mouth of the bird walk, leaned it sidewise on its keel. From our sitting spot inside the window we see members of the residents' committee in high-visibility vests, painting its planks pistachio, shovelling compost between its thwarts and planting the surface solid with primula polyanthus. My father used to own a rowboat. It was much smaller and shabbier than the flowering one, and he kept it moored right there in the bay, roped to a rusted rung along the shore wall. It looked like a box made out of old doors, one of the burden boards even bore the screw holes of an absent handle. I have no memory of my father rowing his boat but he always went out to check on it in stormy weather. I used to think he didn't care very much, now I wonder whether he cared too much, so much he could never bring himself to cast it loose and row.

Next door in the grocer's the ice-cream machine is restored to service, and every morning the grocer or his girl wheel a display cage filled with plastic footballs and seaside paraphernalia onto the street front. There are small spades and flimsy fishing nets, rubber rings and buckets shaped like miniature castles. I've never really noticed the cage before, but now, this year, I think I'd like a football. What do you think?

Some are printed with cartoon characters and popstars, but I choose the one that is patched yellow, blue and grey as though it was tailor-made for you, for your incomplete colour spectrum. I carry it with us in a plastic bag, through the trees and past the oil refinery, over the brow of the barley field and down the hill to the beach. At first, you don't take any notice. When I free you from the leash you set about your business of gallop and scavenge and splash as usual.

I kick the football into the air. It's light but bounceless, and lands with a dull bump and the skew of the sand rolls it into the water. Paw-deep in drift junk, chewing the leg off a putrefied crab, you ignore it. So I chase after the football, kick it out of the small waves and keep kicking the length and breadth of the strand. Now I shout back at you as I go, stupid slogans of encouragement.

'COME ON! CHASE!' I shout. 'GETTIT! GOOD BOY!'

What must you think of me? A giant hurtling about an empty beach with my clodhoppery hands clapping, my black plait beating against my hunch as I run. Now I've disturbed the sludge in my lungs and it swooshes and swirls and makes me wheeze, pant, wheeze, pant, wheeze. So I stop but when I turn back to check the junk, you're hurtling after me. You've conquered your maggot nose, forsaken the pursuit of rotten apples and fermenting crustaceans. Tongue flapping free, you're running, running, running. Snatching up the football, puncturing it with your fangs. Now semi-deflated, it fits snug between your jaws and you can clamp on, firm, and shake.

There's no need for me to chant encouragement. You're nosing it along the sand at a sprint and grunting with joy. Now you're hunting it down as if it were a living thing, a hostile thing, an assailant. Now you're killing, killing, killing.

—

I dream a dream of being born. I slop down onto a bed of newspapers. It's cold and dirty and the headlines are blotted by amniotic fluid. Beyond the end of my nose, I see the pink tips of my mother's teats, and all around I feel the clamour of my litter, the heat of tails and legs and bodies battling to suck.

Do you remember your mother? As a boy it took me years to realise I didn't have one. At the beginning I believed children were allowed to have only one parent. That's just the way it was. Only a rare few, only the children in story-books and on television were lucky enough to have hit the double jackpot. I got a father, that was my lot. By the time I realised I'd misunderstood, it was too late to suddenly ask him what happened to the woman who gave birth to me. By then I'd accepted the chimney was my birth canal, the fire grate was my cradle, my mother was the house.

The first thing I see when I open my eyes in the morning, the view from the bedroom window at pillow level with the curtains open: the high wall behind the stone fence which conceals the grocer's generators, can you see too? Can you see the mass of ivy-leaved toadflax flourishing there? The flowers have violet petals with bright yellow lips, but they are lost amid the plethora of five-pronged leaves and spaghetti stems. Every night it grows and climbs with ravenous force. Every morning it fills a little more of our window. One day, will we open our eyes to nothing but toadflax? Still we'll claw our way through, I promise.

—

On the beach, I stop hurtling and walk even with the tide line and watch you with your ball. After a while you clamp and carry it. You veer away from the sea and head up the strand toward the cliffs and fields. I call you, and you come back. You carry your football in pace with me along the sand. But after several yards, you begin to veer off again. Now I see how you are drawn from Tawny Bay and back toward the hillslope, irresistibly.

What are you thinking? It's hard to judge thought by the life in a tail, by the glint of light in a lonely peephole. And I wonder if it's the badgers.

Is it the badgers, One Eye?

Can you hear them calling you?

simmer

There is singing, singing, singing.

It is sweet and undulating, like a finger licked and drawn around the rim of a wine glass, like a whole chorus of glasses similarly molested. It's rising from the street, fluting through the cracks of our ill-fitted window pane, diffusing about the living room. I remember the song. I learned it from mass as a boy, years and years and years ago. I shut my book, lean forward in the potbellied armchair and try to dredge the words from the stew of my memory and hook them together again, so I can sing along. What do I sound like? Like a toad trying to squeeze inside a song thrush? Out of tune, out of time.

You're at your sentry. Back paws on the cushion of the low chair, front paws balanced on a book heap in the windowsill, eye to the sea. The wet of your nose smears against the glass in the spot where you're pointing, and all around this spot, there are old spots with old nose smears, dried and crusted and yet still glimmering. Like the aimless trails of a night slug, like a whole posse of carousing night slugs. You're watching the gaggle of singing children on the street, little girls in white dresses with white veils clipped into their hair. You're tilting your head to the left, pulling your curious face. The little girls' veils are almost translucent and they skitter in the wind like tiny ghosts. Some are carrying baskets filled with flower petals and the two at the front are holding a plastic arch between them and the arch is decked with artificial roses. Now come the mothers. They're gaggling a few yards behind the girls, keeping guard. They're muttering to each other beneath the singing, praising somebody else's daughter so somebody else will praise theirs back. I peek around the curtain, careful not to lean too far into the window. I don't want to be spotted by the gaggles. I'm just as afraid of mothers as I am of children, possibly even more so. Dominus tecum, they are singing. Benedict tattoo.

It's the May Procession, the first Sunday in summer. I haven't been to mass in almost one year and one half of a year now, I'd forgotten that. Not since the occasion upon which I stood up in the middle of the homily and pronounced the word HORNET. I pronounced it with less force than a shout but precisely enough force to be heard from the pulpit. And because the church was three-quarters full and I was in a pew around the middle, I presume most of the other congregants heard it too, from the woman in the wheelchair at the front to the man who always stood beside the water font holding the collection plate.

I didn't know those people, not really. I knew their mass faces and their mass clothes from decades of Sundays we'd worn down the kneelers together. I'd only ever spoken to a couple of neighbours and only then since my father's been gone, only then in answer to the questions they asked about him. A nursing home in the city, I told them. And I didn't mean anything by it, by HORNET. There was a man kneeling in front of me wearing a jacket with a label on the back, and the label read THE NORTH FACE, and I was making anagrams; that's all it meant. Then I walked out. I cleared the churchyard and was through the gates and in the car before anyone had followed me, if anyone even tried. I didn't stop to check, but I don't expect so. And then I realised I didn't have to go to mass on my own any more, that I'd only ever gone as my father's companion and now that I'd made the old man's excuses several times over, I didn't have to go, and I felt suddenly very stupid for all the times I had.

—

When I was a boy, I used to sit here in this window and watch children with satchels and lunchboxes passing on their way to school. Back then, hard as it is to picture now, I was small, almost as small as you. Small enough to scrunch my whole body onto the sill. Back then, I didn't care about being seen. I'd press my nose against the pane and draw snot trails, just like you. I knew every child by sight and I remember them all: the girl who wore her hair in jade ribbons, the boy with iron calipers up to his knees. I imagined the details of all the parts of their lives I couldn't see, from the contents of their pencil cases to the exact number and colour of stars stuck in their copy books. Even though I'd stare at the crowns of their heads every morning, I never wanted to join them. I was too shy, too frightened. And besides, I didn't really believe I was of the same species as the children I saw passing along the sea front, going to school. Back then, it never dawned on me that I should have the things they had too. I would have to be made again, I thought. I would have to be reborn.

—

I know you're too short to see it, but the picture on our kitchen calendar is a donkey in a sand dune with ribbons fanning from its quadrilateral face like the tails of a kite. It's summer here in the kitchen, even if, outside, it's heartily raining. Outside, every porous thing is turning spongy, every un-porous thing is sluiced and dripping.

Still, people are mowing their lawns and dousing their barbeques with lighter fluid and standing under patio heaters nibbling black meat from toothpicks. I smell their cut grass in the daytime, their charcoal smoke by night. Can you smell it too? The ice-cream van comes out of hibernation and drives in circles jingling *You are my sunshine, my only sunshine* and its fog lights through the gloom every dusk are indeed the sunshine, the only sunshine, as though it knew. People are performing the summer on the summer's behalf, buying flip-flops and body-boards, tricking themselves into believing it's the season inside their TV sets instead, the one from the Australian soap operas. They are pretending, as though pretending alone might a miracle make.

With such little sign of a change in season, how do the plants know it's the right time to flower? Because plants are smart in a way people aren't, never questioning the things they know nor searching for ways to disprove them. All along the road through the forest to the refinery, see how foxgloves split from their buds and tremble over the ditches. And when the weight of their waterlogged bonnets is too much, they keel into the road and their heads are crushed by cargo lorries to a pretty pink pulp.

—

On the beach, most days the mist is so thick that when we reach the mid-point and stop to look, neither end of the strand is visible, each taking its turn to be scarfed up by cloud. Now we must part a channel through the fog like a pair of tiny jets leaving a pair of reverse contrails in our wake.

Through the thick mist a honeycomb collie comes careering down the strand toward us, his great mane crimped by damp and billowing. He's already too close before I see him, and there's no chance to re-shackle you; you're ahead by almost fifty feet. In a flash you've forsaken your football and clamped the collie's muzzle. Now he's yelping and flaying and trying desperately to hurl you off. But you don't budge a hair's width. You're stuck as a mouse in a mousetrap, a fly to a flypaper. The collie looks like a prestige pet and the woman he belongs to looks like she prizes him for his placid face and handsome cantering, for his particular pedigree as opposed to his particular self. She's speedy out of the clouds and to his rescue, speedier than me and my fifty feet. Now she's clubbing your head with a golf umbrella, and all I can do is shout.

'DROPPIT ONE EYE!' I shout. 'DROP!'

It's happening so swiftly, too swiftly for my ordinary fears to keep up with. It's as if the helmet of my spacesuit has been perforated and a flood of oxygen is crashing into my eyes, ears, mouth.

'DROPPIT DROPPIT DROPPIT!'

But you don't, and even though I'm pitching and clumping as fast as I've ever pitched and clumped, flailing like a plastic bag snagged on a thorn in a gale, for a split second, everything goes completely still. The waves stop and the sea turns to cement. A greater black-backed gull mid-flight halts the smacking of his mammoth wings, lies rigid in the sky.

'DROPPIT ONE EYE!' I shout. 'DROP!'

Now the woman manages to sever you from the collie's

muzzle. As I catch up, he scampers for his life and she beats after him waving her umbrella in the air and crying 'HENRY HENRY HENRY' into the fog. Her voice is so high and sharp, it cleaves through me, and perhaps this is the most unsettling part of all, because people never use such an excited pitch in my presence. People always lower and deaden their tone when speaking to me, as though our conversation is immediately unbearable.

You go to chase them but I grab you. Now I feel as though I've left my stomach behind me, as though it dropped out several yards ago and is lying on the sand, quivering globulously. My hands are shaking as I smooth them across your face and neck and back and legs, as I pat you over to check for wounds. My palms come away blotched with red, but there's no sign the blood belongs to you. You're intact, and looking up at me with tongue lolling idiotically, tail skipping. With eye and tongue and tail, you're begging a chocolate treat, expecting my approval.

I don't know what to do with you. I don't know whether I'm furious or frightened or a little of both.

I turn and hurry us back in the direction of the fields. I stop only to scoop up the football before reaching the brow of the hill. Now the beach has vanished again. The mist is sitting in the sky like the froth churned up by angry waves sits on the sea in stormy weather. I can't see the car park on the opposite cliff and I can't see Henry or his woman or the umbrella. But I notice the place where the sand's been churned up by our dashing, hurling, thrashing feet. And the black smear of a gull's wingspan. Flying again. Growing smaller, smaller, smaller.

—

My father had a golf umbrella. It was dark blue, as dark as blue can be before becoming black. And he brought it with him every time he left the house, his house, even if it wasn't raining.

My father always left very early in the morning and arrived back travel-weary and infused with the scent of the pineapple air freshener that swung from his rearview mirror, and some nights he didn't come back at all. When I was a boy, he'd bring me toys and clothes in crumpled carrier bags. The jumpers were usually bobbled with thumb-holes low down in the sleeves, and the jeans were patched in places with slightly brighter squares of denim. The teddy bears were pre-cuddled, the tyres of the dinky cars shorn to their hubcaps, and if anything ever needed batteries, they came either missing or flat. But I didn't mind. The toys didn't need to move; I made them move myself. And besides, I liked to imagine the children who played with them before me. I pictured their faces, made up their voices. Then I shifted my playmates into place around me. I included them in my games.

Oftentimes the carrier bag would be box-shaped and

jagged. These were the ones I liked the best, they were filled with books. The pages were already dog-eared and finger-printed, sometimes there were even crumbs. But I didn't mind. I thought then that nothing could ever be absolutely new. The world was so big and so full of people I was certain that every material thing must be used and reused to its zenith; this was the only way it could make sense.

—

Now I'm afraid to take you out during the daytime. Now I'm afraid to go out alone.

'Quiet now,' I tell you, 'quiet.'

You're at the window, yapping. You yap with your whole body, as if each yap were a volt of electricity, cracking through you from whiskers to tail. Now the schools have closed for the summer holidays. I can tell from the arrival of the boys who congregate along the sea front in the evenings, who frolic around until after dark. They're no smaller than twelve, no larger than sixteen. They number four at least and ten at most, but it changes. Maybe they're the same boys as last year or maybe they're the baby brothers of last year's boys, I can't tell. They all have the hoods of their tracksuit tops raised and the laces of their runners left undone. They all have the same shiftless way of holding themselves, as though their limbs are hinged into their torsos by a network of sagged bungee clips. Always, they're an unsightly bunch, see how the silhouettes of their oversized adolescent heads block the bay out? From now until autumn, they'll be there every warmish night irrespective of the pizzle, as if they're immune to poor weather, as if the blaze of their hormones is keeping them consistently toasty inside. Their presence is the price paid for longer evenings, a reminder that lessened cold and added light is public property, and not ours alone, as I would like.

The summer boys come from housing estates built into the fields and hillsides stretching inland away from the village and the sea. The housing estate houses are as young as the boys and just as indistinguishable from one another. Venetian blinds and block-paved driveways, dormer windows and red-brick cladding. See that woman coming out of the takeaway? She's the mother of a summer boy. I can tell from the way she has the face of a potato and the hair of a film star. See that man coming out of the pub? He's the father of a summer boy, a neatly dressed but beleaguered version of his son, coat over tracksuit and laces neatly tied. These are the people who buy the tool belts and steam mops and magic knickers we see advertised between television programmes, and every day at dusk, their sons trail downslope to the shore wall. They swagger and perch. Snigger and sigh out a language of abbreviated words and exaggerated gestures drawn from experiences exclusive to this itchy, nasty phase of their lives.

They wait until the grocer's shutters are lowered and most

of the curtains along the main street have been drawn. Now they produce cartons of cheap Czech lager and cigarettes stolen from the jacket pockets of their dads. The lit street lamps are casting a spooky pallor to the boy's expressions, a hint of menace to suit their moonlit raillery. Sometimes there's a football and I hear it very late and from my bed, pounding against the salon's shutters like a leviathan crawled from the sea, knocking to be let in. And in the morning I'll see scuffs on the sides of the car, perfect circles in the dust where the leather was kicked, struck. The suction cup prints of a colossal tentacle fastened and unfastened in a moment.

Come away from the glass. It's the most dangerous thing in the world to draw attention to my father's house. You don't understand what those boys could do, how easy it is for them to destroy me, to destroy us. I've always regretted the way the living room window faces square onto their summer territory and can be faced square back into. This is why I always pull the curtains when it's full bright, why we never get to watch the sun set behind the buildings across the harbour. I'm afraid the boys will look up and see me sitting pathetically in front of the television with my pathetic dinner on a plate on a cushion nestled between my pathetic knees. I know how cruel boys can be. Even the one with calipers, when we were both older, joined his friends to chase me, chanting, down the laneway, and I saw that what he really kept inside his pencil case were stones for chucking at my window. Now I'm afraid these new boys will come to know me. I'm afraid they'll call out when they see me on the street. I'm afraid they'll form a procession as I gambol to the shops and back. Can you picture it? All the summer boys pitching and flailing and clumping in unison behind me.

'Come away from the window,' I tell you, 'away.'

———

The temperatures are rising, a little bit, I think. The toadflax swells and stretches. From the walls of the village, valerian pushes through the brick's seams and points unsteadily upward, toward the rooftops. See the buttercups and birds-foot trefoil. See the red clover which is not red, but pink, pink as the valerian. Now is the season of yellow and pink. The days are still grey, but the grey is lukewarm and airtight, like the village and the bay are sealed inside an enormous Tupperware tub.

You sit quietly on the windowsill. In the potbellied armchair, I read. Sometimes you're up straight and looking away across the water, your thousand-mile stare. Sometimes you lie with your beard rested on your front paws, looking in, watching me. What are you thinking? I wish I could teach you how to read. I wish you could understand when I read to you.

———

When I was a boy, before my father brought me books, on my bedroom wall he hung a chart with the alphabet on it. Twenty-six squares with a letter and a picture in every one and sometimes with the picture over-spilling its designated square to intrude on its neighbour. The RAT was rudely flicking his tail in the face of the SNAKE, who was in turn shaking his rattle into the topmost leaves of the TREE. The only thing my father told me about the alphabet was that H was *aitch* and not *haitch*, Z was *zed* and not *zee*. He corrected mistakes I hadn't even made yet.

It was the old neighbour whose name I can't remember who, after she'd taught me to sew, taught me to read. I remember she lived above the grocer's and I called her Aunt even though she wasn't; she was just the woman my father enlisted to sit with me during the day. At the beginning, I read with the index finger of my right hand tracing each sentence word by word, and each word syllable by syllable. Aunt would sit in the rocking chair with her nose poked over my shoulder and shout the whole word every time I hit an unfamiliar sequence of syllables. Aunt's eyes were sharp but her hearing was patchy and her limbs were quaky as a rabbit with myxomatosis. She only knew when I'd faltered because she'd see my index finger had stalled and was tremulously hovering. Then she'd shout it so loud that the ladies downstairs in the boutique could surely hear. 'ENORMOUS!' she'd shout. 'TURNIP!'

Early in life I learned to look after myself as well as Aunt.

I'd see how she was trying to do something – open a can, butter a slice of toast, reach the shelf where the biscuit tin sat – then I'd do it for her. 'GOOD BOY!' she'd shout, and a little more quietly but never quietly enough, 'poor fool', she'd mutter, 'poor little fool'.

What was her name? I can't remember. She looked like a peasant farmer's wife from the nineteenth century, her breast bound in shawls with a puckered face in a gap at the top and the wrinkles in her skin eddying into the folds of her headscarf. It was Aunt who was responsible for the only other poster that hung upon my bedroom wall. It was headed 'Emergency First Aid for Children' and I suspect she intended it more for her own benefit than mine. Beneath the header there was a sequence of panels and each panel depicted a different scenario in which an adult person was in some way struggling for their life and a child person was doing their calm and measured best to rescue them, and now I remember how the persons from the poster used to abscond from their place on the wall at night and insinuate themselves into my dreams.

In the end, Aunt didn't die on my watch. I didn't even know she had and that I'd missed my opportunity to put any of the panels into practice until my father took me to the removal. The funeral home was full of people, there must have been an emissary from every household in the parish, but none of them looked particularly upset, nobody sighed or gulped or sobbed. Back again in my father's house he asked me if I thought I was old enough now to take care of myself. I was nine. I could read fast as a firecracker. I knew First Aid inside out because every night I dreamed up a new emergency. I banked on this being all there was to know. Yes, I said. And in this way, the years passed and passed and passed, just the old man and me and then just me and then you, and now us.

—

Today, we are planting. I know it's already too late in the season. My father's shelf full of gardening manuals would shake their spines in reproach. But every year I plant according to my own unwritten and annually misremembered set of rules, and every year I accept the bounty, however scant or sickly. I pick the slugs off and blast the greenfly down the plughole. Too light to sink, they walk on water like tiny green Jesuses.

On Tuesday, I go out alone and into town. The post office followed by the supermarket, and here I buy saplings and seedlings from the gardening section. Fruit, vegetables and herbs; I've never bothered with flowers. I've always thought it would seem like an insult to the wild ones which every summer arrive unbidden in my yard. Up from the lightless cold they thrust their heads through the compacted dirt and burst into petals amongst the gravel. As though, like the swallows, they've chosen me.

Today it's raining in the yard and on the sea front and all across the bay, and so we're gardening in the kitchen, right here atop the unclothed table at which my father died. Whereas then it was tidily laid for breakfast, now my packets and utensils are lost amidst the queeny frill ashtrays, marmalade jars packed with inkless biros and a whole squad of other stuff I never get around to throwing out. There's half a dozen pea plants for transferring into a grow-bag, now a few trays of tomato saplings and a titsy raspberry bush to go into pots. The pots will allow their suckling tentacles to proliferate, and then they'll stretch and fruit. You sit between the table legs as I work. You examine the trickles of compost. They hit the lino and scarper free in all directions. Under the fridge, the washing machine, the oven. What do you think my compost smells like? Like the kind of soil a man in a factory made, like moistened rootlings and flittered bark but with an aftertaste of chemicals?

I drag the grow-bag through the rain to the stone fence and clear a spot amongst the buoys and bits of buoy which should seize some sun, if ever the sun comes. The raspberry bush can go here too but the tomatoes stay where it's snug on the kitchen windowsill. I clear the tabletop back to its original mess and roll a cigarette which tastes as though there are tiny pieces of compost entwined with the tobacco. Now I lean against the door frame with coffee cup in hand and you sitting on my shoes. Together we regard the backyard's newest arrivals. Soon the pea shoots will be twice as long and their curly tendrils will be grappling for something to cling to. Then we'll go to the forest and gather broken branches and I'll push them into the grow-bag for the shoots to hoist themselves up and clasp the mini trees tight to their stalky breasts. The pea shoots need the pea sticks like the ivy needs a trellis, like the tickbird needs a rhino, like I need gingernuts and cigarettes and you at my feet, sitting to attention, sniffing the breeze.

You shift your weight to lean against my shin. You're dry and warm and soft yet solid. I feel the bulge and fall of your ribcage as you sigh. You seem to do a lot of sighing. I find it strange because I always thought of a sigh as an expression of the sort of feeling which animals are not supposed to be capable of, and I wonder do you sigh because you have the smog inside you, my sapping smog. Does it build within your chest until your muscles spasm and push it out, away?

I don't expect the rain will let up long enough for the plants to need watering. Standing beneath the door lintel regarding our sorry garden, a swallow swoops low, hesitates, flies on. And I wonder was it one of mine. I wonder are my swallows back.

—

Once my father was gone, I expected that someone would come for me. I expected them to lock me up somewhere I wouldn't be able to impede the busybodies, the regular people. I expected to be institutionalised. I mistook the shrieking gulls for sirens and locked myself inside the bathroom to hide from flashing lights. But nobody came.

I summoned every last dot of valour I could scratch from my soul, I swallowed a shot glass of rescue remedy and went to the social welfare office. I filled out forms and ticked boxes. I found that continued survival came down to a simple matter of form-filling, a basic proficiency in the ticking of boxes. And because I managed never to miss a box or make an illiterate mark on the bottommost line instead of signing my name, nobody came.

And here I am still, and here you are.

—

We turn the page of the calendar, from the donkeys to a row of deckchairs in a leafy park with an opalescent pond, a commemorative bench, its inscription too small to read, and a solitary moorhen.

It's two weeks since the clamping of the collie on Tawny Bay. Two weeks of sheltering in my father's house. I can tell you're growing listless. I'm listless too. If it was winter, I could accept the murky weather, the incarcerating walls. But with summer comes hope, and with hope comes disappointment. Now dawn is the only time we can safely walk, and every dawn breaks pale and ungleaming, and every stretch between dawns is ruthlessly long. I want to go out during

the day but I'm afraid. I'm afraid of meeting HENRY HENRY
HENRY and Henry's woman again, of being screeched at and
flogged in the street with a golf umbrella. I'm afraid of being
stopped and asked for my name and our address, of being
shown the bite marks in Henry's princely face and the way in
which the distance between them matches the exact distance
separating your two pointiest teeth. I'm afraid, I think more
than anything, of losing you.

From your sentry on the windowsill, you watch your
unfettered fellows trotting the bird walk. You bark and
bark yet they never seem to see you back. The living room
is cast to darkness by the outside's bright; you're but a
sparkle on the glass. Do you see the mullet suckling at the
water's surface, snatching for midges? And the old men
with girlish fishing rods and packets of white sliced pan?
They're balling bread onto their hooks and floating it on
the ripples, feet dangling over the shore wall like gnomes
by a garden pond. I rarely see them catch a mullet. With or
without reward, they fish. I've seen the bread balls snatched
by greedy ducks and the hooks snap into their beaks as they
try to fly. Only then do the old men reel their broken lines
in and gather their gear, drop their feet to the path and
shamble away.

And the snapped lines collect eelgrass and litter until
the duck grows too weak to cart its monstrous load. Then it
lies down in the ripples, its loyal mate forced to watch as it's
slowly drawn under.

SARA BAUME

See the shelducks and little egrets, the cygnets and swifts. You see every bird the local twitcher misses, although you can't name a single one.

—

At dawn, all the places I thought I knew so well are different countries. Damp and rumpled as though rinsed and shook. Our early walks up the refinery road always follow your aimless course of indecipherable landmarks, from a pigeon feather to a smashed snail, from scent to shining scent.

Today, inside the tree tunnel at the end of the sea front, it's exactly the stage of summer at which the leaves are such a yellow shade of green that they glow, or seem to be glowing. Today, you tow me through the glowing leaves to where there's a slipway and a boathouse. This is the village rowing club. The boathouse is a prefab painted a coniferous shade of green to flush with the foliage. The slip is slimy concrete. While you are sniffing a spool of fox foul as delicately as though it were a fine cigar, I spy through the window to the wooden yawls laid out on racks, capsized, with their oars amputated and removed.

All winter, the prefab stays locked. The window clots with cobwebs, nobody comes. The yawls hibernate, like big brown bears with polished backs in dark dens. But now it's summer, the season of regattas. The boathouse is garnished by bunting and every second Sunday, a marquee goes up, a

76

loudspeaker is nailed to a post, a starter pistol is loaded with blank caps, and the rowers come.

—

My father used to have a shabby rowboat, have I mentioned it before? Have I already told you about the old man's doorbox? It was roped to a rusted rung along the shore wall and it used to dash itself against the stones in wild weather almost as if it was trying to break itself, or perhaps to break away. After he died, I cut my father's doorbox loose and I don't know whether it drifted off or simply sank into the mudflats.

—

From the window we watch the handsome boats skimming across the bay between their markers, the rowers' heads lined up as targets on a coconut shy, pumping time like synchronised pendulums. The markers are gallon drums, strung together into a bobbing boundary. The races tempt a straggle of revellers to the shore wall. I can tell the true enthusiasts from their wolf-whistles and binoculars, whereas most of them are wielding choc-ices and Coke cans instead, more entertained by the sport of putting things into their mouths than the rowing.

Here in our aerial seat, we are ever uprooted and apart. We are ever looking down on life, at sun visors and bald pates and umbrellas. The rowing club marquee sends a perfume of pig meat coasting over the village and up to meet us. Can you smell it? Sausages blistering against barbeque coals. You lift your head to the opened crack, a crack just wide enough for smells and sounds and breeze but not quite so wide that you could dive-bomb an unsuspecting innocent on the street below. You are concentrating hard on the sausages. Your thousand-mile stare stops dead at the marquee. The drool falls, snares on your beard and swings. We can't go out to join the revelling, I'm sorry. The regatta is for families. See the kids in miniature life-jackets all blown up like rubber bath toys? See the parents hanging onto a pudgy arm lest a sudden gust capture their balloon child and send them surfing to the trees? It's for families, not for us. We can only hide here and watch the yawls and the pendulums, the gobblers and gawpers and gabbers.

As evening sneaks in, we go down to the kitchen. I clank the pan onto a hob and fetch a packet of sausages from the fridge. I can't bear the fatty lumps which squeak against my teeth like polystyrene and I can't bear the way each end puckers to an unfryable twist, but I like the ritual of Sunday sausage cooking. I like having a calf-high, furred and dribbling excuse to perform it for. I chop your share into easily swallowable cylindrical segments. I extract all the gristly bits from my own sausages with the filleting knife, drop them to your bowl. Now I lean beneath the lintel of the back door with my coffee cup in one hand, a cigarette in the other and you at my feet. Together we wait for the pan to cool.

The tomato plants are sleeping outside now. Perhaps they look a little hardened, fruitless but in flower. Against the stone fence in their sunless sun spot, the peas have yet to clasp their sticks and probably never will, not now. Their leaves are drab, their roots drowned dead in the gritty black scum of the bag. Why does everything either starve or drown? Always either too much or too little, always imbalance. From the doormat at dusk, we hear the race commentator still calling names and numbers and progress reports, still breathing too loudly into the microphone. I've never seen what he looks like but his disembodied voice is almost godlike in the way it booms from nowhere and reaches everyone, in the way it's terribly indistinct but probably trying to tell us something.

Now the pan is cool, ready for you to slather. The steel scrapes against the lino as you lick, and the sound it makes is like tired boots dragging the last few yards home.

—

My father died of a sausage.

I haven't told you before because it's a stupid kind of death. It's the death of fables told by over-protective parents to caution their children against things which seem humdrum and harmless, to teach them something of the complicated grown-up ways of fearing. There's the fable of the little boy who had his head knocked off by a lamppost because he stuck it out the upstairs window of a double-decker bus. Then there's the little girl who tried to pet a lion at the zoo and had her arm munched, right up to the shoulder. But death by sausage is the fable told by adult persons to their own discarded mums and dads, for whom choking is the only crummy kind of peril left to confront them on a daily basis.

My father is the man you can smell all over the house, his house, but never find. You'll smell his dead skin cells in the leather bind of never-opened books and swept beneath the never-lifted rugs. You'll smell his dead breath, sausage scented, through the cracks in the roof plaster and the draught from the keyhole of the shut-up-and-locked room. You'll smell him most of all in the feet sweat pong of my slippers; here the stench is so strong I can smell it too. The slippers are excessively big for me, have you noticed? Even though my feet are uncommonly long and flat to balance the plundering mass of my limbs and pork of my gut, my father's feet were longer and flatter still; they seemed to reach the full diameter of his unfolded umbrella. When I wear his slippers I must slide my heels along the carpet and grasp my toes to the tatty insoles. Still, I wear them, my incommunicable sense of superstition trumping comfort. Still, I hang two towels on the bathroom rack and stand two brushes in the toothbrush jar. I know the stagnated spit that festers at the bottom is juice of my gums alone, but still.

My father was eighty-three when the sausage segment

stoppered his windpipe. I'd expected that having reached such an age, he'd die of some lazy, predictable thing, in a bed with last words and an emphatic rattle. But life never misses an opportunity to upscuttle us. Life likes to tell us it told us so. Even when we are so very old that nothing is alarming any more. So old we sit and watch, and whatever it is, we see it coming. My father had no last words, or at least his last words were spoken too long before the time he died to be remembered, to be cherished, and instead of rattling he banged his fist on the kitchen table, and with the bang still ringing, he raised his hands to clutch his throat.

My father's name was the same word as for the small insectivorous passerine birds found most commonly photographed on Christmas cards, with orange-red blushed breasts as though they've been waterboarded by molten amber and stained for life. But my father's name is just another strange sound sent from the mouths of men to confuse you, to distract from your vocabulary of commands. It doesn't mean anything; it doesn't matter.

—

Come here, I've something to show you.

I've kept this book close since I was a boy. As a boy, it helped me to work out certain of my uncertainties about the world. *Fairy Tales from Across the Globe* is what the cover title says, now let me show you the page I've visited most. See the mountain and the meadow. See the humpback footbridge. Now here are the three Billy Goats Gruff, and beneath the stone-clad arch down in the damp and gloom, here is the crouching troll. His nose is warty and his brow is bushy. His eyes have a flash of crazy in them. They are cast up to the elegantly skipping goats. When I was a boy and came to this page, I thought of the children passing on their way to school and felt a twinge of camaraderie with the crouching troll, as though I'd discovered my species. There's only one picture, still sometimes I'm convinced that I see him crouching outside of the pages. On the living room windowsill, beneath the log tarp, low down in the kitchen nook.

Sometimes it makes me chuckle and sometimes it makes me queasy to see how closely I've grown to resemble this troll as an adult, as an old man.

—

You sit in the backyard, on the gravel in a scrap of sunshine, your ears ruffling in the breeze and all the rusted roots gleaming through your ragged coat.

I see your maggot nose twitching. I smell the day's confections baking in the grocer's kitchen. The sickly wafts of croissant and apple pie, two different continents together in one oven. What are the other smells, the ones too wispy for my inadequate human senses? Can you smell the compost toasting in the plant pots, the heated wax of the bike tarpaulin, the trace of a cat who passed in the night?

Maybe I was wrong about the seasons. Some sort of summer arrived during the early hours. We woke to the transcendent stillness of a fine day, the first fine day. Bright rays poured through the uncurtained bedroom window, triumphing over the toadflax. We tripped the stairs two at a time, pushed the back door, hopped over the welcome mat. We roused the garden spider who lives between the ropes of the rotary clothes-line and has a gold-flecked abdomen like a tiny amulet. She rose to find the dew already evaporated from the filaments of her flimsy home, a baby bluebottle freshly throttled by her silken entrapments. Dangling alongside the amulet spider, the load of washing I pegged up over a week ago and watched being re-washed by the elements several showers over is finally dry.

For the first time all summer, I carry our breakfast bowls out to the patio table and we eat to the noise of seagulls barking and night lorries roaring up refinery hill, reaching their destination. I lean back in the patio chair. The muscles of my face droop and my jaw cocks open. On the glass of the tabletop, there's a bowl of inappropriately winterish porridge, a cup of pungent coffee, a packet of liquorice-flavour papers stuck to the flap of a tobacco pouch, my Amber Leaf. The first time I smoked, I was fifty-five and three-quarters. Too old for beginning to experiment with injurious substances, but just the right age for taking up a habit that encourages death. I knew exactly how to assemble my first cigarette, I'd watched my father do it ten thousand times. A fat pinch of softly wizened shag, a roll between the middle fingers and thumbs of both hands in smooth coordination. I'd trouble getting the perfect turn. My father always made it look effortless. After a few attempts I managed to seal the paper, to pop the roach in, to light. Then I propped it in the ashtray to smoke itself out. Amber Leaf was my father's brand, liquorice was his dubious choice of papers, and all I wanted was to breathe the companionable smoke. Yet with the smell, a certain dull gnawing inside me eased, and I stopped picking the tough skin around my fingernails. With the second cigarette I rolled, it wasn't enough to inhale the air above as it smouldered itself to a stub. I lifted it to my lips. Sucked, swallowed. And then I felt a little rush, a little swimmy-headed, a little better.

It was only once I'd started smoking for myself that I realised I never found where my father tore his roaches from. When he was alive, I never came across a single piece of soft card with a tiny rectangle wrought from it, whereas I am forever looting the biscuit and cereal and tissue boxes, slowly smoking a trail through my paperback book jackets.

Now the sun's full up and the backyard's a-twinkle. A pigeon settles on the stone fence. Its feathers are palest mauve, the colour of forest fruit yoghurt. It has a plastic tag around its right ankle and seems to be watching, checking to see if I'm the human it knows, if this is the backyard where it left its coop. You don't chase it; you never chase birds. I see how bewitched you are by furred things in the undergrowth and it always makes me wonder, why not birds? You'll squeeze your head down a rabbit hole, convinced your body can be contracted to follow. Yet you seem to know instinctively that you can't fly.

Look, the buoys seem polished again. The sunlight's washed away their slime. Even my dried clothes, my moth-eaten wardrobe of black and brown and grey, even my faded bath towel, look beautiful this morning. The night lorries have arrived, the amulet spider is having baby bluebottle for her breakfast, the business of the salon commences for the day. How strange to think that a few yards through a wall and over a parquet floor people are being shampooed, tinted, plucked, waxed. This makes me remember my calluses, so I remove my socks, take out my penknife and set about the improbably enjoyable task of scissoring the dead yellow meat from my feet. You sniffle them up and chew as though they were chunks of squeak toy, and a child screeches, somewhere way off in the distance, and I wonder was it a screech of joy or a screech of panic, and I wonder how to tell the difference. I wonder if other people can tell the difference. I roll another cigarette, and you breathe deep the second-hand smoke, the croissants and apple pies, the absent cat.

And our pigeon coos, soulfully.

—

Have I told you about my birthday? I've only ever had one, but it happened around this time of year, during summer, on a day of storms which followed the first spell of proper sun. A Wednesday, I think. It wasn't long after Aunt died, and so it must have been the year I turned ten.

My father didn't go to work. He ate his bran flakes, his sausages. Then he told me it was my birthday and took me to the zoo, or was it a wildlife park? Maybe it was a wildlife park. At the zoo or wildlife park, he held his unfolded umbrella up. I could feel the raindrops seeping through my sleeves and even though it was summer, even though the rain was warm, the goosebumps rose on my arms like a cold rash.

There were hardly any other visitors. What few there were we saw over and over as we followed the recommended strolling routes from the aviary through the reptile house, past monkey island to the buffalo plains. All the playground rides were empty and my father told me I was allowed to play on any one I chose. But I wasn't interested in the seasaws and slides and swings. All I wanted was to look at the birds, the lizards, the big cats and tiny red pandas.

There's nothing sadder than a rainy zoo, or wildlife park. All the creatures look either slightly dejected or slightly deranged. The big ones paced their enclosures. The small ones cowered under something and I couldn't tell if they were sheltering from the downpour or trying to hide. I moved on reluctantly from each compound. I wanted to stay there forever amongst all the sad animals. As the rain grew heavier, my father coaxed me into the gorilla house, then left me to go and stand in the doorway and smoke. There was a gigantic silverback leaning against the window of his enclosure. His hands were so humanlike, his nails exquisitely kempt, much more so than my own. Slowly, slowly, he extended the index finger of his right hand and placed its tip against the glass. I lifted mine and laid it level on the other side. And we stayed like that a long while, until my father came back and told me it was time to go.

Once we were home again, my father went to his room to fetch something. At first I thought he was giving me a small cage with an assortment of plastic toys inside, but then I saw its inhabitant. Its eyes were spearing black, its cheek pouches lumpy with stashed seeds. It gripped a bar in either front paw and I remember thinking that all it needed was a stripy jumper to be a convict in a comic book.

'It's a Russian Dwarf,' my father said. But it wasn't. It was a hamster.

I can't remember the exact date of my tenth birthday, but every Wednesday in summer for years and years after I looked out for it, I waited for it to be acknowledged again.

—

Little by little, the pothole tar remembers how to melt. The wind turbines on the further hills cease their impetuous whirling. Their white trunks vanish into the low mist; their blades against the blue sky look as though they've been drawn in Tipp-Ex. The sprat organise into torrents and storm into the bay, mackerel hot on their tail fins.

I watch as you eat the only raspberry on my bush. You smell its ripeness on the breeze and snuffle between the saw-toothed leaves, now nibble it clean to the core with bizarre delicacy, drupelet by drupelet. You're so engrossed by the berry you don't see me watching, behind you in the doorway beneath the lintel, coffee cup in hand, cigarette stuck behind my ear. You don't hear as I let loose a soft snort of laughter.

My father had a laugh like a rainstick, like a thousand grains of raw rice bouncing about inside his throat. He'd blow his nostrils wide and crinkle his cheeks up, but the noise always remained lodged just below his mouth hole, like the sausage. When my father laughed it was mostly over re-runs of comedy shows from the 1970s. Sometimes I laughed with him and while my congenial laugh wasn't exactly false, it was always on cue, it was always stiff.

I'm particularly fond of sitting in the sun, of basking. It's a fondness which shows in the skin of my face, scorched over decades to a permanent tan, dappled by dubious freckles and shape-shifting blotches, no doubt the beginning of leisurely carcinomas. Still I cannot help myself. When I sit out to bask, I feel the sun suffusing my bloodstream and it's like the effects of a tobacco which cannot be pouched. I am instantly revived, inspirited.

Now I see you're a basker too. Together we sit out every

fine day. In our concrete paddock, our yard-sized universe, we watch as the shadow of the roof steadily skulks across the gravel. I haul the patio chair in line with the shrinking light. You follow and lie at my feet. I haul it as far as the stone fence, to the point where the sun slips into next door, and is lost. Betrayed by the roof, now we bob about the yard, now we fidget like litter on the surface of the ocean. You are nibbling the leaves off a vine of poison ivy. There's a mischievous tilt to your head, as though you're consciously mocking death. I notice an ant, another ant; now I count the ants. See how they're suddenly infinite, when just a moment ago there was only one.

I long to go to the beach, not just at dawn when the heat's a little feeble. I long to go now, to walk to the end of the strand furthest from the car park where hardly anybody else ever bothers to walk, and to spread a rug there, to bask. But I'm afraid of being gawped at, and I'm afraid of leading you into a wonderland of things to clamp. Now everybody's on their holidays and willing to travel from all over the green and concrete county to reach the open blue, the beach will be too busy, and a busy beach is a baited trap. I'm afraid of the fair-weather strangers, of their pets and children, of the trouble they make and how it might make trouble for us.

There must be, somewhere, a place left behind by the wearers of swimsuits and pitchers of windbreaks and preparers of picnics. The sun's still high above the chimney pots, so let's strike off and drive around, see if we can find some small piece of abandoned coastline. Into the car and out of the village, we turn down every overgrown boreen which looks as though it might eventually subside into horizon. Sometimes there are private residences and sometimes there are NO TRESSPASSING signs and sometimes there are bulls who mistake me for their farmer, pick themselves up and trundle toward the silage trough. See the butterflies in the road up ahead, their wings swatting the sunlight as they twirl. But I forget to ease my foot from the accelerator, and now the butterflies crash and split against our windscreen. Just for a second before they're gone, I see they're red admirals. They leave two thin smears of gunk and a strange dust on the glass, a glittering dust. Did you see them? Did you see the red admirals?

At last, here's the ghost of a track which tapers into an expanse of springy grass, and collapses away down the clifftop.

—

The clifftop is studded with scabious, chamomile, campion. Ladybirds hug the grass stalks. Hoverflies tread the air. Cuckoo spit slurs through your coat as you bound to the edge. Now here's silverweed, its under-leaves gilded like the scales of a white-fleshed fish.

The track leads downslope. The earth and furze give way to sea pinks and lichen. It's steep, but there's a trawlerman's blue rope bolted into the rock and strung between posts all the way to the bottom. People must have come this way before the undergrowth grew so dense, too dense to push through. I'm stamping it down; you're tunnelling beneath. At the bottom, there's a pebbled beach only as big as a disabled parking space, no good for sandcastles or windbreaks and submerged by several feet of sea at high tide, I'm guessing. It's a beach hostile to holiday-makers, to day-trippers, to fair-weather strangers. My trouser legs are nicked from the furze's tiny fangs, my wrists are nettled. Purple grass-seeds rest amongst your curls and you are sneezing, sneezing, sneezing from the pollen-clogged air. But it's low tide, so it's perfect.

Tomorrow, once our slanted slates have collided with the course of the sun, we'll come back here, I promise. We'll scramble the way of the blue rope. I'll bring sandwiches and gingernuts, a rag rug to spread across the pebbles. I'll wedge your water dish between stones, take my book out, find the page with its corner folded, and bask. The slope's pocked by burrow holes, smattered with dehydrated droppings. Free of the leash, you disappear into the clay at the base of the cliff to exhume the rabbit subways. But the rabbits have long surrendered their old roads to the ravaging roots of the gorse thicket. You don't get very far and now your face is caked in red dust, scrawled into markings like warpaint, like you are the African prince named on your tag. You settle beside me, maggot twitching and eyeball swivelling. Well, what do you think? Will we come back tomorrow, and the day after, and the day after again?

Today, I can't see a soul. There's a row of cottages on the road, about a quarter mile away. I see flowerboxes on the windowsills, swimsuits on the washing line, cars with city registration plates and unnecessarily wide axles squeezed into the cottage-sized driveways, and I wonder why nobody appears to bother with the blue rope. Don't children go adventuring any more? Trampling the bracken in pursuit of secret caves and hidden coves, pebbled beaches at the bottom of puzzling blue ropes? But of course, I forgot how now-adays children are taught to plonk their rugs right at the start of a beach, right beside where the car is parked and all the other families are similarly plonking. These children never had the *Famous Five* because it has since transpired that Enid Blyton was ever-so-slightly racist, or so I heard on the radio. These are the sort of fair-weather strangers of whom we are thoroughly afraid, the sort who rank comradeship over compassion.

I've never read you any *Famous Five*. I should, I think you'd like it. I'm trying to remember whether Timmy ever scoffed lumps of shit or savaged guileless walkers. I don't think so.

———

Every dawn, I expect the weather to have broken overnight. As though it will wait until I'm not watching to break. But it doesn't. We walk the refinery road to Tawny Bay. We eat porridge in the yard. And when the tide is right, we drive to the steep cliff and scramble the way of the blue rope. Now the days are longer than ever before, but like never before, I'm grateful.

I bring a Thermos flask to the pebbled beach and stand it on the flattest rock. It's too hot, I know, but I've always wondered what it feels like to drink coffee on the beach. Are you too hot too? You're pumping out short, fast puffs of breath. I tow you by the collar to a rockpool, hoist you up and lower you in, cup my hands to splash your chest and belly. As the water resettles, you stay as you are. You're watching the shrimp around your feet, snapping at the water, coughing and spluttering it out your nostrils.

You always come back to me in your own time. Now you lean against my crossed ankles beside the Thermos rock. Behind us and beyond the holiday cottages, see the fields. Remember how they seemed to be green as we drove past them? Now see how, from here, they are taupe and mint, emerald and lime.

Interrupting the fields, there's a golf course and a purposeless dispersal of bungalows. Barns, cars, bales and trees. Cows moving as imperceptibly as the hands of a clock, getting there without ever seeming to go. Now look out and see the ocean; the ocean's interruptions. There's a hunk of grassy rock all covered in cormorants. A lobster buoy. Sailboats very far away. A blue gallon drum, presumably attached to

93

something beneath the surface. And a cargoship passing a floating lighthouse on its way into harbour.

Whenever I look at a cargoship, I start to picture all the different things enclosed within each container, then all of the components which went into making the things, and then all of the component's components, and so on, into perpetuity. Like the picture on the tin of Royal baking powder. When I was about as tall as the letter slot and riding in the back of my father's car, we were passing through town one day, driving along the main street, and I remember seeing a woman through the window, standing in her doorway. After a moment, she turned and went back inside, closing the door behind her, and then of course I couldn't see her any more. I know it sounds like nothing much, but it was the first time I realised that other people's lives go on. All of the time, out of sight and without me. It was the first time I realised that everything just goes on and on and on. Regardless, relentless.

—

Don't you ever wonder what exactly people do, all day long, every day? The regatta revellers, April and the Polish hairdresser, the summer boys' mums and dads? We see them power-walking along the shore front, queuing in the supermarket, zipping through the village in their fat cars. Then they pull into driveways and vanish behind front doors.

Secure inside their magnolia dens with the venetian blinds tilted, what do they do?

I can imagine; I do imagine, but my father and Aunt are the only people I've ever actually been shut behind a door with, before you. And of course you're not a person, I always forget that. Now it's forty-seven years since I was shut up with Aunt, and my father hardly counts either. For most of the days each week, for most of my life, he left the house in the morning and didn't come back again until night, and only some nights, not even all of them.

Every morning, he put on an ironed white shirt, a pinstriped tie, suit trousers and sensible shoes. My father was employed by a factory which manufactured confectionery. He was on the production line, and so he must have changed as soon as he arrived at work, and changed back again as soon as he clocked off. He never brought me to the industrial estate in the city to show me his factory, and so the picture I have in my head of little orange men and chocolate rivers isn't real.

My father wasn't an educated or well-heeled man, even if he dressed as if he was. He saved enough money every year to go on holiday, once a year. And every year, once a year, on holiday, he bought a plate. He didn't retire until he was seventy-six. One morning he got up as early as he always had and ate his bran flakes and sausages as usual. He was wearing his shirt and suit trousers, but I noticed he'd substituted slippers for tie. After he finished his post-breakfast cigarette, he went back into his bedroom and closed the door. He did the same thing the next day, and the next. Sometimes I'd stand outside and listen. I could hear pencil scratching, scissor squeaking, cardboard sawing and the tinkling of a paintbrush being rinsed in a jar. After a couple of weeks, he opened the door and showed me what he was making.

It was a board game, colourful and complicated, yet also crude and logistically flawed. It fell far short of what I'd always imagined to be my father's standards of precision, but of course, I didn't tell him that. He made ninety-eight board games in the years between retirement and death, and I never told him. Some of them were reinvented versions of the classics. Cluedo on a cruise liner with a crew's mess instead of a dining room and a guy rope instead of a candlestick. Snakes & Ladders in three dimensions with footstools and waterslides instead. The games my father invented for himself all had names which ended in an exclamation mark and sounded like a fairground ride or an ice-lolly: Scaffold! Golly Whizz! Scramp! I spent thousands of evenings playing his disorientating games with him, losing to my father's ridiculous rules. And for thousands of evenings, I longed to be left to my books instead, to be far away inside their worlds and protected from my own.

I've never really seen the point of board games. They always take too much time to reach the finishing line, and then you either win or lose and that's it. Nothing new is known. The game goes back into its box. Books have always been another kind of safe space, though if I'm completely honest then most of the things I learned from reading I've forgotten anyway. At least by playing the games, by losing, I gave my father some small volt of victory, some sense of accomplishment. I made him feel better, for a while, and that's all the point there is, really. I owed him that, at least.

Before he retired, I knew very little of my father other than what I witnessed for myself. He spoke to me in a practical way, he never really told me things. I knew he always took a conference pear and a packet of custard creams to work. I knew he sat with his right ankle rested against the lid of his left knee. I knew he didn't like the taste of plastic from the new milk bottles. I knew a hundred mundane facts, but nothing of his longings, of his past. Now I wonder if he ate all of the custard creams himself or did he share them? And if he shared them, who did he share them with?

After he retired, my father transformed his bedroom into a workshop for tinkering the board games into existence. There he spent his days sawing sheets of corrugated card, carving counters from bricks of balsa and painting over everything with his soft-bristled brushes. My father's tinkerings left their trace in tiny mountains of wood shavings and flakes of cut card which sat on the carpet or got picked up by the door, swept into the hall and trampled across the house. After he retired, sometimes he'd tell me throwaway things and I'd scrabble them up like a squirrel snatching winter's nuts. *Sometimes on the sherbet line*, he told me, *the sealer would malfunction, then the pressure made the packets explode. The whole length of the belt there'd be a sugar cloud and we'd all be hacking and gagging into our mopcaps.* My father hadn't liked his job. He always made this much clear to me.

In his bedroom-workshop, he ruined a square of wallpaper by using it to soak the excess water from his soft bristles. One day I noticed how it had been dabbed into an intricate pattern, like a coded message. In his latest years, I'd bring him cups of tea and marmalade on toast and I'd see how he'd added a new mark to his square, how it expanded every day. After he died, I locked my father's window, I locked his door. I laid the draught snake out. Now there's nothing more to add. The message is ended and means everything it's ever going to mean. And I suppose I know now everything I'm ever going to know about my father.

—

Come here, I've something to show you.

There are ninety-seven homemade board games inside the shut-up-and-locked room, and the ninety-eighth is here in this box. This is the best one, the only one I still sometimes try to play. It's a version of a real game called Discovering Europe, I think, only based upon a continent of my father's creation. See how he outlined his landmass, then sliced it up between borderlines. See how the name of each country is borrowed from an obscurely titled village or town land or valley or river. Now see how my father gave each country a national anthem, a national costume, a national sport and flag as well as a particular landscape and export industry. Here's Garrowdiff and the Isle of Spence, Moyastree and Ballyooagle. Here's Palace and here's Butts. See how Dyssert is mostly desert and Creggish is particularly craggy, how all the citizens of Elphin wear green tights and the flag of Lisfinny is covered in fish.

It's a game of luck, so you can play it with me if I roll the dice for you, pick up your chance cards, push your counter on a round trip to nowhere. In the low chair on the opposite side of the gameboard, you're sitting up straight, watching intently. Are you waiting to be fed one of the coloured pieces? I'm sorry, these aren't for gobbling.

My father told me that after he died the games were to be destroyed without exception. I expect he was ashamed of the snot-nosed and sticky-fingered child who dwelt within him, who tinkered. He didn't want people to weigh the worth of his life in puerile toys. But I didn't preserve them out of malice; it's just that I don't have a knack for destruction. And besides, I had a hand in them too. He asked for my help, and I helped. I did all the dullest and finickiest and most repetitive jobs. I kicked down the days with mind-numbing tasks on my father's instruction when I wanted nothing but to be reading instead. I know he only came back to remain in the salmon pink house on his retirement because he was old and spent and had nobody to care for him, nobody but me. When I needed him least, he suddenly needed me to sand his balsa and lose at his games. By his eightieth year, my father was scarcely the height of a silverback and he had exactly the same achromatic hair, slouchy gait and pouchy eye sockets. It was hard to hate him then, to treat him cruelly. It would have been like kicking a puppy; it would have made me the troll he'd always led me to believe I was.

I never meant for what happened to happen. I've no more knack for concealment than I do destruction. Please understand, I never meant it.

Who were they? The people my father thought were going to come for his sloppy games and pass judgement on his life? Were they the people who asked me questions after mass, the people he shared his custard creams with, the people alongside whom he inhaled exploded sherbet? Whoever they were, or whoever he thought they were, they never came.

Your counter is in Bunraffy when you give in, curl up and sleep, and I play on alone. I steer thoughtlessly through the game for an hour or two, and after the finishing line is crossed, I feel a little better, for a while.

—

Sometimes, when I was a boy, my father tore sheets of paper from his graphed pad and gave them to me to draw pictures. But instead of trying to replicate items and aspects of my world, I turned the sheet onto its blank side and re-drew the pattern of the graph, meticulously. Hundreds of teeny-tiny squares, without picking up a ruler. Every now and again I'd make an attempt at forms, but curves and shading always straightened and slimmed and led me back inexorably to the grid. It made some kind of sense to me then. It helped to hold the smog at bay. I don't know what happened to those drawings. I think my father threw them all away.

I've never looked through his stuff and I can't explain exactly why it is I'm so incurious. I suppose there are clues about his life there in the shut-up-and-locked room, perhaps even some traces of my mother, but better to be content with ignorance, I've always thought, than haunted by the truth.

—

The sea relaxes into summer, turns from slate to teal to crystalline. The white horses fall back into ripples and until they recommence their watery gallivanting, there'll be no sea-wrecked buoys to find on the rocks and beaches, no stir and shake to smash them, no lob and volley to run their broken pieces aground. It's the season of scantiest harvest for my backyard collection of sea junk. Where the waves have most recently touched, now there are jellyfish instead. No smaller than coins, no larger than coasters. Even though they are beached, traces of poison remain in their floppy tails. Even though they are dead, they can still sting. And there are pine-cones. There are always pinecones.

Now let me show you my junk-treasures. Here are my crabs. Not the severed claws you like to crunch but the shells of their backs, their elegant exoskeletons. I find them knotted into bladderwrack, crisping in the sun on the banks of rock-pools. I bring them home, rinse the stringy meat out, apply a lick of varnish to shield against the bleaching light. The edible crabs are smooth and curved like the red wood of a string instrument. The velvet crabs are fiddly to varnish; my soft bristles get stuck in the down of their carpeted backs. The common crabs have spots and spiked edges, like a pinking shears. Although brown-green under water, once dismembered and risen to the surface, their shells are baked to the colour of marmalade, Seville marmalade. The colour reminds me of Aunt's open casket in the funeral home. Her cheeks had been bronzed by some blundering undertaker and the tanned head on the coffin pillow was a stranger to me, creepy as a ventriloquist's dummy, only without the ventrilo-quist to make it seem harmless, even funny.

Here's my driftwood. I prefer the pieces with swatches of crackled paint. I bring them home and nail them to the yellow walls, each abutting the next, joining the swatches. I think of it as a colossal jigsaw, an abstract assemblage of infinite proportions, and sometimes I wonder if, along with his overlong feet, my father bestowed on me his restless compulsion for remaking.

Now here are my bass lures. They look like fish-shaped toys except for the evil little hooks. Their plastic backs are psychedelic and their plastic bellies rattle like matchboxes. I cut them from great nests of weed wound up with cat-gut and threaded through with tiny, luminous beads. There's something especially wretched about the washed-up lures. It's like the plastic fish have been garrotted by their own line, poisoned by the lead of their own weight.

Best of all treasures, here are my glass pebbles. They're descended from old bottles, shattered and frosted by millions of the water's worker particles. They are mostly wine-bottle green, milk-bottle white and beer-bottle brown. Sometimes they are medicine-bottle blue, but the blues grow rarer by the year. At dawn I sit on the stones of Tawny Bay and sift the shale while you're playing football. And on every afternoon the tide grants us our pebbled beach, I sit and sift again. At home, I fill my jars and stand them in the windows. When the sun shines through, it throws sea-coloured mosaics onto the sill, the walls, the floor. I know what you're rolling about between your teeth. Come here, spit it out.

Now everything holds a diaphanous kind of potential. Now everything is so quiet and so nice and I feel ever so faintly less strange, less horrible. It makes me uneasy. It reminds me how I must remember to be distrustful of good fortune.

—

There is a little boy.

He has frilly hair, apricot skin, symmetrical features. He reminds me of the people in my picture frames, of the posing boys with sweet, smiling faces and a posing parent either side. Only this sweet face is snarled and gulping. This boy is staggering in distress, struggling to reach for his shih tzu and pressing, pressing, pressing his heartbeat into my outstretched palm. We are on the bird walk at last light, and I never meant to touch. I never wanted to touch. I'm only holding him back, with the front of my hand flat to the front of the boy's red T-shirt. Red: the colour of warning, of admonition. But I'm only holding him. My other hand is on your mouth, my fingers pressed into your gums, trying to lever your canine teeth from the tender skin of the shih tzu's neck. And there is blood now. On me, on you. But mostly on the shih tzu, because it's mostly the shih tzu's blood.

The boy's mother must have been all the way back as far as the power station. It takes her forever to catch up with her son. She is fat, too fat for hurrying, and her voice is fat too. A torrent of verbal abuse bulges and rolls from her bulges and rolls. Now she screams and sledgehammers a fist between animals. Her graceless karate chop does the trick. In an instant, I wrench you from your quarry and the little boy scoops his shih tzu back.

I stride away. With you under my arm, I walk as fast as I can without blatantly running. My hips are swinging like a woman's, my bad leg is being left behind. My hands are trembling and the trembles travel through my elbows and shoulders, into my chest. The sighted side of your head is twisted back and you're digging your claws deep into the flesh of my waist, the pork of my gut. Now I lose my grip and drop half of you to the ground. Your front feet are dangling, so I must drag. And as I drag, I stutter angry whispers at the back of your satiny head. 'Sssssstop,' I stutter, 'sssstop ssstop ssstop.'

But you can't hear me, and you don't stop. You're braying, braying, braying a bloodthirsty bray. It seems to come out through every pore of your bandy body. So this is your kill noise, I've heard it only in murmurs before but now here it is at its furious zenith. Perhaps in a different situation I'd appreciate its eerie melodiousness, its piercing resonance. I'd notice how it's like some hopeless, haunted, strangulated form of singing, singing, singing. Out of tune, out of time.

Now the boy's mother is gaining on us. She's just a few paces behind, puce-faced and perspiring. She buys the low-fat cheese, I think. She has a treadmill which stands immoveable as a marble bust in the corner of the spare room. She decides things for her husband and is not worth disagreeing with. Now a sweat mark has appeared at the neckline of her blouse and is creeping down toward the crevasse of her mountainous breasts. The things she shouts, the things she threatens, are clearer now. No longer slurred by shock but whetted by rage.

'VET'S BILLS!' she shouts. 'DOG WARDEN! MUZZLE! PUT TO SLEEEEEEP!'

We pull well ahead, pass the information board and cross the road.

'I KNOW WHERE YOU LIVE!' she shouts. 'I KNOW, I KNOW!'

And even if she is lying it doesn't matter now, for she's about to see us disappear behind the blue metal gate, our gate. The last of her shrilling is carried off on the wind, quenched by bigger noises. By the refinery siren, a passing cargo lorry full of freshly filled cylinders, a curlew calling his buddies to roost.

We fall into the laneway. I slam the gate. Even though you've stopped singing, your song's still reverberating in my head. I bend down to remove the harness. You wag your tail in expectation of approval. You lick your chops in request of a treat, just like before. And I smack you hard across the muzzle, so hard that the bone at the back of my palm makes a sharp, clicking sound as it strikes.

Your eye waters. You shy away. You crumple like a tin can stamped beneath a hobnail boot.

I should never have adopted you. You bring trouble and then just when I think the trouble has passed, you bring trouble again. Caring for you is like keeping a nettle in a pretty porcelain flowerpot, watering its roots and pruning its vicious needles no matter how cruelly it stings my skin, until I'm pink and puffy all over yet still worrying the old welts back to life.

I find the key and open the front door. I step into the hall, but you don't follow. You stay where you are. You cringe into the coarse brush of the mat.

And now I think of how I was my father's nettle. His big lump of an embarrassing son. A son with no life of his own, no apparent trace of intelligence, of personality. A son fit only to be kept indoors, away from people and from light. Where there's nothing to sting but himself.

—

I'm sorry. I didn't mean it. Come in and let me clean the blood from your beard. It's almost time for supper.

At certain stages of the summer, the bay is fringed by a phlegm of dirty white weed. The top gets crusted by the sun, but underneath, it's soup. Parsnip, no, cream of mushroom soup. On hot days at low tide, the soup smell steeps the village. Do you get it? Of course you do, you can smell everything. You can smell feelings; you can smell time.

Now we sit behind the window. You on the sill, me in the armchair. Outside it's dark. The tide's coming in and all the birds are gone; gone wherever it is they go at night-time and high tide. Out to sea, the bird book says, as though 'Out To Sea' were some immense country unfastened and cast off to drift alone between continents. In the mud still barely visible below the wall, see the traffic cone buried to its third luminous band. See the golf umbrella wasted to its contorted joints. That's my father's golf umbrella; there's the spot where I threw it. See what is maybe the blunt bow of his doorbox and maybe just a bow-shaped hump of bedrock. See the concrete cavity block. Inside it's brimming with common crabs preparing to shed their softened shells. And across the bay, see the lights of a livestock ship pulling out of harbour. Inside there are hundreds of individual crates, and inside each crate, there's a calf. I picture the calves are tan, white, black, mottled, and the ones with window cabins are staring out across the bay. But they can't see as far as the bird walk. They didn't notice what went on while they were watching. They don't understand what's happening to them and they are mooing, even though we can't hear them from here, they are mooing tragically for their mothers, for solid earth beneath their hooves.

—

The livestock ship sails from the harbour every Wednesday. It's bound for Italy, I think.

Thursday passes, Friday, now Saturday. We don't walk to Tawny Bay. Not even at dawn. We don't scramble the way of the blue rope. We venture no further than the backyard. We can't. We have to stay here, out of sight.

In the backyard, I rake the gravel. I'm careful to rake around the tufts of grass you like to nibble. And the weeds, the weeds which chose me, which chose us. I uproot the poison ivy, chuck it away. Next spring, I'm going to scatter grass-seeds. I'm going to see how much of a lawn I can plant before the pigeon eats it, our soulful pigeon.

A bee is circling the buoys, trying to figure out what sort of flowers they are. It isn't one of the chubby bumbles which everyone loves. It's a wasp-like honey bee instead; it carries baskets of pollen hooked around its backmost legs. I stop raking to watch. You're chewing a piece of gravel. Even though I've told you ten times not to, still you are chewing. Now you swallow and watch with me. The honey bee chooses a blue float and touches down for just a second before flying on again, indignantly. I read in the newspaper that they can see blue and lavender, but none of the other colours. None of your greys and yellows, none of my everything. And they are dying, so the newspaper said, the bees. Perhaps next spring, I'll plant flowers as well. Every open bud is a bee fed, I'd forgotten that.

Avoiding the weeds and tufts and buoys, the rotary line, the patio table, I'm trying to rake the gravel into smooth lines. I want it to look like a Zen garden, like the picture in my library book, remember? A floor of stones in a swirling pattern of perfectly parallel ridges. But it doesn't. There are so many obstructions it's just a mess. Now one of the jackdaws from the chimney pot hops down to the gutter, peers over the edge of the roof and croaks, as though it is taunting me, taunting my dismal attempt to impose order.

Now I kick your football against the stone fence, against the wall. It smacks into buoys, upsets pots, desolates my ridges. You try to prance behind it but the yard is too small. You lose interest, bit by bit. You cock your leg to piss against the tarp of the log pile and I pick your shit off the gravel before it gets levelled by the ball. I handle it in the way butchers handle raw meat at the deli counter, a plastic bag tied in a knot around my wrist. But I don't mind because the weather is hot, the turds shrivel into liquorice sticks.

I'm guessing by now the calves have arrived in Italy. Would it take three days, or not that long, or longer? Is it only three days since we ventured out? It feels like a lifetime, like the lifetime of a creature which lives extremely long, like an ornamental carp in a Japanese Zen garden.

———

You on the sill. Me in the armchair. Facing the bay.

We see a car with four bicycles strapped above the tow bar, a kayak straddled across the roof rack and a caravan bumping along behind. It jostles up like a shiny-shelled beetle bent out of shape by its alien attachments. Now it jerks to a stop and gobs a family out. The mother takes photographs of the horizon. The children sit along the shore wall tossing fairy bun crumbs to the gulls. And the father adjusts his strappings, bends his attachments back into shape. See the summer whose arrival we waited for so patiently; it doesn't belong to us. It never belonged to us.

The salon's shuttered and locked. The hairdresser's gone

on her holidays and taken the hum of hood dryers with her, the tap of high heels, the tittle-tattle of female voices. I'd always thought these noises irritating, now it suddenly seems they were a kind of comfort. The phone in the salon is ringing, ringing, ringing through the floorboards, jingling like a giant wind-chime suspended in a draught. I try to drown it out by talking, by telling you about the dreary things we do and the blandest of changes beyond the window. I used to tell my father things like this, later when he chose to remain mute and it was left to me to chip away at the surface of our shared silences. Even though I knew he wasn't listening, it was still hard, it was a bit like stinging myself, over and over. After he died, I continued to ramble. I'd point my face to the ceiling and address him, but it was easier because I knew he couldn't really hear. And now it's easiest of all with you. Now there's no need for the weighing and measuring of words, no need to listen to the way they stand in the air after my voice has finished. I tell you of the new rib tied to a rusted rung, the tower crane raised over refinery hill, the man who practises casting his lead off the pier at high tide. I tell you anything, so long as it staves the smog off, so long as it gags the sentence that shrills in my brain. I KNOW WHERE YOU LIVE, it shrills, I KNOW, I KNOW.

What do you suppose she meant by that? What form of fear was she determining to instil, and am I fearing it as I should be? I'm fearing a poisoned sausage posted through the letter slot, catapulted over the stone fence into the backyard. I'm fearing the piiing-ponnng of the doorbell and a uniformed official standing on the coarse brush, wielding a pole with a modifiable collar sticking out the lowered end. I'm afraid of losing you, I never expected I could be so stupidly afraid of losing you. I see the fat woman on the undersides of my eyelids, her spittle and her sweat. Her words circle inside my skull like a sock trapped in a washing machine, the knob jammed on spin cycle.

Now see the slim skids of shit down the side of our house, below the roof cranny. Even though I can't see through the flaky mud, it must mean my swallows, that they've chosen me. They've chosen us.

—

In the yard, I gather all the dead things. Each hummock of solidified earth falls from its pot like a sandcastle, peaked into imperfect turrets. I make a row of earth castles along the stone fence. I stick a few square-ish pieces of gravel into their facades, as windows. I stab a pigeon feather into the centre top of the tallest. Now I realise a castle would never be laid out like this, with its towers all in a tidy row. I should push them together, into a cluster, a fortress. But I don't. I turn the tap on and unspool the garden hose. I spray my castles down, and as I spray, you snarl and snap at the jet of water, as though it were a living thing. A hostile thing. An assailant.

She knows where I live, yet I've no idea where she lives. But then everybody knows where I live. You've seen how they're always perfectly polite, but this is a pretence; they are pretending. They've long since marked me down as strange, a strange man, I am a strange man. And it's because of my strangeness that they make a special point of knowing where I live. And they wait, and have been waiting all the time I've been in this house in this village, all my life, for strange things to happen for which they can finger me, for which they can have me and my threatening strangeness removed.

Her words are spinning in my brain. Spinning, spinning, spinning without ever making it to the end of the cycle, without ever reaching the stage at which everything goes still, and the door can be opened again. And now the castles are demolished, you dig a shallow hole for yourself in the yard, a wallowing pool. And you lie in the wet mud. You wallow.

——

I'm going out. I won't be long, not even an hour, I promise.

It's Sunday and my father used to bring me to mass on Sundays, have I mentioned this already? In the later years, I used to bring him, and in the latest years he'd place his palm over the back of my hand as we crossed the churchyard and lean down hard as if I was a walking stick. My father was raised a Catholic, I presume, but he didn't abstain from meat on Fridays or put up a crib at Christmas. He didn't have Jesus in a picture frame with a tiny red bulb for a sacred heart, as Aunt did, and he didn't stop what he was doing at six o'clock and bow his head for the Angelus bells. I don't believe he believed. He only went to mass on Sundays because he liked to grumble and smoke by the gates after the communion notices. I'd leave him with the neighbours and sit in the car. I'd wait, and always, he made his own way back.

I don't believe either. It takes all of my energy just to have faith in people. I went to mass and knelt on the cold lumber beside my father every Sunday only because he expected me to. During the service, I'd bow my head and un-tether my thoughts. And if there happened to be somebody sitting in the pew in front with a visible coat label, I'd reconfigure the letters into anagrams, as many as I could think of, until it was time to get up again, to go again to the car and wait.

Have I told you about HORNET? I think I already told you. Hornets are enormous wasps, you know. They eat bees because bees taste like honey. The church is beside the post office and I must have passed its gates a hundred times since then, one year and one half of a year ago. I've seen the church-going neighbours, my father's fellow grumblers who asked me questions after he was gone, in other places around the village and in town. They always seem somehow incongruous; they always catch me unaware. And even though I know who they are and they know who I am, I've never spoken or saluted

SPILL SIMMER FALTER WITHER

and not one of them has ever acknowledged me either, not even a nod. It seems that outside the church gates, we are strangers again.

I'm going to put your chair in the bedroom and close the living room door so no one can see you at the window. I'm going to lock the metal gate so no one can reach the letter slot.

'Back in a minute,' I say, and you are a good boy, and so I tell you.

'Good boy,' I tell you, 'good.'

—

I get stuck in the mass traffic. I'd forgotten there's mass traffic. The hedges are covered in red blackberries and amongst the berries, here's willowherb, wild mint, meadowsweet.

I can't bear the prospect of having to retell the nursing home story and so I let everybody else file in before me. From the woman in the wheelchair to the man who holds the collection plate, all wearing their mass clothes and pulling their mass faces.

The interior walls have been repainted. Now they are limp green, the colour of central embankments in winter. The statue of St Joseph is missing several of his digits, as if St Joseph were once the victim of a ransom that took too long to be paid. The plastic posies above the tabernacle are caked with dust, the Jesus face on the Eucharistic tapestry is a redhead, and the altar carpet is flattened along the pathway of the altar boys' duties, as though they move on tiny steam-rollers beneath their gowns. It's odd I don't remember these details, I must have looked at them Sunday in Sunday out for decades and decades. I must have scrutinised them clean out of existence.

I'm kneeling at the back with three rows between me and the closest congregant. All the things I've forgotten, yet I remember the words of the prayers and responses. But I don't join in. I'm not here to cut bargains. I'm not here to make anagrams. So why am I here? I can't remember why I came. It seems suddenly rash, stupid. Maybe I just wanted to have a spy at them, at all of these people who think I am a strange man, and know where I live. Every now and again someone glances around and shoots me a look of misgiving. Now it's the kiss of peace and there's nobody nearby enough for me to shake hands with, to wish peace upon. I stand with my wrists at my sides and chin rested against chest, pretending it is some kind of contemplation.

Come communion everybody gets up and queues toward the priest. I stay as I am, as still as I can, as though I might be invisible just as long as I don't move. The procession kinks around so people can walk back down the aisle and return to their seats. Christ is melted to a wafery gloop on the roof of their mouths and their faces are pointing in my direction. Now I see the fat woman and her little boy. She is marching. He is scurrying behind. His fingers are pressed together and pointed to the rafters. His photo frame smile is demurely pursed.

I flee. I don't stop to genuflect. I don't stop to drop coppers into the collection plate or dip my fingers into the floating dust of the font. I clear the churchyard's paving slabs, pass through the iron gates and rush to the car. No one catches up with me; no one tries, just like last time. I leave the church door open, and inside the car I can still hear the communion hymn. I can still hear all those ladies in shoulder-padded jackets with purple perms, and they are singing, singing, singing.

You're waiting inside the front door. 'It's okay,' I tell you, 'I'm home again now.'

You're grunting your greeting grunt, wagging your tail ecstatically as though we'd been separated for forever. I know it's too early for supper, but let's have sausages anyway. I know it's too late for dawn, but let's go out and walk. Up the road past the refinery, over the fields to the beach, to our beach, to Tawny Bay.

—

As we approach the edge of the slope, sandmartins lift into the sky. It's as though someone's standing below the line of the cliff, holding the birds scrunched in their palms, now flinging them upwards, fast, their wings only opening once they are high in the air. I remember finding a stunned sparrow, as a boy, and doing just that, holding and flinging, watching for its wings to open. Only they didn't, of course, it fell straight back.

And once we're over the edge, we are running. Because it is too steep, because we cannot help but run.

—

Do you hear it? The piiing-ponnng of the doorbell.

Now you have to follow me. I have to leave you here and go downstairs. You have to be quiet. You have to wait. 'Quiet,' I tell you, 'wait.'

There's a uniform standing in my laneway. Inside the uniform, there's a woman. A smallish, oldish woman. I hadn't expected that. She has the look of a John Dory about her, moon-eyed and frowny. There are dark speckles of stubble either side of her upper lip. Leathern patches encircle her elbow bones and her hair thins from the crown, exposing a kippah of vanilla skin. For what feels like a long time, the woman just stands there and says nothing. As though she knows I know exactly why she's here, exactly what she's going to say. And even though I do, it takes me some time to register the thing she is carrying, the pole. Only now do I see the modifiable collar sticking out its lowered end.

I do not imagine the contents of her breadbin or the providence of her Christian name. I have only a second to think, and in that second, I think: things are never so immense when they happen as they were in my head. And so the woman warden asks me if I am who I am.

'Yes,' I say. I'm ready.

'I'm afraid I've received a complaint,' she says, but she doesn't sound very afraid. She sounds like she's tired of being at work. She sounds like she just wants to go home for the day. 'I believe you were involved in an incident last week, along the village bird walk . . .'

Now she hesitates, perhaps giving me a chance to chip in, but I don't. Behind me in the hallway, I picture the clutter of fallen coats, wellington boots, cockle shells, driftwood, plastic bags, woollen scarves. I wonder has she noticed your muddy paw prints on the flat-weave rug. I wonder if she thinks I'm the strange man the fat woman told her I'd be.

'. . . in which a local boy and his pet were both injured . . .' she finishes.

Now my fists jump to a white knuckle grip on the door frame. I register at once the gravity of the thing she has just said. For perhaps the first time in my life, my internal metronome is not several beats behind. It is on beat; I am unbeaten. My heels dig into the welcome mat, the not-actually-welcome-at-all mat. 'HE DID NOT BITE THE BOY,' I say, and she sighs. She sighs with all the unstilted force of several years of dwindling job satisfaction. And I say it again.

'He did not bite the little boy,' I say, but already the strength is gone from my voice. Because maybe you did bite the boy. I can't remember. Maybe your teeth grazed his hand in the scuffle, even if you didn't mean it. Maybe I can't remember because I don't want to.

Life never misses an opportunity to upscuttle us, I think. Life likes to tell us it told us so.

'I'm charged with the authority to seize your animal,' the woman warden says, 'and to detain it until such a time as a decision's reached on its behalf.'

'He isn't here,' I tell her. 'He's with a friend.' I'm ready. I've had five days to fear this, to prepare. I've learned my lines by heart. I've locked you in the bedroom wardrobe and turned the radio up loud to muffle your discombobulated hollering. Now she's thinking, so I go on.

'I haven't been well,' I say, 'I've been bed-ridden all weekend. So I haven't been able to walk him and he's staying with a friend until I'm back on my feet.'

She's still thinking. Is she thinking she can hear a smothered sort of woofing? Is she trying to make out whether it's coming from inside the house or somewhere in the distance, down the street, an adjacent building?

'He didn't bite the boy.' I say again, quietly, I implore. If I straightened my spine to its fullest, I'd be half the height of the pole taller than the woman warden, or thereabouts. But because I'm bent like a man in a pillory, we are standing almost exactly eye to eye.

'Okay,' she says, clearly, carefully. 'Here's what's going to happen. You'll collect him tonight and I'll come back first thing tomorrow. I'll take a full statement, your version of events.' I'm nodding, nodding, nodding.

'If you don't hand him over to me without fuss, I'll have a warrant to search the premises.'

She turns to go. The gate swings. I expect she'll leave it to bang, but she doesn't. She stops and turns around. She fiddles with the faulty handle until she's solved its knack. Now the latch clicks softly into place and the sound of the woman warden's footsteps become the sound of her growling engine. And I stand on the coarse brush of the not-actually-welcome-at-all mat, and wait. I wait until her engine has dissolved into the day. Now there's only your muffled barking, the radio pealing diddly-eye music, the dinging of a metal rung against the village flagpole, the soft rap and roar of the restive sea.

White sliced pan, I think, and a name like Orla or Gráinne or Margaret.

As I open the wardrobe door, you topple out head first and I catch you up. You seem to have forgotten it was me who locked you in there. You grunt your greeting grunt. Gratefully you beat your stumpy tail against the carpet.

—

Tonight, I do not dream. I sleep in spells, waking every few hours at different stages of the night, as if there were different stages of the night as there are the day, as if for a meal or a walk or a radio programme. But in the dark, there's nothing.

I go to the bathroom and stand on the tiles to cool my feet. I stand over the toilet bowl and try to piss. But I don't need to piss, and so it only makes my bladder ache. You get up too. You lie in the hall outside the beaded curtain. You wait for me. I wait for the morning.

And as we wait we listen to my father's house, and as we wait and listen, I realise that the rats are gone. I cannot remember them going or say whether it exactly coincided with you, but I realise I haven't seen them scurrying the perimeter of the yard, whiskers brushing the stone fence, or heard their scratching against the skirting boards, their affrays inside the roof, not for weeks and weeks and weeks. Standing on the cold tiles in the middle of the night, I realise my spate of rats is ended.

At last, it's morning enough to get up. I cast the bed covers off. I put my clothes and shoes on.

—

It's Tuesday. But there'll be no trip to town today, no post office.

Instead I'm walking from room to room, slow but purposeful. I'm surveying all the flaccid things which fill my rooms. They churn up pictures in my head but the pictures only smudge together, intermingle into brown. If you take more than two colours and blend them, they always make brown, a hundred different yet similar shades. Now I pick up thing after thing after thing. A margarine tub full of incense sticks, a pottery zeppelin, a lamp without a lampshade. These are my father's things. I've never used, never needed them.

Now I draw two columns in my mind. On the right, there is Everything That Doesn't Matter. On the left, there is Everything That Does. Now I start to divvy up all of this stuff which isn't mine but for which I am responsible. And you follow my slow steps, look each way I look, sit at my feet every time I stop. There's a flake of something pale stuck to the wet of your nose. It looks like an infinitesimal communion wafer. It mocks the seriousness of your face, the worried tilt of your head. I knock it off.

'It's okay,' I tell you, 'it'll be okay.'

In the kitchen, I set the switch on the kettle to boil. I lean against the work-top. Already there's such a compendium of items bulging against my temples. The right column's an abstract smush, whereas the left is almost empty. I try to remember item by item, but before the kettle has tripped its switch, I realise there's hardly anything worth crouching down to lift. Hardly anything worth lugging the length of the laneway. Hardly anything worth its weight in expended petrol as we drive. I realise that all these particles of matter don't matter, that not one is capable of expressing grief as I abandon it. Down the blue rope, from our sit-spot amongst the pebbles, do you remember the lichens, limpets, barnacles, periwinkles, anemones? The sea pinks and chamomile? Do you remember the rocks? Now remember how everything clings to them, how every surrounding life-form must hold fast to the nearest solid thing in the modest hope it will sustain them. Like the pea tendrils to their dead sticks, like me and my unfeeling objects.

We're back in the bedroom when the first smidges of dawn illumine the toadflax. See how its leaves and flowers have dried up and died back, as if overnight. Now it's discoloured into umber, wilted into paper. I sit in the rocking chair beside the fireplace. The grate is empty but for some twigs lost from the jackdaw's nest. I rock.

To the right of my mind, there're the draught snake and the board games, the ash stump and the rag rugs. There're the souvenir plates; the stupid plates from places the world over but not one place I've ever been and not one plate I've ever carried home with me. They follow the trail of a life lived before I was born. The only places I've ever been are in the books I can't bring either. To the right, it's just card and wood and wool, and the house is just plaster and brick and board, and it's a sad place, don't you think it's sad? And it didn't give birth to me and it isn't my mother. It is inert, immoveable. Whereas I am alive, unbound. We are alive, unbound.

My mother is dead. I always knew from the twist in my father's face, from his fundamental coldness, that she had died and bequeathed him a tragedy with which to define himself for the rest of his years. And me, of course. I was paramount to his tragedy. Now I go to the door of the shut-up-and-locked room and I stand outside fingering the handle. I look down to the draught snake and I look up to the cracks in the ceiling plaster. I feel as though there's something I was going to say, but it escapes me. And so, I go back to the rocking chair.

To the left of my brain compendium, there are a few practical items: underpants and the camping cooker, kibble and gas, my father's slippers, a pebble jar, the low chair and the football, your precious food bowl. To the left, there is you. Of course there is you.

Now you hop into my lap. And together, we rock.

'It's okay,' I tell you, 'it'll be okay.'

falter

We are driving, driving, driving.

Over hillslopes and humpback bridges, through loose chippings and potholes wide as children's paddling pools and deep as old people's graves. Past lavender hedges, betting shops, sports grounds. Past countless closed doors behind which are countless uncaring strangers, their lives going on and on and on, relentlessly. We are heading inland, keeping to the back roads as much as possible. You are looking out the rear window where the view is best, or perching on the passenger seat with your maggot pressed to the air vents. What do you smell? Fox spray and honeysuckle, pine martens and stinkhorns, seven different kinds of sap? Riding in the car is like watching a neverending reel at a wraparound cinema, complete with the surround-sound of engine putter, the piped scent of petrol fumes and passing countryside.

We are driving, driving, driving.

And the wraparound car screen is reeling off monkey puzzle trees and peeling eucalyptus, parish halls and handball alleys. Here's a pair of running shoes tied by the laces and slung over a phone wire above the road. Here's a steel grain silo at the edge of a farmyard, nose pointed to the moon like a shoddy rocket. Now here's a crucifix set in concrete with a vase full of shrivelled stalks in front, a roadside memorial shrine. The plaque's too small to read but what it means is that some stranger died here, on this most seemingly non-treacherous of corners with a cow field either side. What it means is that even the tattered verges are depositories of celebration and devastation in unequal measure.

We are driving, driving, driving.

And every time the engine stops, you expect we've reached the end. But each stop is never an arrival, just another pause along the way. A snack, a walk, a smoke, a sleep, and off again. Now we piss in the hedgerows, side by side. Shit in the dykes under the cover of dark, side by side. I understand you're confused, that you had settled into a routine and now it's hard to fathom the new nook where your food bowl lives, the altered angle of your safe space and the way the view is ever rushing, changing. It's hard for me too. I hurt to the core of my bones from trying to sleep in the rolled-back driver's seat. I still haven't found an efficient way to fold my limbs, nor decided which is the more comfortable side to lean on. My body snaps and creaks louder than the radio and I tend to nod off on dual carriageways. The car wavers onto the white lines and the cat's eyes bonk beneath our wheels. BONKbonk, BONKbonk, BONKbonk, and I wake to the red twigs of the dogwood shrubs clawing our paintwork. But it's not only sleeping that's hard, it's everything. It's hard to learn anew how to make it through from dawn to dark without all of the props and pointers inside my father's house. Without plant-watering, yard-pottering, chair-rocking and channel-zapping. I expected it would be exciting; I expected that the freedom from routine was somehow greater than the freedom to determine your own routine. I wanted to get up in the morning and not know exactly what I was going to do that day. But now that I don't, it's terrifying. Now nothing can be assumed, now everything's ill-considered, and if I spend too long thinking it makes my eyes smart and molars throb. I tense myself into a stone and forget how to breathe. I pull the car to the side of the road and put my flashers on. I list aloud all the things that are good and all the reasons I must go on. Glass pebbles are good, games of football on deserted strands, oil refineries by night, jumble shop windows, gingernuts, broken buoys, nicotine, fields of flowering rape. And I must go on because of you. Now it's okay; I can breathe again. And on we go. I put distance in front of my face and my body has no choice but to follow, unthinkingly, and your body too. Is this how people cope, I wonder. Is this how everybody copes?

We are driving, driving, driving.

And the wraparound car screen is reeling off fields and fields and fields, of wheat and oats and barley which have all died now, and in death, turned to gold. Torn filaments of their gold blows to the ditches, sticks in the prickles, dangles and glitters like premature tinsel.

We are driving, driving, driving.

And the car is our house now, home. The boot is our attic. The loose chippings are our floorboards. The sun roof is our balcony. The back roads and hinterlands are our ceaselessly surging view.

—

My father didn't teach me to drive until I was in my forties and he'd started to suffer from gouty feet. It was the twinge in each gigantic foot that caused him to foresee a time when he'd require a personal chauffeur. I used to grant him nobler reasons, now I see this was the only one. Learning to drive was the most gruelling thing I've ever done. I mastered the simultaneous operation of pedals, gear-stick, steering wheel, indicator and mirror easily enough. I trained alone by patting my head and rubbing my belly. The difficult part was sitting in a confined space with my father looking on as I made mistake after mistake after mistake. He'd bellow instructions and mutter and smoke in the passenger seat. He'd slam his heels to the floor every time he feared I'd fail to break, every time I grazed the undergrowth because the passenger window was obscured by smoke. He'd grasp the door handle and squeeze so viciously his fist left a dent in the supple upholstery. Because I was allowed barely any opportunities to practise, it took me three years before I was confident enough to sit with a licensing official in the passenger seat instead of my father, before I obtained my first ever document of identification. The official was a bald man with librarian spectacles. He barely spoke and appeared to be immensely distressed even before he climbed into the car, which set me somewhat irrationally at ease. I imagined he had a wicked wife who had dramatically walked out on him just before he came to work. His state of shock was such that he overlooked every mistake and carelessly passed me. It was a Monday and the date was September 19th. That was the day I became a person; I still believe I owe it to a licensing official's unfaithful wife.

—

The season of falling foliage kicks off with falling rain instead. And a wind so ferocious it shakes down leaves that aren't yet dead enough to drop. It wrenches away stalks still green to the tips, still being fed by mother trunk, and off they blow. Somewhat less decorously, old, fat and rotted branches belly-flop into the electricity supply lines. Now all the surrounding houses are swamped by dark. The people inside are eating their dinner out of yoghurt pots and going to bed un-showered. They're lying awake listening to the plip-plip-plop of petits pois and chicken drippers musically defrosting. It's a power cut, but then I don't suppose you ever understood where the small ceiling suns in each of my rooms came from in the first place. I don't suppose you ever pondered the working of the magic switches.

Now there aren't any ceiling suns. I used to care so much about incandescence and now all I have is a bag of tea-candles and two torches. I forgot to bring spare batteries. I forgot lots of things. I remember them gradually as we go. Now home is only one room big, I'm surprised by how much stuff we still seem to need, and by how much rubbish we are creating. I sort through our rubbish, apportion it into bags small enough to shove through the slot of a public bin. And every time I see one, we stop and shove, scattering little clues of our passing behind us as we go.

The car bounces, rolls and jitters like a steel orb in a pinball machine, with no right way to go and no particular destination. We round an everlasting succession of hairpin bends, bump through ten thousand bottomless ruts. Every day we see abandoned traffic cones and signposts heralding road works which never materialise. Now the ditches are distended by blackberry brambles, ferns, nettles, fuchsia, knapweed, elderberries and rose hips, so overgrown they narrow the road to a single lane for travelling both directions. See how the hedge-trimming tractor has left a trail of massacred vegetation in its wake. Flowers with their throats slit and berries chopped, popped.

But between our windscreens, everything is in its right place. My bed-things, a single duvet and a feather pillow, are pummelled into the cranny below the passenger dash where once you cowered. The duvet cover is midnight blue with a motif of stars and spaceships, a coffee stain somewhere, a splodge of toothpaste somewhere else. On the passenger seat, there's the camping cooker, a flask and a carrier bag of assorted snacks: sesame sticks, granny apples, comice pears and gingernuts, of course.

The back seat belongs to you. Your food bowl and water dish on the floor, the low chair wedged between back and front seats, the tasselled and chequer-boarded blanket slung over its grimy wicker. Your football, gnawed and deflated, is always on the loose somewhere, roving and jumping to the motion of the hairpin bends and bottomless ruts. The boot is three-quarters filled with gas canisters, blankets, toilet paper, a sack of emergency kibble, two gallon drums of washing water. The pockets and compartments are bursting with a muddle of things both useless and useful, from crab shells and bass lures to wet wipes, pencils, loose change, a tooth-brush and my penknife. Laid across the sill between the back seat and the glass, there are the tomatoes, twenty or twenty-five at least. I picked every last one before leaving. Then they were still pea green and hard as passion fruit; now they are almost ripe. The tomatoes bring out your inner thief. You can smell their exact phase of ripeness and as soon as I'm not looking, you snatch and pop and swallow. Whenever I leave a window lowered, the last of summer's drowsy wasps sneak in and fumble between the snipped and shrunken tomato branches. With weary antennae they fondle the fruit, feeling out tiny fissures through which to siphon juice. You snap at the wasps, irritated. They sting you in the mouth and your upper gums expand and lift off your teeth into a Cheshire cat grin.

Every dawn, we leave the car to walk, to follow your directionless route of indecipherable landmarks. Over a drumlin and a bog, past a saltwater lake and a shooting sanctuary, through a patch of magic mushrooms and a fairy circle. Now here's an alien thing which might be a lizard and might be a stranded newt. You lick its dead belly. What does it feel like? Like boiled, cooled leather, like licking your own tongue back again? You learn each new stopping spot detail by detail, by its symphony of smell, and never by its signpost. Still I read them out to you. BUNRAFFY, the signposts say, DOWRASH, CREGGISH, LISFINNY. And every dusk, I place a row of tea-candles along the dash and watch until the longest-lasting wick is drowned by wax. Spit spit hiss. This is our power cut.

—

They are mostly villages, the signposted places, some hardly even that. Did my father realise every last one of them was inland? And if he did, what does it mean? But meaning doesn't exist unless you look for it, and so I mustn't look, and so things will not mean.

After several villages we stop at the sight of a post office. 'Back in a minute,' I tell you.

I slide my savings book and driver's licence beneath the safety glass to a girl with an armload of copper bangles. I ask her how much I'm allowed to withdraw at once. She says 'What?' three times before she hears me properly, and each time I repeat myself, I feel smaller and smaller and smaller.

I drive from the village until we are between cow fields again. Now I pull over and rummage in the rubbish parcel for last night's sardines tin. I rinse it into the ditch with the washing water from our gallon drum. The lid is only peeled back a fraction, just enough space to fork the fish out. I dry it with a tissue and fold my notes and poke them in. Now I hide the tin in the kibble sack and lock the kibble sack in the boot.

———

A village becomes a town when somebody builds a super-market, a library, a secondary school, a third or fourth or fifth pub, a retirement home. And we are avoiding them, the towns.

Here's a thatched and ruined cottage, a couple of slime-walled farmhouses surrounded by shit-caked yards. Here come the featureless bungalows, each with a couple of gar-den ornaments distributed about their neatly trimmed lawns.

Squirrels, gnomes, wild cats, wishing wells, nymphs. Here's one with a stone eagle atop either gatepost, painted an inauspicious shade of peach and turned in to face one another across the cattle grid. Now here's an electronic gate with a keypad mounted to a post. At the far end of the extensive driveway, see the unfinished palace. Naked plaster and a lake of mud where grass-seeds ought to have sprouted. Count the front-facing windows. There are no fewer than twelve, plus three dormers and a skylight.

You can guess the size of a village by the grandiosity of its grotto. Blonde Marys, black Marys. Marys in blue, Marys in white, but Mary always draped in rosary beads, standing on a serpent and holding her palms open around the height of her crotch.

This village is a row of stuck-together houses, just enough to call a terrace, and the same again on the opposite side of the street. They are pebbledashed and painted beige, cream, wheat and buff. What smells are wafting from them? Soup and gas and bleach and bread and tea and turf? As our car passes in the dark, we see clearly into their brightly lit rooms. We see a china tea set displayed on a dresser, trophies in a trophy cabinet, cooking knives planted in a block and the steam that rises from an invisible saucepan on an invisible hob.

In almost every village there's a shop, and almost every village shop is attached to a pub with a sign over the door bearing the full name of the original proprietor: JAMES

O'SHEA, they say, JOHN T. MURPHY. The shelves are dusty. The merchandise is bizarrely organised. A box of powdered custard sits next to a can of engine oil, which sits next to a tin of marrowfat peas, which sits next to a tub of nappy powder. In the stationery section, there are multicoloured elastic bands but no red biros, and greeting cards for a Holy Communion but none for a Happy Birthday. Now these are the only places we stop to shop. They never stock exactly what I think we want, but there's always something close enough to compromise.

And I like the cramped proportions. I like the cold and clammy air, the surplus of useless clutter; it puts me in mind of my father's house.

Tonight it's JACK P. RUSSELL, and I can see over the counter into the part that is a pub. It's dim and dank and quiet there. It makes me crave a hot, sweet whiskey and a packet of salty nibs. Now I drop my batch loaf, chicken noodle soup and bottled water into the snack bag on the passenger seat. Now I go in through the pub door and rest my hands against the bar.

The shopkeeper is the landlord. He tells me it'll take a minute and he'll bring it out once the kettle's boiled. I can tell he was butch as a youth, but now he's sagged like a lumpy old sofa and the tattoos on his forearms are engulfed by body hair. I go back to the car and harness you. I tie the leash's handle to the leg of a picnic bench and together we sit beneath the patio heater. The barman brings my drink and nuts and a cardboard mat printed with the picture of a beer I haven't ordered. Tonelessly, insincerely, he wishes me well, and closes the door. It's a soft night, rainless and calm.

I sip slow and you catch peanuts in your mouth. How smart you are not to miss a single one. I'd have thought the partial eyelessness would affect your depth of vision, but apparently not. I sip, you chew and we watch the sycamore's crashed helicopters dithering in the dirt, trying desperately to lift into the air again, ignoring their broken rotors.

The villages we pass through and sleep by, whose marrowfat peas and corned beef we purchase, whose pubs we sometimes sit outside; I read out their names to you. DYSSERT, the signposts say, SUCK, BINDADA, TOSSIT. They are, all of them, middle-of-nowhere countries, left-behind countries, dead-end countries, no countries at all, really. They are sad places. Don't you think they're sad? But then I suppose this is how I always expected them to be. But then I suppose I always expect everything to be sad until proven otherwise.

—

A boy, a waifish boy with prematurely skimpy hair, asks me to stand by the gate with my arms outstretched so his cows will know which way to go. He's carrying a switch, twirling it between his fingers like a majorette's baton. He caught us walking through his field, his father's field. I thought he'd ask me where I came from, why I'm parting a path through his beet. Instead he asked if I'd help him herd.

They are black and white and mud-caked. There are twenty, twenty-five. I can tell from the swollen udders that they're milking stock, heifers.

I tie you to a fence post and stand beside the gate with my arms spread. From fingertip to fingertip, as long as my unstooped self. Now the cows come plundering toward us. They are disconcertingly fast for animals so thickset, so poorly streamlined. My role is to act as a human hedge, to bar the straight-ahead path so they'll know to bear round the corner toward the parlour.

The leading heifer waits until her snout is inches from my chest to swerve. I smell a puff of hot fog from her nostrils. It is sort of sweet, almost cidery. Do you smell it too? Behind me beside the fence post with your hindquarters backed into the ditch, you're unusually abashed. Now all the other heifers follow. Feel the thunder of hooves as they pass.

The boy comes last, twirling his baton. He thanks me, locks the gate behind himself. Now he follows his cows along the field boundary toward the farm.

I untie you, and as I do, I don't know why, but I feel euphoric. And you hop up and down in excitement, as though the cows were something we survived. You rush and skip into the beet again, as though you are euphoric too.

—

The radio plays, almost incessantly. I tune to the speaking station first thing. We listen to the news bulletin over and over, to the newsreaders' accentless voices. I wait for them to sneeze or sniff or clear their throats, but they never do. Every day there's a succession of experts on the radio, telling us things. Today an expert is telling us how people choose pets they feel reflect the way they see themselves, and in time, the person and pet grow to resemble one another. After the speaking is ended, I turn the volume very low and switch to the classical station.

Your maggot nose intersects the rearview mirror. Your head's held erect to catch smells breezing through the opened crack of the passenger window. Your ears have fallen back and open. Inside, they're white and bald and twisted. What do you think of the classical music? Of the chimes and pops and strums and biffs, of the drum rolls which mount into grand cymbal smashes? You seem to be listening, but I can't be sure.

Now I glance at the side of my own face in the mirror's foreground, and I wonder have we grown to resemble one another, as we're supposed to. On the outside, we are still as black and gnarled as nature made us. But on the inside, I feel different somehow. I feel animalised. Now there's a wildness inside me that kicked off with you.

—

The sun's out. It saturates the distant dual carriageway with watery quivers. Inside our shell of steel and glass, sheltered from the nipping autumn wind, warmed by the sun and lulled by the bump and sway, I can feel myself pitching toward sleep. Now our wheels err onto the cat's eyes and the BONKbonk wakes me up. I roll the window down and hang my elbow into the cleansing car wind. I keep my hand poised to spring into a shield should you attempt to leap out at a pigeon or a cat or some other piece of prey, into the whoosh and crush of the speeding road.

We've already seen enough dead creatures since the driving began, of all shapes and phases. From creatures still drenched by internal fluids to creatures pancaked and sun-dried to a ship's biscuit of their former selves. Do you see that neat little pile of mush, no more than a balled rag in a puddle of scarlet? It's either a burly rat or a baby rabbit, impossible to tell. Now here comes a fox with both its eyeballs popped. See the peculiar angle of its dislocated tail bone and the place where a snapped rib has prodded free. Do you remember the tortoiseshell kitten, how it wore a dainty collar and the dainty collar's dainty bell had been pressed into its throat like a dainty cookie cutter? Do you remember the badger, the badger who forgot to use its designated underpass? He was too sturdy for properly squashing; he lay supine on the side of the new dual carriageway, as though napping.

Hares and mice, wagtails and rooks, squirrels and mink. Every kind of creature every kind of killed. Eviscerated and decapitated, lobotomised and disembowelled. Sometimes the only remains are a puff of uprooted plumage, pale down dancing in the whoomph of air from passing vehicles, no sign of the bird from which it was bashed loose. The people inside the grim reaper cars don't care, they have places to go, they keep going. Now we circle a roundabout and circle again, and as we circle, I watch the traffic. I wonder where everyone is going. And I wonder if any of the road-kill creatures actually wanted to die and threw themselves beneath the speeding wheels. A lethargic swallow who couldn't bear the prospect of flying all the way back to Africa again. An insomniac hedgehog who couldn't stand the thought of lying awake all winter with no one to talk to.

I indicate, pull onto another dual carriageway. Up ahead, there's an indiscernible thing obstructing the traffic. For at least a hundred yards, vehicles queue to pass the obstruction in single file. We creep closer. I squint into the sun, trying to make out what the fuss is. You press your face between front seats and squint with me. There's a car and a motorbike pulled awkwardly into the hard shoulder. The car has its flashers flashing, its hazard-triangle propped inside the yellow line. Now we see it, lying in the middle of the road. A swan, a mute swan. It looks like an offcut of organza, crumpled around the edges, twitching. As we pass we see its long neck has buckled into its body like a folding chair. We see its wings are tucked back as if the tar is liquid and the swan is swimming.

There are two men and a woman in the road. One man

is standing on the tar, the other is directing the traffic. The woman is kneeling down beside the swan. I think she is crying, she seems to be crying, and this makes me suddenly angry. I think of all the other creatures we've seen since we set out. I think of the rat, the fox, the kitten, the badger. I think of the jackdaw, did you see the jackdaw? We passed it in the queue to pass the swan. Its beak was cracked open, its brains squeeged out. Why didn't anybody stop for the jackdaw? Because the swan looks like a wedding dress, that's why. Whereas the jackdaw looks like a bin bag. Because this is how people measure life.

From the radio, an expert is telling us how the extinct and endangered animals and birds and fish must be brought back, or the planet will slowly fall to pieces, bit by bit by bit by bit.

—

We stop at a petrol station with a sign for a public toilet. I find the bag containing my soiled socks and jocks, I squash it small as it will squash.

'Back in a minute,' I tell you, even though I know, all going to plan, it will take ten at least. Sometimes I take liberties with the things I tell you. I know you understand this phrase means I'm leaving and not bringing you along, but every time I leave I guess you don't understand when I'll be back again, or if I will be back at all. You may be able to smell time, but you cannot tell it.

There's nobody else inside the gents. There's hot in the hot tap and soap in the soap dispenser. It's the powdery sort. It comes out in feeble coughs. It slows me down. Still I've managed to wash everything up to the final sock when the door swings and a man comes in. I don't see what manner of man; I bow my head as he passes. I feel his eyes travel down my plait and across my hunch to settle on the gap between sinks where my underwear's heaped. Now he goes into a cubicle. I hear the slide and clack of the bolt, and a second later, an ugly, jagged splash. Now I squeeze the heap, slop it back into the bag and make for the car park.

A mile or so along the road, I pull in and drape my washing over the rim of the back seat. You examine my socks as though they're somehow exciting. You sniff my under-pants crotch by crotch until I shout at you to stop.

'You're horrible,' I tell you, but I'm laughing.

—

It's the oak that goes first; the beech that holds on for longest.

Last night, the in-between leaves dropped altogether and at once, as though a herd of nocturnal giraffes came sweeping through, stretching their prodigious necks into the treetops, stripping the branches bare and then scattering the stripped leaves over their footprints so no one will know who to blame. This morning, now freed, the stripped leaves skip and soar and shapeshift. They scuttle like pygmy shrews, flutter like common chaffinches. They spread across the road and contort into letters of the alphabet, miniature whirlwinds, religious apparitions. Did you see it? Did you see the Jesus face? They always look so much like something else from a distance, and up close, I'm always disappointed when they transfigure back into leaves, just leaves. Now I'm snatching the air because it's supposed to be lucky to catch a falling leaf. I'm jumping, jumping, jumping and still I can't get any. But they're landing on my boulderish back and sticking to my greasy hair, and maybe this is lucky too.

It is the most absolute of autumns. See the tractor-lawnmowers riding out for the last cut of the year. Smell the freshly severed stalks. The slow-to-start summer clung on throughout September, but now it must be October, or nearly October. How long have we been driving? A month, at least. Six weeks, maybe. Soon I think I'll need another post office.

What else is wafting through the air vents? Wind-fallen crabapples abandoned to rot? Bonfire smoke and rowan berries? Here's a rusted iron water pump, handleless and unpumpable, so there's no need to stop and test it, to try and fill my drums. Here's a fugitive straw bale lodged in the ditch brambles, estranged from its fellows still clustered in their field like a herd of motionless highland cattle: oblong and exquisitely brindled. Now these are last year's stacked point-to-point jumps, birch twigs bundled, cast aside. The cotoneaster and its waxwing in his Zorro eye mask, and everywhere the blackberries are undersized and inedible after the superfluity of summer rain. See how every berry is the runt of the briar's litter, rotting in its receptacle.

Here's another grain truck. We've spent the whole of harvest season getting stuck behind strange farming contraptions, listening to the clatter of threshers and shearers and spinners as we drive. But now it's only grain trucks, a new truck round every corner, and every truck sending pale chaff flurrying from their open tops into our windscreen. I never overtake them. Why bother, what's the rush? It's good to be able to roll a cigarette and hang my elbow out the window, to watch the pumps and bales and jumps pass as I smoke. See in the distance, the mustard-coloured apex of a hillslope perfectly centred inside a V of greenery? It doesn't matter what month; it's exactly the time of year at which everything is mustard-crested. It's the most absolute of autumns. But soon, slow, autumn will lose its radiance. Autumn will be threshed and chopped and spun back to brown and bole and dun.

Now all the ditch's tiny celebrations and devastations proliferate and fill me, buoy me, and in this way, the fear subsides, to some degree. I realise that you were not born with a predetermined capacity for wonder, as I'd believed. I realise that you fed it up yourself from tiny pieces of the world. I realise it's up to me to follow your example and nurture my own wonder, morsel by morsel by morsel.

See here, a banana skin skewered onto the spike of a

fence. Do you remember the walk up the road through the forest and the banana skin which lay by the refinery gates below the intercom? Remember how the world was then that small. See how, now, it's a limitless expanse of liberated bananas.

—

At last, a village shop that stocks the right batteries.

I can see where the old fireplace has been shoddily boarded up. And the bench which stood in front is pushed against the wall and piled with multi-packs of toilet paper. The grocer's next to my father's house used to have an open fire in winter, way back when I was a boy, long before the era of tags for measuring loyalty and robotic checkouts. Today I load up on batteries and jumbo oats. I take an eight-pack of fish fingers from the freezer for our supper and balance a bag of barley sugars on top.

The tall, concrete counter is paved with broken tiles and I can see the borders of lost coppers twinkling between the cracks. The man behind the counter is easily old enough to have lit fires inside his shop. He asks a lot of questions. He asks if I'm just passing through and where did I come from. Am I from there originally and what was the weather like when I left. He eyeballs my toilet paper and batteries and fish fingers and barley sugars as though he's never seen them before, as though his own goods are suddenly as alien to him as I am. Both his palms are laid against the broken tiles and he gives no indication that he's going to charge me until I answer.

'Yes,' I say, 'the south coast, yes, and it was dry, but windy.'

Now he starts to chunter about the prevailing souther-lies as though they're somehow my fault. He doesn't like the wind, he says. It makes a howling noise in the telephone wires and keeps him awake at night. Now he forgets to be nosy and starts telling me of his struggle against sleep.

'The older you get the tireder you are,' he says, 'but the harder it is to go to sleep.' He shakes his head sadly, and I picture him lying in a dark room with wood-panelled walls and a china chamber pot under the bed, and I recognise him as a person who is lonely as opposed to solitary, who did not choose to be on his own but involuntarily lost people until he was. Now he digs his nails into the counter's cracks.

By the time I get back into the car, the fish fingers have started to defrost. There's a soggy patch on the cardboard, just underneath Captain Birdseye's lapel. And you lick the lapel, wagging.

—

Tonight, the windows fog. The fan grumbles and the wipers moan. It's raining and we're lost. The bulb of the left headlamp is out, and so it must seem to oncoming traffic as though our car face is winking. See how all the cars have car faces, headlamp eyes and a shiny-toothed number-plate smirk.

The road tapers into a single lane and a succession of roundabouts. Each has a signboard bearing the name of some obscure saint, and almost every second roundabout is encumbered by road works. Now the workmen have gone home and left their machinery slumbering for the night. Portable barricades and flashing arrows draw us into yet more erroneous detours and abandoned traffic cones. Do you remember the traffic cone buried in the bay? When the tide went out, it poked up as far as its third band. Then when the tide came in, it was again submerged and I'd forget that it was there at all. Still buried, just out of sight. I'd again forget that things continue to exist even though I cannot see them.

A wrong exit off the roundabout of St Gobnait brings us to the outskirts of a city, a former village subsumed by metropolis. We pass a Mary in a perspex box beside an ATM machine. Now, on a street too dark to see the street sign, I find a couple of empty parking spaces in front of a shuttered shoe shop, an empty unit with a TO LET notice and a brightly lit fast food takeaway. I'm hungry and dreadfully need to piss, this is why we're parking. There's nobody on the street, only the lampposts plotting a passageway through the dark. Come here and let me clip your leash on. Now we leave the car and walk up the footpath and into the shadows. You sniff and raise your leg against a drainpipe and once you're finished, I bring you back. I lock you up safe with a window ajar, your water dish replenished.

'Back in a minute,' I tell you, and now I go into the take-away on my own.

I don't like urinals but there's no one else here so I hurry up and use it. I glance around the bathroom as I piss. There's a collage of old tissue glued to the ceiling. Sopped and flung, now it's dried to creased splats. It reminds me of flat fish only without the sideways eyes. Like flounder, turbot, dab, like Dover sole. Back in the over-bright restaurant, I order a coffee and two large punnets of chips from the brown man behind the till. The brown man is smiling and I notice how his smiling jaw is mottled by spots, and I realise I hadn't realised before that black skin could pimple in just the same way pink does, and I wonder if Chinese people pimple too. Now I'm fidgeting with the change in my wallet, too embarrassed to look again. I count out the exact price, take the cup I'm being handed and as I pay my fingertips brush the brown man's palm. I keep my eyes low to my cup. I see the coffee's weak and watery brown, exactly the same colour as the cashier's skin.

I wonder if the cashier sleeps at night. I wonder if, when he hears the wind in the phone wires, he thinks it sounds like a howling thing. Like a wolf or ghost.

I sit at an empty table in the empty restaurant. I wait on our chips. The chair's uncomfortably slippery, the seat of my trousers squeaks against the moulded plastic. There's a picture on the wall showing a smiling child, and the child is recommending various accoutrements to my chips. Bacon tenders, curry coleslaw, chicken nuggets. In the next picture, the child has been joined by a full set of smiling parents, and altogether they are sharing a Chicken Family Box. Now I look away and out the window. I remind myself that they are just models told to pose, that in reality, they aren't even related. From where I'm sitting, I can see through the restaurant's glass front to where our car is parked. I can see the silhouette of your head and ears and neck, your crushed velveteen paws resting against the dashboard, the glint of the tag on your collar, the glint of your maggot nose and the glint of your lonely peephole. Out the restaurant's glass front and through the car windscreen, I can see all of my family at once, glinting all over. And suddenly you seem so small and faraway, and I realise we haven't been separated for more than a few moments in weeks and weeks. Since the beginning of autumn, since the driving began.

'SIR!'

The brown man startles me. I take the paper bag and bolt through the door without looking up again. Inside the car, the smell of chips is deliciously suffocating. We eat so fast we wound our tongues. Now you lick the grease from the empty punnets. You propel them up and down the back seat, and up and down again.

—

From the radio, an expert is telling us how most of our waters are unlicensed, as though they ought to be licensed, as though every grounded thing is licensed. The trees and bogs and heather and hills and mountains. And now I remember that you should be licensed. I remember I never licensed you.

—

We sleep in gateways, a new gateway every night.

And every evening, you watch the wraparound cinema screen until the mulch and stretch has warped into our lacklustre reflection. Until, in the arid light, the most familiar things grow sinister. The roving football becomes a mannequin's head and the sound of the tomatoes softly nudging one another becomes a mutinous mumbling. Now you cave into the hollow of the seat and rest your beard against the blanket. You sigh, laboriously, and I take your laborious sigh as a cue. I begin my look-out for a tangled boreen with a gateway: a left-behind gateway, a dead-ended gateway, a safe-seeming gateway. The gates are mostly welded metal slats. Sometimes scabbed by rust, sometimes wired into an electric fence and ominously droning. Now here's a gate which is hardly a gate at all, just a symbolic barrier. It's slapdashed together with disintegrating pallets, chicken wire, the disparate pieces of a fallen tree. Here's penny-cress, angelica and a hare over in the field. Stiff as a garden ornament. Now it barrels off, breaks into a succession of long vaults over the stubble of harvested grain, between the bales. Did you see it, did you see the hare?

I shunt the car a little back, a little forth, a little back, a little forth. Tonight, it takes forever to get properly tucked in from the road. I feel the unstable ground caving beneath the wheels and I wonder if we'll be able to get out again in the morning. Now you're up from the seat hollow and standing to attention. You're making your excitement noise. This is your favourite part of the evening, my favourite part of the evening too. Now I let you out to explore the night's gateway and its nebulous surrounds. While you are exploring, I fetch our groceries from the boot and set up the gas cooker on the flattest part of the bonnet. I take out the saucepan, plates, fork, spoon, tin opener. Tonight it's peas, baked beans and spaghetti hoops, a French baguette with orange cheese and marmalade. It takes a couple of tries to ignite the hob in the wind. I pull the side of my cardigan taut to shelter the lighter's flame. On rainy nights, I do this on the passenger seat with the door open. I know it's careless, even dangerous. The first time I lit the gas cooker inside the car, I made sure you were outside. But nothing happened, and I've grown reckless with the cooker since. Sometimes I don't bother to push the passenger door open and roll the window down. In this way, the heat's trapped inside and our car home remains warm as a burrow for much of the night.

But this evening it's dry and only gently gusty. Blue jags spring out from the hob and contentedly purr. I always buy the ring-pull cans and cook everything together in one pan, the only pan I brought. I tear fistfuls of bread from the loaf and apportion the cooked gunk between two plates. One you-sized, one toppling. Now we scoff, scoff, scoff in the name of all our missed meals.

I rinse the supper dishes and utensils in the ditch with water from a gallon drum. We are running low on washing water. I need to find a roadside pump, a stream, a public toilet. NON POTABLE the public taps say, and so I buy bottles of the mineral stuff as well. But you don't like the taste of minerals, you drink from field streams and mud puddles. Now I stack the supper things back in the boot. I parcel the rubbish. You lick your private bits in the grass. With your pointy incisors you comb the wirebrush fur of your paws and I sit on the bonnet and smoke until it's too cold to stay outside. Now I line tea-candles along the dash, open my book, prop it against the steering wheel, read to their twizzling light. And you climb into my lap and lie, semi-sleeping, with your dominant ear at half mast, your eyelid always raised to its sentinel slit. I read until the light has spat itself out.

'Time for bed,' I tell you, 'bed.'

Bed is one amongst your one hundred and sixty-five words.

Now comes sleeplessness. I wind the driver's seat back, unroll my duvet and clout my pillow into place. On my left side with feet tucked together and hands pressed between thighs: this is as close to comfortable as it comes. I lie awake and smell your malodorous snores slowly filling the air, and I wonder can you smell me as strongly. My smoky, yeasty, heinous breath. And I wonder which organ is putrefying inside me and how it generates so sickening a stench. Every morning it sits thick and fetid between the walls of the car. It's like all my bad habits are fermenting in an infernal pit below my mouth hole, rising up to taunt me when I'm fresh from sleep and at my most defenceless. Your snores are almost sweet and biscuity in comparison.

Is this what my father's house smelled like? Not garlic and coffee and cigarette smoke and bins, not the old feet sweat in his slippers, not the draught through the keyhole and cracks in the ceiling plaster, but like my heinous breath instead?

—

It's hard to find Amber Leaf in the village shops and petrol stations where we stop. Liquorice-flavour papers are even scarcer. I buy Drum instead; they always have Drum. I don't like the taste but I tear my tiny rectangles and smoke it anyway. I suppose this means that addiction has superseded sentiment now. I suppose this means I'm an addict.

—

Sometimes while we're driving, I kill the radio and we listen to the passing world instead. Most outside sounds are smothered by the rapping of raindrops against tin, sputters rising from beneath the bonnet, a ticking here and a rattle there, the scour and chump, scour and chump, scour and chump of the wipers. Sometimes a chittering magpie peals through, the panicky moo of a ravenous cow, the angry revving of an overtaking vehicle, a faraway siren and I feel a cold flush of fear. Everybody always overtakes me, do I really drive so slowly? Sometimes when I'm thinking and sometimes when I'm not thinking, my accelerator foot relaxes, retracting from its pedal so the car barely ticks along, the gears straining. Sometimes it's several miles or more before I notice my tailback.

The outer noises are important to me. It doesn't matter what form they take or how loud they are, but I need to keep them always sounding. I depend on them to gag my thoughts. My thoughts are rancorous, ruinous. They throng through me like a shoal of sharp, silver sprat whenever the outer noises aren't loud or plenty enough to keep them at bay, to keep them out of the bay, the bay of my brain. I need them most of all during the hours of sleeplessness, the only time at which I can't play the radio because it would run the car's battery flat. In the gateways by night, unless it's raining, there's little noise, and all the noises are little. But they don't sound little. Cats skulking in the hedgerows become lions. And the rustling mice they hunt, the rustling rabbits and shrews, become wildebeests and warthogs. On my left side with my feet tucked, interminably pursuing comfort, I think about my father's house; I think about my father. I analyse my regrets in unnecessary detail with unnecessary force, and I wonder how I wound up with this life, and not somebody else's. For a while, it's a topic of tantalising possibility, and then, all of a sudden, it grows sickeningly boring and I'm left with a tension headache in place of an answer. A dull pounding which runs from the blades of my shoulders to the backs of my eyeballs. When I can stand the throng of sprat no longer, this is when I start my commentary.

In the latest years of my father's life, he misplaced all of his small talk. Have I told you this already? Have I told you how, gradually, he stopped making his usual humdrum enquiries: whether the post had come yet, or if it looked like rain, or what we were having for supper that night. Maybe his mind had gone. Maybe he was an imbecile. Maybe he just didn't see the point of wasting what breath he had left on such meaningless niceties, I can understand that. Once he had completely stopped talking, that was the point at which I began to gabble. 'The postman's passed without leaving anything,' I'd say. 'It's surely going to rain soon,' I'd say. 'What do you reckon to a chop tonight?' I'd say. And now I address it all to you. You who never spoke anyway. You who misunderstands almost everything. I describe the things we pass even though nothing is interesting, even though I've already mentioned it several times over, even though I know now I sound like the imbecile.

See how each road sign has its own name. JOHN, this one's called. It's because the county council men abuse their spray paint when they are bored. Now MARK, JIM, R153, now JOHN again, or maybe a different JOHN. See how the farmers abuse their paint too. They spray the sheep so they can recognise members of their flock when they're dotted across the hillside. But the damp air disperses the paint through their wool and the sheep end up pink and blue almost all over, like the sort of gigantic cuddly toys people win at fairground stalls. See a faded teddy bear slumped in the upstairs window of the tumbledown farmhouse, back turned, shunning the view. Now see the nasturtiums. The leaves are like tiny green parasols blown inside-out and the flowers are terrifically garish. In every village we pass through, see how they are everywhere, how they fill every gap in every wall, every crack in every path.

The nasturtiums have it figured out, how survival's just a matter of filling in the gaps between sun up and sun down. Boiling kettles, peeling potatoes, laundering towels, buying milk, changing lightbulbs, rooting wet mats of pubic hair out of the shower's plughole. This is the way people survive, by filling one hole at a time for the flightiest of temporary gratifications, over and over and over, until the season's out and they die off anyway, wither back into the wall or path, into their dark crevasse. This is the way life's eaten away, expended by the onerous effort of living itself.

Now, I'm gabbling, I'm sorry. I catch sight of you in the

rearview mirror. You're watching the side of my face as I speak. Head tilted left, you look perplexed. I know you don't understand, and so I bellow a sentence made up entirely of your words.

'WALKIES, BICKIES, BEDTIME,' I bellow, 'ALL GONE, WAIT, FOOTBALL, BOLD,' I bellow, 'SPEAK, ONE EYE, SPEAK.'

—

It seems almost incredible, how far we can drive in a country so small, without ever really reaching anywhere. But then I am slow, I suppose. I forget I am slow.

How many weeks now? What day is it, what month? Sometimes you look so much as though you're about to talk, as though you're trying so hard to answer me. October, of course. Now it must be October. See the primary school with paper chains cut into witch shapes and strung across the windows. See the white pillowcases slung over balloons and hung by their heads from the trees at the edge of the playground.

Soon the grocery shops will be selling fat pumpkins too floury-fleshed for eating, monkey nuts roasted in their knobbled shells and elasticated plastic faces with the eyes cut out. Soon it will be the time of year when it's vaguely acceptable to be crepuscular, to be wonkety.

I don't know where we are, and I wonder if I took the handbrake off would the car remember for itself and roll us home again to the footpath outside the terrace of the village that hums, but I haven't the courage to put it to the test.

I stopped following the board game weeks ago, now I've stopped reading the signposts too. Even though we're lost, it seems as if you're at ease in our car home now, as if your safe space has spread from door to door and devoured the entire seat. Now our backyard is the limitless countryside. Now our neighbours are grazing stock, hedgerow birds, hibernating mammals, an infinity of insects. No longer are we creatures of routine; now we're creatures of possibility. I think of all the years I spent living in so many rooms and how I used to believe I needed a different room for everything. A room for preparing a meal, another for sitting down to eat in, another again for shitting the digested meal out and flushing it away through a network of pipes secreted within the plasterwork. Do you remember all of those tiny rooms between rooms with no use at all? The hall, the porch, the corridor. Rooms just for passing through, for cluttering up with a panoply of objects more purposeless than the tiny rooms themselves, do you remember? Even though I'm at ease in our car home now too, still sometimes, I miss my father's house. I miss it more the further we go and the less I know where we are going. Everything I remember is caught in the void between its stained carpets and slanted slates. All my memories are cast to a honeyed hue by its yellow walls.

I remember how my father used to hum. He hummed

even after he'd ceased to talk. The hum was a soundtrack for whatever it was he happened to be doing: for moving, for thinking, for sitting, for smoking, for tinkering. From the needless room adjacent to his needless room I'd hear his humming leach through the plasterboard between us. It was always the same tune but I could never exactly identify it, and I never asked. Maybe my father was just repeating it wrong, like the way I always mishear the lyrics of songs which play between items on the talking station, and make up my own lines instead, substituting noises that aren't even words. Or maybe my father's tune was from some phase of his life which preceded fatherhood, from so many decades ago he couldn't have identified it even if I'd summoned the question. Maybe my father's humming was drawn from no fixed point of reference, but as involuntary as a yawn.

This might sound strange to you, but now when I think of the house, I picture it precisely as we left it, except that my father is still alive. I picture his unslippered feet planted firmly on the carpeted boards again, and he's humming and shambling between rooms, even though the lights are out, the curtains drawn and all the appliances switched off. I picture the painted men in painted Puerto Rico bartering their cockerels on the wall behind him, the bathroom beads gently knocking against one another in his wake. And Mr Buddy behind the washing machine with his button nose pressed to the cold wall, listening as my father passes.

I lose you.

At first light in a manmade forest. Most of its trees have been felled; between each slim copse there's an expanse of sorry stumps. Here in this clearing, there's a solitary Scots pine left standing. Branches severed, bark stripped. It looks like a lightning bolt driven into the earth and turned to wood.

I'm contemplating the surface of a stump when I lose you. There's some strange substance growing from it; strange because I can't decide whether it's a plant-like mushroom or a mushroom-like plant. After a couple of rainless days, the mud of the forest floor is pale and dry and the stump's dead roots push through the pale, dry mud like a network of veins on the back of a skinny hand. Now see here how the old rain has made a pond beneath the upraised roots of a fallen beech.

But when I look up I can't see you. I turn to where I think I saw you last. The clump of undergrowth where you were rummaging still holds the indentation of your disturbance. Now I kick through it, trying to go the way you could have gone, calling your name. There isn't any path here, and I don't know where I'm going, and I can't see you anywhere.

'ONEEYE ONEEYE ONEEYE,' I shout.

How can I know for sure you went this way? I can't. You could have gone any way. You could have gone on. I go on.

'ONEEYE ONEEYE ONEEYE,' I shout.

I use my angry voice, my angriest voice, even though I'm much more worried than I am enraged. How many minutes? Ten, fifteen, twenty? I feel sick with panic. What if you're looking for me now too? What if you went back to the car, and are waiting? I go back.

But there isn't any sign of you in the clearing where the car's parked. The only different thing is a mess of bird shit across the windscreen. I stare into the empty branches of the overhead tree. I think it's a eucalyptus, and I wonder how it ended up here and what sort of bird has made this foreign species its home. I sit on the edge of the passenger seat with the door open, facing into the forest. I wait. I know there are lots of things I could be doing as I wait. I could make coffee, read my book, check the oil, shake the blanket out. But I don't feel like anything but sawing the hard skin from my fingertips. I don't look at the time on the dashboard, and the minute hand of the clock inside me grinds as though towing a grain truck in its wake.

It's only now you're gone I see how you're my reason for doing things. Now I'm a stiltwalker with the stilts removed. My emptied trouser legs flap in the wind and I can't remember how to walk without being precipitously propped.

Now I hear a soft tinkling coming toward me through the ferns, a grunt. Now I see your black head pushing through the green fronds.

'BOLD!' I yell, but I don't mean it.

—

Up ahead, there's a man standing with one foot on the tarmac and the other in the ditch gully, and he's swaying in the wind like a bendy tree.

As we approach, I see his grey head's bowed against the horizontal drizzle and his right hand's stuck out into the roadway with a crooked thumb raised. It's early in the evening on a wide stretch of back road. There's nothing interesting on the radio and the rain's too weak to stifle the blare of my thoughts. So I slow down, pull in just beyond the hitchhiker. I shove the gas cooker and snacks from the passenger seat into the back. I pummel my bedding a little deeper into the cranny beneath the dash.

The hitchhiker is a man about my age. Too old for starting over, too young for giving up. He's chunky around the waist yet gangly in the limbs, sparse of hair and puffy of face. His nose is particularly bulbous and purple, scribbled with thread veins. He's wearing no jacket, just a woollen jumper worn to thousands and thousands of fluff bobbles. 'I'm local,' he says, 'just a few miles home along the road here.' He points west. 'Thanks very much.'

You're yowling, nipping. Within the confines of the car, the hitchhiker smells like stout, sweat, rancid butter. As he reaches for the seatbelt, your teeth graze the cuff of his shirt. 'BOLD,' I tell you, and you sit back, swallow your yowls and press your face into the gap between front seats. Now

SPILL SIMMER FALTER WITHER

you grumble like a kettle brewing, poised for attack. The toes of the hitchhiker's boots scuff dirt onto my duvet, cow shit and ditch mud amongst the spaceships and stars. He looks out the passenger window and chunters away without listening to himself. His manner is noticeably looser and less calculated than a person in an ordinary state and this is how I recognise that he is drunk. He tells me of the softness of the rain, the early coming of the dark, the poor condition of the back roads. His fingers move in time to his words, tracing squiggles in the air like unlighted sparklers. Whenever they sweep too suddenly, you take a snap, growl a warning.

'SSSSSHHHHHHHH,' I tell you, even though I know you can't grasp what form of command this reptilian hissing is supposed to be. You throw me a glance and I wonder if you're checking to see if I'm punctured.

The hitchhiker doesn't try to buckle his belt again but rides with his back flattened to the seat as though pretending to be belted. His chunterings don't need to be stoked by responses; he asks me no questions, makes no enquiries, polite or otherwise. I wonder if he even knows I'm here; I wonder if he even knows he's here. He doesn't ask about you; he doesn't ask where you and I are going. He doesn't remark upon the mishmash of belongings rolling and juddering around the car. His eyes drift off across the soggy ditches and I keep mine to the left of the white lines, but I am listening, nodding. I listen with unforeseen intensity, and so there is no need to picture the absent details of his life because he tells me in his loosened, uncalculated way.

He used to be a pig farmer, the hitchhiker says, and now he isn't. But he hasn't retired, he'll never retire. Now he manufactures the wood chippings horses sleep on, and lots of other animals too, of course. His former sows slept on chippings in two enormous sheds equipped with a complicated system of electronic feeding compartments. They were fed on anchovy fishmeal from Peru, bred for an average of six years and the length of each pregnancy was always exactly three months, three weeks and three days: three, three, three.

'Did the sows ever go outside?' I ask quietly while he's pausing for breath. I want to know whether they saw the sun, all their lives long.

'No need, the pig sheds were only massive. INDOOR FREE RANGE is what ye call them.'

'Pigs are smart,' I say. I suppose I read this in a book.

'The second smartest,' he agrees, 'after primates.'

'Keep any animals still?' I say.

'Just a cupla your fellas now.' He warily inclines his head toward you. 'Rhodesian ridgeback and a lab. Never lock them in. It's proper cruelty to have them locked in.'

I plunge back into silent nodding. It's jackdaws and swans again, the perplexing way in which people measure life, but I let it be. I follow the hitchhiker's directions, down a circuitous driveway to his farmhouse. There's grass growing along the middle of the road, tickling the car's belly as we pass. There's a jeep parked on the lawn. It has moss in the blades of the wipers, moss encircling the window frames. The house is run-down and every front-facing sill is utterly empty, no vases or books or figurines, not a single personal item to make a home of it. It's a sad place, don't you think that it's sad? There's no sign of a Rhodesian ridgeback running free, no sign of a labrador either.

The hitchhiker doesn't ask me in. He doesn't offer me supper, even though it's supper time. He doesn't even suggest a cup of tea.

'Thanks very much,' he says, tonelessly and insincerely. 'All the best.'

Now he slams the car door and sways off across the splintered slabs of his driveway, into the dark of his slumberous house.

—

We stay as we are with the engine ticking until the hitchhiker has his key in the hole and is wiping his boots against the front step. The evening has already piddled most of its light away. But the sky's cleared to pink and is covered in straight lines as though the clouds have been doused in amaranth, and ploughed.

I'm tired, so tired. From the effort of being attentive to the presence of another human, of having to say things to someone who isn't you, to someone who might actually listen. I don't feel like driving around for hours to find an appropriate gateway, not tonight. But there's no real need, we're already well out of the way of civilisation, save for the hitchhiker in his tumbledown farmhouse. I picture him slumped at the bottom of his staircase; he only meant to sit down for a second to remove his shoes but now he is drunkenly snoring, dribbling into his collar.

Both sides of the road are frilled by dead ragwort, dead montbretia. Beyond there's nothing but field upon field of harvested tillage. We drive on through the dead flowers and the dark. There's a rat high up in the hedge, can you see him? He's scaling the scrawny branches of a hawthorn tree. With his lardy arse wedged into a crook, like an ugly bird with its wings coiled into a pointy tail, now he's gorging himself on hawberries. I've never seen a rat in a tree before and I wonder why, if rats can climb, they never climbed down the step-ladder in the shut-up-and-locked room? There was a time when I could hear them constantly, running and jumping and scratching about in the roof. There was a time when I used to constantly listen and constantly wait for them to come down on me.

Further along, there's a chunk of old fortress collapsed to a landlocked spit, bearded all over by creeping ivy. There's a great mob of rooks scavenging a freshly shorn field, delving for gold nuggets amongst the gold spikes. Now they rise altogether to the ear-splitting pop of an invisible scarer.

There must be fifty of them, maybe even a hundred. See how they fill the sky with tiny brains and tiny hearts, so many tiny pairs of feet.

You're watching your reflection gathering definition in the back windscreen. You're still watching as I find us a gateway and park for the night. A little back a little forth, a little back a little forth. Dinner is powdered mash watered back to life, corned beef shavings and chocolate biscuit fingers for dessert. We're almost out of washing water again; tomorrow I'll have to find a stream or tap. The last of it goes toward brushing my teeth, the only way I know of quelling my horrible breath for a few hours, at least. I'm too tired to bother with the tea-candles tonight. I roll out my bedding, brush the hitchhiker's toe-prints away. Now I try to smoke myself to sleep, and once the tobacco is all gone too, I yank up the duvet, draw it tight around my iron-filing stubble, which isn't really stubble any more but a beard, my Brillo Pad beard.

I lie awake on the old seat foam and two fields over from our gate, I see a trailer with a portable billboard attached. The field is otherwise empty, fallowing, and the billboard looks so out of place, like some alien creature that had been dropped there and abandoned. I suppose it must be visible from the main road, which is perhaps another few fields over, I can't remember exactly. The words of its slogan are barely visible through the dark. It says something like: MAKE WAY FOR A WHOLE NEW YOU. But it took me fifty-seven years to become this me, I think, and I just don't have the stamina to make so many mistakes all over again.

At night, the sheep look like walking headstones.

—

You're quick to guiltless sleep, shifting through a sequence of dream positions. Now crumpled, now sprawled, now foetal. Now with elbows akimbo, paws pushed forward and bunched together as if bound, as though you are a dead boar swinging from a hunting sling. I extend my hand to touch you, just to check. You are the only living thing I dare touch. And you like to be rubbed dry with a towel on rain days, to feel your skull patted when you have been good, to be stroked from ears to tail whenever I am reading. Now I run my big hand over your neat ridges of muscle and fat, your sporky bones, your wirebrush coat. And I check your heartbeat, just to be sure.

The leaves overhanging the car are jostling in the moonlight, tossing their shadow-puppet shapes across the dash. Through the slits of my half-closed eyelids, they look like trapped insects swarming on the floor mats, scooting beneath the seats. Now a bat dips and pitches over the bonnet before continuing down the road. For a while, I watch the place where it faded out and I wonder whether it was a bat, or maybe just a light leaf surfing a bouncy piece of wind. It is now, and only because I'm already watching, that I see an owl, a gigantic barn owl. Its face is apple-shaped and onion-coloured. Its wings are huge and mottled. It moves in thoughtful strokes, dives for something, disappears. It's the most splendid thing I've ever seen.

You're awake as fast as I can raise the lock. We fall from the car and set off in ungainly pursuit of a bird-ghost. We gamble and trot over a field of square bales and startled mice, smashing the spikes and nuggets as we go. The owl flashes back into view, just for a second before vanishing again, this time into a patch of forest. Now it's properly lost, impossible to trace its route through the black canopy. Still we trammel to the edge of the bale field, and here I pause for just a blink, but you push on alone, and so I follow you.

The dry, bare branches high ahead clop against one another. They make a sound like timber horseshoes on hard ground. In the dark, you are no more than a jagged stripe of white beard. It's only a short way over the crackling floor to a ruined house. Inside, the windows are veiled by filthy nets and lacy cobwebs. Here's a picture frame with its glass shattered, the photograph bleached out. Here's a broken mug with a cockerel on the outside and somebody's old tea stains still tarnishing its base. The roof is off, and high up on a rafter fixed into a nook, there's a box. A wooden box exactly the size of an owl, with a few coloured wires trailing from it, leading to an identical box lower down. Now here at eye level, there's a sign emblazoned with the words: WARNING: FILMING IN PROGRESS. DO NOT INTERFERE WITH OWL BOX.

On our way back to the car, we trudge more than we trot. It's not until you're tucked into the low chair and I'm back beneath the duvet that we hear the owl. It sounds nothing like a hoot, nothing like a too-it-too-woo. But even now, even at a distance, it is startling: it is livid. And I remember what I'd forgotten all throughout our night adventure up until this point. I remember that the owl is a harbinger of death.

—

There are barns and slatted sheds behind us, water troughs beside. There's an electric fence and a mud track. How many suchlike cattle paths have we walked now, between fields at dawn? The fence is switched on and sizzling. I'm stopping, starting, leaning into the bramble hedge to reach the ripest berries. There's a bag swinging from my wrist carrying at least a half-mile's worth of fruit, now crushed and leaking black blood through a prick-hole in the bottom. You're at my feet, scoffing your way through the knee-high berries. I wonder how is it you can tell red from black amongst all your yellow and blue and grey; now I remember that ripeness has a smell.

One second you're beside me scoffing, the next you're rocketing away up the cattle path, and I glimpse a ginger-coated thing rocketing inches ahead.

A fox? I call your name even though I know you won't

hear me, won't come back. The ginger streak dives into the undergrowth and you lunge after it. I hear it howl, you yelp. I'm running to catch up, though I've no idea what I'm going to do once I get there. Now I see it catapult into a tree, and because rats aren't red and foxes can't climb trees, of course, it must be a cat.

The cat crouches in the low branches, raises its hackles to hiss. Now you're sniffing hasty circles around the trunk. You don't appear to understand exactly where the cat has gone; it doesn't seem to occur to you to raise your head upwards. Now I reach you and hold you still. There's a red scrawl across the bridge of your muzzle, a few dabs of blood on your forehead, but the cat missed your eye. Thank goodness, it missed your eye.

I re-attach your leash but you're obstinate, and now I'm dragging, dragging, dragging. Back on the cattle path, I lift a stone and turn around. I take aim and fling, hard as I can. Now I do it again and again, until I clip the cat's back and it scrambles higher and blends into the unfallen yellow leaves. It is a sycamore tree; it seems to be marking a field boundary.

'Come on,' I tell you, 'brekkie.' And you come.

What happened to our blackberries? I must have dropped them. Now see how the bag's exploded in the dirt. We leave them for the birds and bugs.

—

The road meanders. There's a river to one side and a wood to the other. Another wood. I didn't expect that for every shell on the coast there's a tree in the midlands.

From the radio, an expert is telling us how some blackbirds have a tendency to imitate car alarms. But what does the car alarm mean in bird-speak, and what do the other birds say back? Or do they say nothing and shun the alarm bird? Do they point him out to one another and remark that he's strange? The expert doesn't say.

You're not listening anyway; your thousand-mile stare pierces the woods. The river is really only a stream. Still, good enough for refilling our drums. In some places there are shallow meres and squitty waterfalls. Elsewhere the ditch is too thick to see through. The wood climbs a hill away from the river and the road. Most of the slope has been deforested and there's nothing but gorse to hold the loose logs back, to prevent all the rejected bits from ricocheting into the traffic. Not that there is any traffic, just us.

Now we come upon a clearing at the river's edge which looks faintly as though it might once have been a designated parking space. Here the river pools, so once my drums are filled, I set to washing my socks and jocks. I empty my soap powder into the water without thinking. It's not until I gather my slop pile for its final squeeze that I remember the river creatures. Some bubbles escape my washing pool and infiltrate the current. And I feel suddenly thoroughly terrible that I might have poisoned them. Remember the radio expert who told us about the male roach who developed eggs as well as sperm, because the water he lived in was polluted by insidious endocrines, do you remember?

Here's a footbridge with rope handrails and decomposing planks. You've already crossed and found something to sniff on the opposite side. You seem especially panicked by the meaning of this smell. Now I hesitate to follow, just for a second. I think about the wood where I lost you or you lost me, where we lost each other. I remember *Billy Goats Gruff* and I lean over the handrail to check for a troll. Below, now my bubbles have been carried on, I can see minnows, sticklebacks, baby rainbow trout. See these brittle stone caskets; they are sheltering the larvae of the caddis fly. And these triangular ripples are the tracks of a whirligig beetle who's just skated across the surface to reach the further bank. See the silty mud at the pool's very bottom. Down there I'll bet there's a family of frogs preparing to sleep out the coming winter. But there isn't any troll, of course not. I am the troll.

A trail looms from the forest floor and rises up the hill before us. It disappears beneath the forest's ceiling of dying leaves and thriving needles, of ripening conkers and burgeoning pinecones. There's a handwritten sign nailed to a stump in the shape of an arrow pointing to the trail. RINGFORT, it says. What do you think, would you like to see a ring fort? It'll probably be overgrown and disappointing even if we manage to find it, but I've never seen a ring fort before, and hundreds and hundreds of years ago, people used to live inside them. They built earthen banks and raised huts and dug chambers and clad the chamber walls with flat, smooth stones. Then they squeezed themselves inside to hide from death.

—

Up, up, up we scramble.

You're drawn on by your panic-worthy scent, I'm drawn on by the low autumn sun winking through the scraggled branches, the promise of an earthen rampart. Past cobnuts, lords and ladies. Past a magic toadstool bent and macerated like an ancient man, a tiny ascetic taking refuge in the woods. You leap and tear through the tangled stems. I've never seen you so messianic. Does the forest make your brain buzz with memories of digging out in spring, of bounding with the baiters? Now you clamp something beneath the knotweed. A dormouse, a field mouse, a bank vole, a shrew? I watch as you mercilessly nibble it to death, now stand with a paw entrapping the tail, waiting for it to betray a sign of life. It appears to be breathing even though its organs are surely pounded to pieces. Now the last nerve-ending in its acorn-sized body short-circuits, and with the flick of its tail you recommence death-nibbling. I see it's a shrew, poor shrew. It should have kept still, but it's too late now. The shrew only knew to fear buzzards, foxes, owls, mink. How could it have imagined such a thing as you? Its lost life was worth no more or less than yours or mine, than the man in the popemobile or the sardines in the sardine tin. You might at least have killed it quickly.

And almost at once, you are off again, and I must run after you. Pitch and clump across the pliant ground, flailing the buckler ferns down, cracking twigs with my planky soles. This time I will not go quietly to the car and wait. This time I will not lose you.

I find you in a bank. I find not you but a burrowhole and know that you have crawled inside it. I know from the sound of your muffled braying. I know from the shrapnel of mud shooting free from the mouth of the hole as you dig.

I am an imbecile. An imbecile for never having you fastened on the leash and an imbecile for bringing you here to this forest filled with irresistible burrowholes. And the only way to redeem my imbecility is to dig too, is to out-dig you.

I find a fat stick. I press my fingers together to make shovels of my ungainly hands. I prod and break and scrabble and fling and claw. I work so hard I forget my ungainliness, I replace it with a reserve of strength I didn't know until now I'd been reserving, by a wildness that I learned from you. Animalised, I am digging, digging, digging.

An oblivious blackbird shouts from the buckler ferns. *Hurdy-gurdy hurdy-gurdy hurdy-gurdy hurdy-gurdy,* it shouts, and so it must never have heard a car alarm. It sails my thoughts back to the barn owl and even though I know of course it's a blackbird and not an owl, not a harbinger, I shout into the ferns 'IT WON'T BE HIM!' And then I shout into the hole 'IT WON'T BE YOU!' Do you hear me? It won't be you, okay? I promise.

Now I brace my strongest shoulder against the bank and shove my arm as deep as it will shove. Now I feel you. The scraggled stump of your amputated tail. I drag you up, dragging against me. I wipe the mud from your mud-drenched face.

I know you are mad. I've known from the start you are both kinds of mad but this time I see it's mouth-frothing, eye-popping anger. You might easily bite me, free yourself, crawl back in. And yet you don't. Why don't you bite me, One Eye? We are lying on the freshly dug mud and I am holding you to my chest. I check your heartbeat, just to be sure. I can feel it battering; I can feel my own battering too. I hold our battering hearts together and you do not bite me, and I see how your wiped face is only as incomplete as I've ever known it to be. And I realise the earthen bank we just dug down was the rampart of our ring fort.

—

It's barely distinguishable. There's a set of raised, curved ridges, inside which the forest floor is flat and carpeted by old foliage. In the very centre, an oak stands fifty feet tall, at least. Its thick branches sprawl in every direction like the legspan of a giant octopus. It stands intractable, as though as a reminder to the forest that it was the first tree and will endure to be its last. At the edge of the bank on the furthest side, the forest ends and opens onto fields. A green crop I can't recognise by just the leaves stretches unimpeded for several miles before the green's again adulterated by houses and roads and pylons, by people. At first it was a beautiful view, but suddenly it seems like a sad place, don't you think it's sad?

We sit on the field-facing bank of the ring fort. I roll a cigarette. I always carry the tobacco pouch with me while we are walking, along with the car key, the leash, some chocolate buttons. Now the smoke runs through my blood vessels and I unclench. I offer you a button. You are back on the leash now, sniffling the wind, tilting your ears this way and that. Can you smell a trace of badger, can you hear them calling you? I place my palm across your shoulders and stroke your warm back. Your silver tag jangles in the wind. Your chest swells and deflates in neat bursts, a string of drool hangs off your chin from the place where your lip is missing. I see the mud already dried into your fur and the threads of grey worming through your curls in the place where I wiped your face clean. And I wonder are you old? I'd forgotten that you might be old.

—

Now I'm beginning to dream again. I'm sinking to the black-most layer of sleep, remaining there for longer intervals.

Tonight I dream of your badger, of the badger who took

your eye. I dream myself down, down, down an unfathomably small hole. Deep, deep, deep through a bone-crunching tunnel. I dream the air wrung out of my lungs. I dream the smell of an earthworm mausoleum. The spindly ends of tree roots combing the long hairs of my back. The wet of the earth permeating my skin, its cold tongue licking my spine. I dream the muted shouts of men from somewhere up above and far behind. The only clear sound is the grate and slither of my uncertain progress. The only light is shrinking, shrinking, shrinking. Now I dream the flash of the badger's teeth and a sound like a violent collision of fur and flesh. I can't see anything any more and now I know; one of my eyes is filled with blood and the other is inside the badger.

When I wake, I am me again, and you are you.

You're outstretched across the back seat of the car, grunting and waggling your paws as though you have picked up my dream and are again running, running, running. Your right eye is closed and on the other side, your eye-hollow is closed too, so that, in sleep, you look almost symmetrical again. You seem almost unscathed.

—

Sometimes when I'm descending gears to turn a long corner, the car begins to fail. The engine dips and coughs and I lean my head and shoulders and chest in the direction of the corner's curve, as though I might impel the car myself.

Mostly the putter perks back up in an instant, pushes us on again.

All I know of maintaining cars is the very little my father taught me for my driving test. I know to check and occasionally replenish the oil. I know my front left tyre is going bald because the impact of a mighty pothole several weeks ago threw the tracking of the wheels into misalignment. And I know my bulbs are blinking out, first the indicators and soon the brake lights, one by one by one. But I don't understand about the dip and cough, and I am waiting for the day the car fails altogether.

See the funeral home with crucifix-shaped windows. See the tile warehouses and fireplace showrooms. See the homemade signpost hammered into the mud of a roadside flowerbed. COLIN & MARIE'S WEDDING, it says, the words underscored by an arrow. Do you think Colin and Marie are really inviting us to their wedding? I've never been to a wedding before. You're gnawing loudly on your most recent stick. Ten minutes ago it was the shape of a flamingo's long neck with a bump for the head and a curve for the beak. Now it's splinters flittered across the rag rug. I say your name again but you are not listening.

—

A yellow circle slides into my dream, a face appears pressed against the window. It's an old woman's face, her bottom lip's crusted with cold sores and her nostrils are prickled with echoing pores. Dandruff falls from her scalp onto her shoulders. It shows up like glitter through the dark, as if she is sporting a sequinned mantle.

Now I try to open my eyes, and they're already open. The yellow circle is a torch beam and the old woman is real; we are touching noses through the glass. Now she raises a bony knuckle and knocks.

You wake up too, we wake up together. You're in my lap and yipping. I push you onto the passenger seat, grope for the leash, twine the handle loop around the headrest and clip the other end to your collar. All the while, the old woman is scouring the car with her yellow circle. It sears my leaden eyes as I roll the window down.

'What are ya at?' she says. 'What are ya doing parked up here?'

There are two bungalows a couple of hundred yards up the road from our gateway. They seem suddenly much closer than they seemed when I parked. You're stomping all over the gingernuts. Calm down.

'I was just on my way home,' I say, quietly.

'What's that? Speak up!' the old woman says, as though she's a school teacher and I'm the mumbling boy at the back of the class. I picture her as a school teacher back in the days when they were still allowed to use a cane. I picture the pigment restored to her hair, the dandruff twisted back into a face-stretching bun.

Now I don't know why I said that.

'I was just on my way home,' I say, ever-so-slightly less quietly.

'You're not broke down or anything?' Now she's narrowing her eyes.

I wonder how long she watched us for and from where she's mustered the courage for confrontation. Is there a huddle of grandsons crouched in the ditch behind her, clutching broom handles and shoe horns and hurleys? Is this why you're ballistic?

'No,' I say. I'm dazzled and blinking. I'm tired and meek.

'Then you can't sleep here,' the old woman says, 'you're not welcome here.'

She steps back and signals with a swatting hand for me to pull the car out. I fumble my bedding into the back seat, push my toes down to the caps of my boots, wind the handle which raises the window up. The woman stays as she is and continues to shine her torch into my eyes, watching. Why isn't she afraid? I'm twice her size and you are fierce, and of course there are no crouching grandsons in the ditch. But she can see you're fastened I suppose, and perhaps I'm not so big now as I was when we set out. For just a second, I feel intoxicatingly reckless. I want to let you out of the car with your mouth unshackled so you can maim the rude old woman. Maybe I even want to maim her myself. But I don't, of course I don't. I'm not the kind of person who is able to do things, remember? I'm not the kind of person who could go to Colin and Marie's wedding, even if I was really invited. Instead I rev and shunt until the car's back on the road again. I suppose Colin and Marie are all married and done with now. Instead I drive away.

After a while you remember the gingernuts beneath your feet and stick your nose into the trampled packet. Why did I tell her we were on our way home? I wonder if it's because now I want it to be true.

—

On a long corner, at last, the car fails.

I get out and push it to the ditch. Now we sit and wait. I don't understand why, but after an elapse of exactly eleven minutes, it simply starts again, miraculous.

—

I sleep through the dawn. I never do that. I wake to the sound of inclement grumbling.

It takes my mind several seconds to catch up with my ears. For several seconds I'm waking up in my father's house again. I'm watching the slothful light spear through my bedroom window between the leaves and stems and flowers of the rejuvenated toadflax. It idles about the rugs and cushion covers, the coal bucket and kindling basket. It illuminates the dust, speck by speck. Now I remember I'm under a duvet in the driver's seat and we're parked in a lay-by which seems much larger this morning than it did last night. There's a gurgling lullaby rising from somewhere. I pull myself up, look beyond the car over a fence and through the trees to a river. Yes, I remember the river. The river's why I stopped here, to fill my drums and slosh out my underwear. It's much fatter and slower than the stream in the ring fort's wood. Even through the windscreen, I can see fins breaching the ripples like tiny sharks.

There's a blanket of deciduous debris trodden into the surface of the lay-by. I can single out ash leaves, horse chestnut and sycamore. I can see keys, conkers and samaras. Over the fence beneath the trees, there's a conclave of rusted appliances. A chrome microwave, a hairdryer, an electric keyboard and a toaster. They're huddling together beneath a sign that reads NO DUMPING: CCTV IN OPERATION. On the other side of the lay-by, there's a picnic bench and a padlocked chip van. Last night, through the dark, the chip van looked like a portable billboard, a long skip, the rear end of a transportation truck. The lay-by is set back just off the main road and there's already a trickle of rush-hour traffic. Now I see how I've been careless. I feel a flush of danger, like acid reflux in my head. I need a cigarette.

The inclement grumbling is you, of course it's you. Across the lay-by, a clapped-out Volvo has pulled in and parked alongside the chip van. A man in blue jeans gets out. He pays no attention to the presence of our car. He takes a signboard from the Volvo's boot and pitches it amongst the trodden leaves. HOT DRINKS MINERALS, it reads, CHIPS CURRY BURGERS BREAKFAST ROLLS. Now he props the van's awning out, fiddles with the padlock, pulls the door and disappears inside.

Swiftly, swiftly, swiftly, I untangle myself from the duvet, clip on your leash and we tumble from the car. You tow me to the ditch and obligingly piss, now I loop the leash into the lever of the door's lock. With my hands my own again, I fiddle my loose tobacco into the shape of a smoke. I tidy our night things away, making ready for the road, for another day's driving. The leeway of danger's befuddled my head, and my heart's in my ears again, beating down the sound of your warning growl. My pillow's only half squashed beneath the dash when, all of a sudden, you yelp and jolt toward something behind me I can't see. Now your leash is drawn into a trip wire, and as I spin around, I fall hard onto the concrete.

I land flat on my front like a domino, like the last domino. I ram the heel of each graceless hand into the ash, the horse chestnut, the sycamore, so hard that the blood rises instantly into my cuticles. I feel more than winded; I feel split in two. From the gash that's opened in my chin, clean down the centre, like an axed log. I picture the bruise, from forehead to toes, as though my biggest vein has burst blue ink beneath my skin.

It's decades since I've fallen. As a boy I was forever falling, and every time I picked myself up again without fuss.

I wore short trousers all year round and all year round my knees were scabby and the scabs were as ordinary a part of my legs as were my god-given knobbly kneecaps. But now I am old. In the reflection of the car door as I lie like a domino on the ground, I am an old man. I've completely forgotten what my bare legs look like and my clobbered jaw hurts with every ounce of consciousness, with the united intensity of every fall I never felt in boyhood.

You're facing away from me. You're pulling against the leash. You're histrionic. Now I look to where you're looking, now I see what you're seeing. Advancing toward us across the lay-by, there's a little girl. She's snot-nosed and soft-shaped and dressed like a story-book witch. She has a tall hat, cat-patterned petticoats and a pair of patent leather shoes with pointed toes. Now I remember, it's Halloween, or thereabouts.

'Ouch!' the little girl says on my behalf. 'Y'okay mister?'

She is four or five, I can't tell exactly. She's extending a hand to my crumpled frame. She's trying to help me up, even though she is tiny. The weight of a tumbleweed, the strength of a moth. Hasn't anyone taught her how to recognise when a man is strange? Hasn't anyone told her to stay away from strange men? Now I heave myself up, wrench myself back.

'You shouldn't talk to strangers,' I say, 'didn't anybody ever teach you not to talk to strangers?'

She must have come out of the Volvo with the chip van

man. She must be his daughter, yet too young for school and brought along to work instead. Why isn't he watching her now? Why hasn't he called her back? Now her eyes skip from me and settle on you.

'We'd one like him before,' she says, 'can I pet him?'

She takes a footstep closer and reaches out again. In a flash, you snap at her hand. I know you don't mean it. I know you're only protecting your property, which is the car, and your family, who is me. You miss, but I know you'll snap again and so I'm on you. I'm hobbling and bundling and chucking and slamming. I'm pulling the car fast, fast, fast to the mouth of the lay-by and indicating into the traffic.

But I have to stop, I'm forced to stop. As I wait for a gap, I curse rush-hour. I look up and see the little witch girl in the rearview mirror. She's a solitary splash of colour against the grey sky and mud. She glissades around the lay-by, having forgotten us already. The tip of her hat is drooping slightly and the cats on her tights are splattered by dirt. What posters has she on her bedroom walls, I wonder. Has she stars in her copybooks, stones in her pencil case? Suddenly she stops and raises a palm. Look, the little witch girl hasn't forgotten, and is waving.

The car kicks up a cloud of ash keys in its wake. Blood drips from my chin onto my trousers. I thrust the gear-stick into fifth as we speed down the main road, away.

—

My hands shudder against the steering wheel. I feel like I swallowed a free bird and it's lashing its wings against the bars of my bones, trying to find the way back up to my mouth-hole. But this time the free bird isn't fear. This time the free bird is rage.

When I used to feel angry in my father's house, I boxed cushions, flung knick-knacks, kicked kickboards. But I never broke anything and always tidied up afterwards. My anger was a tea-candle, one more useless sensation amongst a snowslide of useless sensations I suffer but never act upon. Now it's a whole cathedral of tea-candles, an inferno. I'm angry at myself, for being careless, but I'm angry at you too, I'm even more angry at you. Because of the little girl. Why did you have to snap? She wasn't trying to hurt you. Because the pain in my walloped jaw is blighting my sense of reason. And you are the only animate thing at which to direct my anger. You are the only thing; you are the only.

I drive. For several miles down previously uncharted back roads. Ballistic, directionless, I drive. Now, on a road between two hedgerows of dead honeysuckle, I skid the car to a halt. I climb out of my seat and flip it forward, violently. I grab you by the scruff and drag you from the shelter of the low chair. I haul you from your safe space. The tasselled blanket is caught on your back paws. I snatch it away. The leash is trailing from your collar like a polyester umbilical cord. I pull it off and drop you to the ground. Now I get back into the car and slam the door. Now I drive away, and leave you.

When I was very young, too young for riding in the front seat of the car, I remember a journey home from town one murky evening. I remember the tonsured back of my father's head as he drove and the radio playing wordless songs, and I remember crying. I bawled and screeched and sobbed and snivelled because I'd dropped Mr Buddy on the floor and couldn't reach to pick him up again. All of a sudden my father yanked the handbrake and stopped the car. He leaned over and lifted me from the back seat. Then he placed me into a tuft of grass at the side of the road, and drove away. Young as I was, I remember thinking this wasn't the sort of thing fathers were supposed to do. I remember thinking he would soon come back, he would definitely come back. But he didn't. And I remember the exact stretch of road and how promptly the daylight died that day, how the crows went off and the cats came out, how the car faces lighted their eyes. I grew very cold, my fingers turning numb, my nose leaking unstoppable runnels of snot. I remember worrying about Mr Buddy and what my father might have done with him. Eventually a neighbour passing in her car saw me and stopped. She picked me up and I remember the rustling sound her jacket made against my legs and I remember how she took my hands in hers and raised them to her lips and I thought that she was going to bite me, but she only blew on my freezing fingers. Then she drove me home and rang our doorbell, and when my father answered, he looked surprised; he pretended to be surprised. He sent me to my bedroom and I never heard what he said to the neighbour, how he explained it away. But after that day, I never cried in the car again. I never cried anywhere. With or without onions, I never cried.

You stay as you are in the road, at exactly the point where I dropped you. Is the air not thick with new smells? Are you not surrounded by new fields and hedges and ditches untrammelled? Yet you resist, and stay as you are. I watch you in the rearview mirror, your small shoulders black and hunched against the green and vast. I watch until the car rounds a corner and I can't see you any more.

Now all my rage transforms to panic. I do an unwieldy U-turn on the too-narrow road. I thwack down the nettles with my number plate. I speed back. It's been only a moment. You're still as I left you. Your lonely peephole's fixed on the precise spot at which my taillights disappeared. Now you're on your feet. Now you're beating your stubby tail with all your strength. I'm sorry. I'm so sorry. I should never have blamed you. It's my fault. Everything is my fault.

I'm tired now. I want to go home.

—

Together, on we drive, with all the windows open, even though it's cold. Together we breathe deep the cold, fill our lungs with fox spray and dead honeysuckle, pine martens and stinkhorns, seven different kinds of sap.

We are driving, driving, driving. Heading for the coast, keeping to the back roads.

wither

Things are freezing, freezing, freezing.

Dew drops on furze bushes and rain drops on mud. Gutters, cattle troughs, mill races, puddles, potholes, garden ponds. In the boot, the mineral bottles and gallon drums. On the windscreen, condensation. And beneath the bonnet, the tiny plastic gauge for feeding the wipers with washing water.

What day is it? It must be the beginning of November at least. It seems too early for the first frosts, for such face-aching cold. I still don't know exactly where we are even though I know now where we're heading. We're following the straightest route back to open sea. We're keeping close as I can keep us to the line which the crow flies, and all of the other birds too, of course. Watch out for people who say it's only the crow who flies straight. They'll have you believing the pigeons and starlings and waxwings and gulls are all crisscrossing idiotically, weaving and winding and never quite getting there.

I wonder if my father's house is freezing too. It wasn't ever warm, but the smallness and clutter made it seem somehow cosy. Do you remember last winter? The lowest temperatures for half a century, the meteorologist said. We didn't know each other then. It was the first winter without my father and the first I felt the full bitterness of his house, the first it drove me back beneath my duvet during the thrifty daylight hours. Through the flimsy single-glazing, I could feel the wind and hear the rain softly tapping as though begging to be let in. Every morning I built a fire in the bedroom grate and every day I kept it crackling until I was back beneath the duvet for the night, and every night the bedroom ceiling froze and the freeze crept up from the sharp bones of my toes and stopped to take me by the shoulders and shake me awake. Then I'd see the ceiling plaster twinkling like a clear sky, as though the roof had been lifted clean off by an enormous godhand.

One freezing winter years and years ago, one morning after my father had left for the factory, I snuck into his room and yanked the pull-string that swung from the trapdoor. It seemed to me such a paltry device; I couldn't imagine it might be capable of drawing a folding stepladder down upon my head. But it somehow did. And so I climbed into the roof and there I saw for the first time there was no trace of any insulation, no yellow pillows of spun glass.

I never considered my father a poor man. He worked

every weekday of his able-bodied life and he was paid rent in a monthly bundle from the lady who managed the fashion boutique, then the Polish hairdresser after her. My father never spent a reckless copper or owned a frivolous thing. He never showed an interest in money nor any of the spangly things it might have brought him. I don't understand why he didn't have the roof insulated, and I wonder if the house is freezing now, even more severely so than last winter without the small warmth of my breath and the jittering fire. I wonder about the bedroom ceiling plaster. I wonder about all of the fluid things I left so carelessly exposed. The suds in the soap dish, the damp earth in the plant pots, the oblong pool at the bottom of the toilet and the vetch's stagnant water in its unemptied vase. I wonder is my father's house a salmon pink ice palace now.

—

In the winter, Aunt couldn't take the cold in my father's house so she'd bring me next door. Down the grocer's passageway and up the rickety stairwell to her low-ceilinged flat. The smell was TCP and chicken-stock, and it was always warm. A sticky, cheesy kind of warmth. I can't remember what the source of heat was, though I remember how Aunt kept the curtains drawn so not a wisp could squeeze free. I was already acclimatised to the chill air and ubiquitous draught of my father's house and I didn't like to spend the day sealed inside Aunt's flat. It was too clammy and there was nothing to do. Even though many of Aunt's belongings resembled toys, she never let me play with anything. She had a whole mantelpiece crammed with porcelain cats and porcelain girls in porcelain skirts and bonnets with porcelain frills. She had a picture of Jesus with a three-dimensional sacred heart and a tiny candle-shaped bulb that constantly flickered. Her only books were the Bible and a mass missal with a leatherette cover, if these can even be called books. I'd sit cross-legged in the central circle of the concentric circles on her living room rug. I'd make believe I was a baby Buddha like the one I'd seen inside a story book. I'd stay still as I could, and pretend to be meditating.

There was a fish bowl, I'd almost forgotten the fish bowl. It was big as a motorcycle helmet and there weren't any fish inside, nor any water. Instead there was a fistful of marbles; they were the brightest things in the whole flat. As a boy, I'd pretend Aunt's goldfish had turned to glass, and as I meditated, I'd stare at the marbles. I'd will them to swim again.

———

Since I forgot to bring the kitchen calendar, I've come to measure time in weather, in walks, in passing wilderness, in miles clocked on the dashboard dial.

The weather and walks and miles and wilderness between us and the lay-by with the little witch girl accumulate, so that it seems long ago, even if it isn't. Now whenever it was, it troubles me less. It troubles me with only the same ferocity as all the other things that trouble me. With your nose glued to the air vents, your thousand-mile stare boring through the windscreen, I wonder: what are the things that trouble you?

I notice, on the index finger of my right hand, a skelp of skin gone from the knuckle leaving a patch of pink, the vivid pink of chewed bubblegum. There's an extremely fine strand of your fur lodged in the wound, and I wonder how I wounded it and what force of nature carried this particular strand to my finger and deposited it there. Now I tug the free end, but the strand resists. And I see that I'm too late, that it's already set into a scab, that it's part of me now, that you're part of me.

———

You're in the low chair on the back seat and I'm pushing. There's a knoll in the road like a tarmac tumour and I'm struggling to get the car over it. You're looking through the rear windscreen and watching me push. Your head's tilted in confusion.

Now a transit van ticks up the road behind us, slows and parks on the grassy verge. A man in a boiler suit climbs out. He's eating a packet of hoop-shaped crisps. Now he's coming toward us.

'D'ya need a hand there?' he calls, and I pretend not to

hear. I don't see what he does with the crisps, but the packet's gone by the time he reaches the car and he's brushing dust from his hands onto his suit, greasy orange dust. 'What's the trouble?' he says, bending down to push uninvited alongside me.

Inside the car, you are apoplectic. I have to raise my voice to be heard over your barks. 'No trouble,' I say, 'just cuts out sometimes. Give it ten minutes and it'll start again, no trouble.'

Unfazed by you, by your hysterics, the man chuckles. 'Doesn't sound right though, does it?' he says. 'Want me to take a look?'

'No,' I say, 'thank you and that, but no.'

Now the car summits the tumour, tips into the ditch, rolls a little and comes to rest. The man and I stop pushing and straighten up. What if he goes around to the front and tries to lift the bonnet? Again and more firmly this time, I say 'Thank you but no. No. No thank you.'

There aren't any other cars passing on the road and over the hedge, perhaps the winter wheat is rustling softly to itself and perhaps the birds are singing, but I can't hear anything but you, your implacable warning call. Now the man seems to look into the car for the first time. I suppose he notices the blankets and the rubbish bags. The gas cooker and the football. The low chair and food bowl. You. Everything.

'Right-o,' he says, 'only tryna help.' Now he holds his hands out like a Mary in a grotto, with his greasy palms up.

He walks back, climbs into the seat behind his steering wheel, starts the engine. SWIMMING POOL SOLUTIONS says the sign on the side of his transit.

As it passes, a crisp packet blows into the air, falls down again. Now I hear the whisper of the winter wheat, the rattling call of a magpie in the distance. I wonder how a man might attempt to solve a swimming pool. And I feel suddenly terrible. He was only trying to help us, and I drove him away.

—

Through the spirit-rotting cold, we are driving. The mileage clocks, time passes. I feel as though the further we descend toward sea level, the ever-so-slightly warmer the nights will become. Things will stop their freezing, or at least freeze less and remain softish in the centre, like a custard cream, one of my father's.

We pass the last and most resilient of the terracotta beech and melon-yellow sycamore leaves. We pass pheasants strutting the tractor rucks. Fertiliser sacks undulating against the hedgerows. Takeaway boxes turned spongy by rain. Sugar beets fallen from trailers with their heads smashed and tresses ripped from the scalp and strewn. For a time, we pass all of the things we already passed, only in reverse. And so I suppose I know where we are again, not by name but by association.

Do you remember the monkey puzzle trees and peeling eucalyptus, the shoddy rockets and neglected crucifixes? Now here's the same pair of running shoes slung over the same wires still walking on air above our heads, and the same straw bale rolled from the same hill stuck in the same ditch, only now, it is wizened and black. See how it has been burned out, as though it were a joyridden car.

For a time, we sleep in the same gateways, car pointing in the opposite direction. Now the nights are astonishingly cold. I have four jumpers and a coat, and blankets, even one with sleeves and a hood. I should be acclimatised after so many winters in my father's house, still everything aches and I don't know whether it's the cold or the position I'm trying to sleep in, or both, probably both. At night I feel the old familiar creeping from the sharp bones of my toes up through my spine to shake my shoulders. Now I'm awake and shivering, and you are woken too. I switch on the torch and relight the camping cooker. I boil a cup's worth of water, and while it's boiling, I spoon honey from the jar and pour whiskey from the bottle and cut a wedge from a lemon and stud each segment with a clove. It's fiddly work for a fat-fingered man by torchlight, but a double shot is certain to settle me back to sleep. While it's cooling, I rinse the saucepan and heat a dish measure of milk. You know what's coming and dribble with anticipation as you wait. You press your face close to the blue flames, so close your eyebrows and whiskers are singed to brittle kinks.

For a time, we stop in the same villages and buy food in the same grocery shops. Except for a bottle of whiskey here and there, a net of lemons and a jar of spicy twigs, I choose all the old reliable items. I think I could travel as far as Tasmania and still I'd stop in the first little shop I stumbled upon and try to buy gingernuts, margarine, fish fingers, spaghetti hoops. Then I think I'd find a salmon pink house in a place by the coast where the shore birds wade, and I'd go about every day in exactly the same way I've always done, and the only thing different would be that we'd be in Tasmania. Yes, you could come, of course you could come. How could I ever manage without you now?

Passing bungalows after nightfall, see the glow of strangers' kitchens. Smell the wood smoke from their chimneys. Now we pass a house with an illuminated B&B sign swinging over the mouth of the driveway, and because the kitchen glows and the chimney smells of wood smoke, because I ache from cold and sleeplessness, I'm almost tempted to stop. But all the guesthouses will be guestless at this time of year, and I can't stand the thought of trespassing on a family, of paying strangers to be kind to me, of lingering in the foothills of their domestic tiffs. I can't stand the thought of eating from their crockery, of sweating into their bed-sheets, of patting myself from bunions to brow with their bath towels, of being watched through the dark as I sleep by the glassy eyes of their sentimental geegaws. I can't stand the thought of being steadily infused by their smell, because every house and every family, however scrupulously clean, has its own smell. Of course I know you know this already, that every smell is ten times bigger to your senses, that you can smell history, that you can smell time. My father's house smelled of black mould, cigarette smoke, fried garlic, hand-wash, damp dust, sweaty slippers, my own heinous breath and the fetid draught through the cracks in the ceiling plaster, the keyhole of the shut-up-and-locked room; but they consolidated into what was simply the smell of home, which no one word can describe and nowhere in Tasmania can ever smell exactly like.

—

I don't ask, but she tells me. A woman of thereabout my age with a little boy's pudding bowl haircut. Her voice is tone-less, insincere. From the opposite side of the indoor window where the air is purer, life-prolonging, she tells me 'That's the last of it now. It's a bit of a mixum-gatherum.' I gather my notes and wonder where the coins came from. And the plastic casing of my savings book makes a low squeak like a plaintive mouse as she slides it back to me over the counter. Or maybe it's my driver's licence that's the plaintive mouse; I cannot tell.

—

We drive on. It doesn't get any warmer. Instead, rainstorms come. Wind buffets the car and the wipers fling themselves to and fro until they are exhausted. We stop in petrol stations, as we must. In the queue for the till, I inspect the chocolate display. I locate the position of the Fruit & Nuts, and if I can reach them without stretching too far and becoming conspicuous, then back on the road we'll share a bar. Fruit for me, nut for you and the chocolate between us.

We pass a hillside of windmills like medieval spindles in the sky, spinning the cirrus clouds into cumulus. We pass sick rabbits with limp ears and socked expressions hopping circles in the ditch. We pass sheep's wool torn by barbed wire from the sheep who grew it, tussling to bust free of its spokes.

We see a glossy ibis, a spoonbill from southern Europe, Portugal or Spain. An elongated raven with a curlew's beak, rare as a bank vole. He is delving in the brown puddle of an overflowed field. He flies away as the car passes, did you see?

First thing every day, I wind down the windows to evacuate the stench of our morning breath combined. Now the nights are so cold, so astonishingly cold, I faintly expect it to have frozen inside the car, into a solid clot of lurid green, an ugly embodiment of foul dreams and sleep disturbance. SLOW THROUGH VILLAGE, the signposts say, but I rarely heed them. I keep on until I know from the angle of the trees, from the way they shy their limbs from the brunt of the sea gales, until I know that we are nearly there.

Look, the sidewise branches.

'Nearly there,' I tell you, 'nearly.'

—

I dream I'm tied to a post and standing up to my chest in snow. Even asleep, even inside the dream, tied to my post, I know the picture-making part of my mind has borrowed the dream's landscape from an article I read in the newspaper roughly this time a year ago. It was about a group of greyhounds who were left tied up in their compound and froze to death. Without kennels, they lay on the concrete and were buried the first night of the blizzards. The article's photograph showed a scene of wheelbarrows, shovels and ropes which trailed off into the drifts. Now I can see, in my dream, greyhounds on their backs with their legs standing high and rigid as the post I'm tied to. I can see tongues stuck to fangs and turned a powdery blue, the colour of cornflowers. It's a cruelty I never even witnessed, yet I associate it with you, I dream it into your past.

Sometimes I notice tiny scars beneath your coat, tiny claw slashes and teeth prints. A few bits of your ears are missing, a few bits of your face. Can you remember how you lost them? Do you dream about it, as I do? I see how you move your left brow up and down and left and right in coordination with the expression on your face. I notice how still you blink your hollow. Do you miss your missing eye, I wonder. Have you even realised it's gone?

—

The concreteness and geometry of the scenery is building, building, building into a town, a seaside town.

First come the bungalows, always the bungalows. Each surrounded by a lake of lawn, by swan-shaped flowerpots and terracotta cherubs, perennial shrubs and flatpack sheds. See the palm trees; I never expected there'd be so many. The palm is a tropical tree, as out of place in this wetland of cows and fog as a bullseye in a bag of apple drops.

Next come the Italian and German supermarkets. Now a secondary school with three storeys of bored and pimpled faces peeking through the slatted blinds. Now come the narrow streets and shops and pubs, a library and town hall. Buckets on the footpath in front of a flower shop, bouquets of gerbera and gypsophilia looking strangely cheerful against the bleached winter. A rail of second-hand clothes wheeled out of a charity shop onto the street, a sea gale knocking the mothballs out of capacious cardigans and chintzy frocks. Now come the apartment blocks, all taupe and steel and stifling close together, with balconies too narrow to open a newspaper, never mind a folding chair. The apartment blocks are abutting a plaza of wide, smooth slabs. Now here on a pillar is a statue of some dead sea captain. There's a herring

SARA BAUME

gull perched on the crown of his admiral hat and a splattering of milky crap down his epaulettes. In the town by the sea a man in a sandwich board pronounces that it is Friday, and Friday is market day. And I wonder if, when he was a little boy, he wanted to be a man in a sandwich board when he grew up. The slabs of the plaza the length of the shore front are pitched with open tents, billowing with canvas canopies, bustling with browsing bodies. Beyond the Friday market, the bay curves like a beaten horseshoe.

I get the car stuck in the town's illogical one-way system and drive us in circles until you begin to look sick. Now I stop at the first free parking space and shunt into the drain gully. As we climb from the car, I remember the muzzle far away on its apron hook. I know I promised never to mention it, but I feel as though you should be muzzled now, as though it's dangerous for us to walk about this sea town with your mouth unshackled. But I brush the feeling off; today I am strangely buoyed, strangely brave. Perhaps it's the sea gales, the inspiriting salt air. Perhaps the months of driving have peeled back some of my strangeness, my horribleness, and replaced it with pluck.

FARMERS MARKET, the sandwich board says, yet few of the stallholders look like the farmers I've known, like the old men I used to see at mass, like the pig-farming, horse-chipping hitchhiker. These farmers have woolly scarves and placid, unscrunched faces. Their stalls hold potted heathers, rooster potatoes, plaited and sugar-dusted loaves of bread, iced sponges on paper doilies. The market pleases the bower-bird within me at every swivel. Here are baskets of green, red, yellow apples and glass bottles of clouded juice. WINSTON, JUPITER, the baskets say, EGREMONT RUSSET. Now see the cages packed with poultry of every squawk and plumage pattern: bantams, rosecombs, quail. Plump, white ducks with plump, white eggs arranged in boxes stacked on top of their cages.

Of course you see them. I have to bind the handle loop of your leash around my wrist as we pass and you nearly saw my hand off with your tugging. I know the market's disorientating; it's disorientating for me too. All of this colour and movement and sound, after so many weeks just you and me in the quiet capsule of the car. The smells are of stoneground flour and ripe cheese and broken eggs and lavender and shit-coated feathers. So many new smells that you're tossed about by the whimsy of your maggot nose, from cured hams strung up on hooks to feathery creatures innocently scratting. Now a girl with a stud through her upper lip like a silvered beauty mark proffers a tray of tiny breads.

'Would you like to try some tapenades, sir?' she says. Her voice is sing-song.

The tiny breads each carry a tiny splodge of grainy paste, in faded black and brilliant red and anaemic green. I know I should keep walking. Ordinarily I'd pitch and clump away as fast as possible. But I don't. I take a red, the colour of warning, of admonition. The taste is vivid. It seems to gush into all the parts of my mouth at once, and is good, so good.

'You like that one?' the girl says. 'That one's my sun-dried tomato. Here, have another.'

As though faintly inebriated by sun tomatoes, again I accept. I take a second red bread, and without thinking, I drop it to you. You're watching, waiting dutifully at my feet for a little taste of whatever it is I'm eating.

'Treat,' I say; this is your favourite word, foremost amongst your one hundred and sixty-five.

You gobble the bread and lick your chops, and the girl laughs, sincerely. Just for a second, I feel like a regular person, doing regular things, in a regular way. I look around at the crowd, at the peddlers peddling and browsers browsing, at mums rallying three-wheel buggies and teenagers slouching against each other and old folk baby-stepping behind their walking frames. And I feel faintly ordinary, faintly incon-spicuous, faintly unsuspicious. And it's good, so good.

'I'll take a jar,' I say, 'of the sun tomatoes.'

The girl laughs, but not in an unkind way. From a wad in my shirt pocket, I unroll a note and hold it out and she hands me back some coins and a jar-shaped paper bag.

'Thank you,' I say, 'thanks very much,' and off again we wander, in the direction of open water, feeling all vivid inside, all sun.

———

At the stop of the slabbed-stone plaza, there's a railing running along a step which falls into the sea. I'm leaning against the railing and you're standing on your two back legs with your front feet rested against the step like a tiny man, like the two-year-old child you match in intelligence. Straight away it feels as if I can breathe better, now the view is blown open, now the land is drowned. And even though it's a different bay and a different ocean, you smell the cloy of rot and fish and tang and wet and seem to recognise a trace of home.

The waves are breaking against the concrete, but it looks like there's a measly beach beneath the step. What stage of tide are we at? It must surely be the highest. I always used to know, yet somewhere in the scrum of countryside, I lost track. Now I tow you along the shore front in search of sand, past the last of the market stalls and away from the crowd, following the footpath which follows the curve of the bay until we come upon a solitary caravan.

The caravan is a strange distance from everything, everyone else, as if it's been nudged to the very limits of the town. Through the broad rear window, I can see three seated women with white-gold hair and thick shoulder spans. They're facing a huge screen mounted to the low wall above their heads. On the screen there's another gold-haired but slimmer woman facing back out at them. She's speaking through her smiling teeth and jiggling her hands and bouncing her empty gaze about to include everyone and no one all at once. She's wearing a Madonna blue dress, and on a short shelf alongside the mounted screen, there's a Mary, a scapula and a crystal vase of fresh carnations: a homemade grotto.

I turn away, I don't want the women to see me. As I do I notice you've rammed your claws into the concrete and will not budge. What is it, what's wrong? I look into your eye to try and tell what you're feeling, but it's black as your fur. All pupil and no iris, no white. Now I remember from somewhere that these are the kind of people who bred you, the kind of people from whom you ran. Is this why your chest's dropped low to the concrete, why you're pulling, pulling, pulling? I steal a last look at the caravan and as I do I understand how these people are outcasts too, pariahs, and I know I should feel some throb of kinship. But I don't.

I turn around and allow you to tow me all the way back through the plaza, the market, the town, to the car. I lock our buttons against the world, against the peddlers and browsers, the slouchers and strollers. I look out the windscreen at all the people walking on the street and sitting on high stools in cafes and queuing beneath the shelter beside the bus stop sign. I know each person is carrying a tiny screen in their pocket. I know each screen holds a list of the names of other people who are not here but somewhere out there also carrying a tiny screen. I know that inside each pocket there's a gold-haired woman whispering to the person who carries her, telling them they are included. Sitting locked inside our quiet capsule, I try to picture the details of these people's lives, in order that they'll seem less unfamiliar, less unsettling. I try to picture the colour of their walls, the clutter on their kitchen tables, the view out their front-facing windows. But no matter how hard I try, all I can see is my purest egg-yolk yellow, my inkless biros, the mud of my bay.

I'm still holding the jar-shaped paper bag in my hand. I place it down beside me. But as I place it down I start to wonder if maybe I didn't seem regular in the market after all, inconspicuous, unsuspicious. Maybe the girl at the tapenade stall was conniving against us all along. Maybe what we've been given is a poisoned dose, a jar reserved for those who seem strange, those who walk the streets unarmed with tiny screens. Now I knock the bag onto the floor mat with a sweep of my fist, now I lean over and push it beneath the passenger seat. And we drive out of the seaside town and away from the main road, away again in search of a reassuring dead end where the drowned view is ours alone.

You understand. I know you understand.

—

See the black-headed gulls in the fields, picking the naked soil for earthworms. They're listening with their earless faces for the muffled shuffle of a careless crawler. They're stabbing the brown glop with their hatchet mouths. See how the gulls' plumage has returned to its winter pattern: a smudge of dark feathers behind the eye. Is that how much time we've let slip past inland? I hadn't realised.

Now we find a narrow back road which leads to an even narrower track. Our wheels amble through hollows and weeds and brooks for a half mile at least. Now we arrive at a clump of houses, an unsignposted strand and a shell cottage facing the sea. I've heard about such cottages but never seen one. I park and out we climb and go to look. The cottage is completely covered with cockles and limpets, hundreds and hundreds, even thousands. Each shell is shallowly set into the plaster; each is blanched and sullied. Time and weather have transformed the shell cottage from an august monument to a tumbledown thing all barnacled by hard, dead blobs. Who lives here, I wonder. Who would you guess lives here? But you're busy sniffing, always sniffing. Now the thistles stretching up through the rungs of the wrought-iron gate, the pillars either side, the whiskery moss. The path is covered with algae and the shrubs have grown errant. An old woman, I think. An old woman too frail to hoick a lawnmower across the grass or lift a power-hose to her limpets. She has a paunchy son, I think, of thereabout my age, who keeps promising he'll come and do a job on the garden, but never does. I would willingly hoick and mow and hose for this old woman. I'd chop off my plait to have an old woman of my own who'd let me sit at her kitchen table with a steaming cup and a gingernut. Maybe she'd let you sniff the overgrown garden, to excavate her flowerbeds for buried pats of shit.

But it's too late, I'm sorry. Now I have no idea how things begin, nor how to know that they are safe, nor how to show strangers we are safe too.

There are other houses here. It's not so extremely left-behind. One house has a granite-chipped driveway leading past a laurel hedge, a fuchsia bush. Another has a sculpted stone head sticking up from a gatepost. Remember the peach eagles? This one looks like a tigress, but I can't be certain, perhaps a leopard. We're still standing outside the front gate of the shell cottage as a boy in football socks stomps down his driveway to retrieve a wheelie bin. Now we watch as he drags it up through the laurel and back to the house. All his gestures are exaggeratedly huffy, though there's no one to witness his protest, no one but you and me, and the boy didn't even see us.

We walk from the thistles to where the cliff drops into open Atlantic and there's nothing but luscious, jumping blue all the way to America. I'm still thinking of the boy in the driveway, of how he doesn't realise how lucky he is to live here where there's space to run and the salt wind ruddies his cheeks each day, how he takes it all for normal and considers himself entitled to be huffy with the wheelie bin. Now I wonder was I lucky too, and never grateful? Sometimes a little hungry and sometimes a little cold, but not once sick or struck and every day with the sea to ruddy me. Perhaps I was lucky my father took me back when the neighbour woman rang his doorbell, lucky he never drove away and left me on the road again. But it's too late to be grateful now. It's too late now for everything but regret.

I'd like a coastal cottage of my own, of our own. What do you think? I'd cover it with seashells, only we'd have queeny frills instead and I'd piece our windows into place with my sanded glass, pebble by pebble. We'd have a lawn for you to lick the dew from and a patch of bare earth where I can raise my faulty crops straight from the ground. Our cottage would be down a narrow track with an unsignposted strand and an unbroken view of jumping Atlantic, just like here. And I'd carry a patio chair to the end of our lawn. I'd put it there, see there? Right there. And I'd face it to the uncluttered horizon.

But it's too late, of course. And suddenly, it's a sad place, don't you think? Suddenly the shimmer of possibility is blotted by the shadow of a soaring gull. The gull scans the tide as it passes, and seeing that it's not yet low enough for mud worms, it flies back inland, to pick the naked fields again, to root the brown puddles alongside the ibises.

—

We scrabble down the cliff face.

Below the shell cottage, choughs are nesting between the juts and scrub, the chamomile and samphire. There's something sinister about choughs, something impious about their witchity cawing. There's a bird book in my father's house which spells the sound they make as *chuff-chuff-chuff*, like a jaunty steam engine. But the book is wrong. The real sound is raucous, like the choughs chuff sixty smokes a day and are warning us to stay away from them, from their juts and scrub, samphire and chamomile.

The lichen here is different from the lichen at home. Instead of blistering yellow, see how it's globby and white like the surface of a moon a child might draw. Below the cliff face, here's a plot of rubbled strand, and now sea. The water is dungeon dark and the way the ethereal weed moves beneath the surface makes it look as if it's a living, swimming, struggling thing, as if it's the long black hair of a head held under by an invisible manacle.

Now I let you free of the leash and you take off without a tic of caution. You stick your nose into several different holes, gobble an unidentified object, cock your leg on a patch of dead clover and still reach the bottom before me. On the strand, you stop and push your face into the stones, twist your neck after your face, twist your back after your neck. Your legs lift into the air, the pads of your paws face the sky and waggle. Now I stop my downward scrabble to admire your spontaneous little jive, the ecstatic thwacking of your upside-down tail. Does this place remind you, as it reminds me, of the pebbled beach where we picnicked every rainless day in summer? Now I'm sorry I don't have my rug and flask and parcels of picnic food. But then you were always afraid of the aluminium foil, so it doesn't matter.

I sit and take out my tobacco pouch. I pinch and turn and tear and roll and smoke into the setting sun. You and your maggot nose continue with the pressing business of sniff and scoff. You scale and comb the rocks, leaving no pool unpaddled, no inlet unslobbered. You're watching all the new things and the way they are quivering. You're waiting for some part of it to rise up, to configure into prey. I see how clumsy you are, how your balance is affected by your lopsided sight. You stumble and fall, chip your knobbled bones and bruise your pallid skin. You disappear for just enough time for me to worry. Now you reappear, dragging a strange bulk over the pebbles. It's longer than you by a yard and trailing kelp fronds, tens of tiny crabs, a regiment of goose barnacles. It's an enormous spine.

I laugh. I say, 'What are you going to do with Moby Dick then?'

And you drop the spine at my feet and wag your tail. It was maybe a dog fish or maybe a spur dog or maybe even a basking shark. Now it's a gift.

'It's a good gift,' I say, and you settle beside me, and I roll a smoke, another smoke, and smoke.

And we stay like this until the sea has risen to the tip of the dark stain on the cliff-rock which marks the line of highest tide. And I note the time. I memorise it. Now I'll never let myself lose track again.

—

There's an angler spinning for bass on the *further* rocks, picking his way between the lofty jags and yawning hollows, over the wet weed and moon lichen. Now the white horses are gathering height, their froth licking his boots, and they are heavy boots, designed for drowning men.

I wonder why he takes all that trouble for a fish, just to break its neck against the sandstone, chump off its head, scrape its organs out and bake its sides for supper. Maybe he isn't doing it for supper but for the sport of killing, for some small spilling of blood to satisfy his internal Neanderthal. It's hard to understand when you're a man with no knack for destruction. But maybe it isn't for supper or sport but for the thrill of the girth of the gap between his drowning boots and dry land, and this I understand, because as much as I crave the sea I crave its openness. I need to know that even though I'm small and land-bound, right in front of my face it is enormous, endless. Can you smell it; can you smell the endlessness?

We watch him for a long time. You patrol the quivers and I smoke, at first, and now forget to smoke. Now I grow as rapt by the spinnerman's task as the spinnerman, as intent upon a catch. We watch his slow-yet-certain progress across the distant rocks, how artfully he flicks the rod, dips and swishes his jellied lure. Now I begin to feel what he feels, a vestige of the force that compels him to fish even though it's cold and dangerous and disappointing. Across the wet weed I am whispering, *Just once more, Just a little closer, this time, almost.*

Come the sun's last stand, the spinnerman hauls a beast of a sea bass from the froth. Fat as a baby crocodile. He holds it up, admires it. The fish bares its teeth, swats his wax jacket with its great tail fin. Now we watch as he tosses his beast back to the toppling waves. It breaks the surface with an almighty splosh. And the spinnerman continues on his way. Sashaying across the rocks, wiggling his worm. Beginning again, for nothing.

—

We pass playgrounds. There, that's what that is, there. See all the contorted structures, ply planes connected by rubber-coated bars and painted. Whatever happened to straightforward swings and slides and seesaws? There's something menacing about these newfangled contraptions, these rungs and nooses and pony heads mounted to the sharp end of thick springs. If it wasn't for the bold colours, they'd look like medieval instruments of torture. Here's the rack, the stocks, the breaking wheel, the Witch's Closet and the Judas Cradle. The playground's surrounded by wire and railings to keep children in, paedophiles out. There's a regulation notice outlining the rules and restrictions of play: NO RUNNING, NO JUMPING, NO PUSHING, NO DUMPING. Alongside the notice, there's a bench for guardians to supervise from, to ensure that fun is never allowed to list over the line into depravity. They watch us as we

SPILL SIMMER FALTER WITHER

pass. They make a mental note of our registration number. 93-OY-5731.

How many weeks now since we turned around? How many gateways revisited? Now we pass a lay-by with a man dressed in steel-capped boots and a high-vis vest. He's manning a canopy-covered car trailer alongside a display of bundled sticks and reused fertiliser sacks of rough sawn wood. STICKS, his sign board says, BLOCKS. It must be fulsome winter; now we pass Christmas decorations in place of tree ghosts and rotted pumpkins. See the bulbs hanging from the leafless branches of a streetside beech, white light prickling the perpetual grey. See a spray-painted Santa in the chemist's window, waving at us from between the anti-ageing potions and protein shakes. Now here's a car with a red nose attached to the bumper and a felty antler stuck out the windows either side. How puzzling people are.

We are heading south, I think. Getting lost, retracing roads and finding south again. I seem to miss a lot of cul-de-sac signs; now I'm master of the six-point, three-point turn. We are keeping the sea in sight as much as possible, sometimes veering into barns, streams and slurry pits, almost. I never expected it would take so much reversing to make a straight line. It's still so cold, and still I wake at night and relight the gas, and still you wake with me, lean in and drink the blue flames. I make hot whiskey, warm milk and something stodgy to eat, to heat the blood about our bellies.

'Treat,' I tell you, and you wag.

See the hairs, your hairs. See how they accumulate in the car's interstices, knit together into fuzzy rope. I strip the upholstery and shake our blankets out. I scrape the ropes from their interstices. I lay them on the wind to fly. From the radio, an expert is telling us how birds will gather loose hair and use it to cushion the lining of their nests. But now I remember, of course, it isn't spring. It's December. I'm months and months and months too early, too late.

—

I wake to a face at the window, again.

This time it isn't a grizzled old woman but the sheen of a child's flawless skin, a boy. Not the boy whose shih tzu you spectacularly maimed nor the boy who directed his huffiness toward the wheelie bin nor any of the boys with raised hoods and unlaced runners, not even the boy with calipers around his calves and a weaponry of pebbles bulging his pockets, his pencil case, yet familiar somehow. In my lap, you tweak a sleeping paw. I look down, just for a second, but you don't wake. And when I look up again, the boy's face has changed. The brow seems to have bushed, the nose seems to be breaking out in pimples, scales, warts. I watch as it changes, bit by bit, into a troll's face instead of a boy's. And I forget that it's only a trick played by the moon, a distorted reflection of my own face. Just for a second, I forget, and am terrified.

SPILL SIMMER FALTER WITHER

—

I was standing at the sink with my back to the table.

Are you listening? I'd like to tell you this now. I'd like to tell you about what happened on the morning my father sat choking in the kitchen.

I was standing at the sink with my back to the table.

Then I heard something behind me like the noise a bicycle pump makes when the bicycle tyre is as inflated as it possibly can be. Then I heard the bang of his fist against the Formica. All the crockery hopped and dinged and I turned around.

My father had moved his hands up to his neck and wrapped his fingers around his throat. Because he was not speaking or coughing or crying out, it took several beats of my internal metronome to realise there was something wrong, that he was somehow in trouble. For several beats I stood and gawped and tried to bring to mind where I recognised this gesture from, and then I remembered.

It was the International Choking Symbol from the Emergency First Aid for Children chart. I could have lumbered up to my bedroom wall to check but there was no need, I knew each panel off by heart. Whether by accident or design, my father was acting it out. I knew absolutely that he was choking, and I knew exactly what I was supposed to do. I was supposed to lean the adult person forward, to administer five firm blows to their back with the heel of my stronger hand and once this hadn't worked I was supposed to enfold the adult person with my arms until my hands were able to hold one another beneath their breastbone. I was supposed to drive the knuckle of my thumb into the flesh of their belly, over and over and over, until the sausage was dislodged.

I knew, I knew, I knew. To do all of these things. But I didn't. Not one.

I stood at the sink facing my father with my arms dangling at my sides. I allowed the only opportunity I'd ever had to practise my panels slip past. I watched as his lips and fingernails turned blue. The blue began pale, with only the intensity of a sea aster, but then it continued to intensify through harebell and into forget-me-not. And I wasn't paralysed by fear or stunned into spontaneous memory loss. Nothing like that. I didn't do anything because I simply decided not to.

—

For years and years, the flat above the grocer's has been used as a storage space for the goods sold downstairs. Now I see boxes pressed against the window, bottles of fabric softener and sunflower oil. Next door, there aren't any lights left on inside my father's house. At least, not in either of the rooms which face front.

So here we are now. Two wheels abutting the footpath. Home.

I haven't been able to remember whether I remembered

to switch them all out. The lights, my precious incandescent bulbs. Every day these past nine or ten or eleven weeks, I've wondered, I've worried. Now we're back in the car's old parking space outside the terrace, but it's such a bright morning and all the curtains are drawn, so I still can't tell for sure, about the lights. Now I think I see the curtain twitch, the curtain of my father's old workroom. The brushstrokes-on-the-wall room, the shut-up-and-locked room. Did you see it too? There's the weakest glow, I'm certain, a circular beam pointing down into the street, moving over the shore wall, scanning the bay. And I wonder if he's somehow sitting up and manipulating his desk lamp, searching for us. Now I hear the boom of a ship's horn. There's a cargo vessel coming in to dock at refinery pier, a great tanker with tens of circular reflectors twizzling from its cranes and pulleys. A cloud slings itself across the morning sun and when I look back at my father's window, the searchlight's gone, of course it's gone. Of course it was just the sun bouncing between the ship's reflectors and the window pane. From the apron hooks to the chimney pots, the house is every bit as dark and somnolent as it ought to be.

It's almost noon. Last night's rain has stopped and the bay is as brilliant and blousy as the day in spring I drove you home from the kennel compound and coaxed you out of the cranny beneath the dash. Remember the cherry's confetti and the flowering embankments, the blinding yellow of the rape? But now it's December and I'm the one refusing to climb from the car. I can't stop myself thinking about the halo-headed boy and his barraging mother, about the woman warden with her collared pole who swore she'd come back. I KNOW WHERE YOU LIVE, but they all know where we live, and that's why I can't get out.

So here we stay. Here we watch people come and go with their bags and boxes from the grocer's, their choco-crispy breakfast cereal and bottles of discounted Chardonnay. They are the people who buy tool belts and steam mops, remember? The people who visit fireplace showrooms on Sunday afternoons. See the icicle lights strung from the grocer's awning, the wreath of polyester holly batting against the door each time it bangs. Now the Polish hairdresser arrives and raises her shutter. See the notices Sellotaped inside her window. GHD STRAIGHTENER SALE, they say, HALF PRICE GELI-CURES. Behind the notices, there's a stuffed reindeer. It's tall as a child with several Styrofoam robins perched along its speckled back. Now the twitcher pitches his twitching stool along the bird walk and unfolds a tripod to support his gigantic binoculars. There's a little egret on parade, a couple of curlews and a clatter of redshanks, the same decorous old heron. The summer boys are gone now; they're hibernating behind their mother's venetian blinds and there's a Christmas tree in their old slouching spot. See the noble fir with gift-wrapped boxes tied to its branches. I can tell by the way they quaver in the wind that the presents are empty, just for show.

We sit outside. We watch everything proceed oblivious to us. I know I should drive away before somebody recognises the car, and remembers. But I want to sneak in. I want to check if I turned the immersion off and hit the oven switch on the wall. I want to gather some of the stuff I offhandedly left behind, stuff that never seemed precious until I was without it. The brass egg-timer and the pencil-sharpener in the shape of a panda bear eating a bamboo shoot. Then there's the cushion with an embroidered Indian elephant on the cover, a log splayed between tusks. I read somewhere that elephant motifs are supposed to be lucky, but only if they are facing outwards. What if I left the cushion upside-down, the elephant smothered? Then there's Mr Buddy. Now I feel terrible I left him behind the washing machine so many years alone. And I want to collect the swallow's nest from its roof cranny because maybe if I have their nest then the swallows will somehow still know how to find me.

I want so badly to sneak in. I want to stand beneath the scorching gush of the showerhead and feel the filth of nine or ten or eleven weeks wash from my skin, my hair, and down the plughole and through the secret pipes. Now I feel as though I'm crawling with tiny worms, and as I slice them with my scratching nails each slice becomes a new worm. Each slice is burrowing, burrowing, burrowing.

I look up at my father's house. The sun has shrugged its cloud off and turned the window panes opaque. I think of all the books inside I left unread. I think about the marmalade mouldering, mouse shit collecting in the presses, mouse-bitten bran flakes leaking onto the beauty board. I think about all the planes of soft card with tiny rectangles torn from them and I think about the tin of baking powder with its picture of a tin of baking powder, with its picture of a tin of baking powder, and so on, into infinity. I think about the bathroom sink, about the furiously blue watermark, the blue of forget-me-nots, of my father's choked lips and choked fingernails. It pinpoints the exact spot beneath the tap where drip hits enamel, over and over and over, and I wonder how much more furiously it will have blued.

What will happen if they come and break the door down? It's only a flimsy door. It won't take much breaking. What happens if they go rifling through all my offhandedly left-behind stuff? Toss the panda into the bin, smash the frail glass of the egg-timer, kick the draught snake from the threshold of the shut-up-and-locked room, find my father's shoeboxes and snort with laughter at his homemade games. What happens if every last thing is cleared out, lobbed into an industrial bin bag and left on the side of the street to spill? The neighbours will come poking to see what utensils or appliances might be worth recycling for themselves, and then they'll quickly move on again, empty-handed. Shocked by how a life might come to be so wretched as ours, so insignificant.

What happens if they find some small trace of my mother? For all I know she was there all along. If our life was a film, it would be a photograph in a locket, a love letter, a tress of hair. What happens if they decide to take a look in the roof?

Strung from the left-side hanging basket, there's a length of clear plastic, the sort that comes off the goods pallets delivered next door. It's long as a lamppost, strangling the facade of my father's house, flapping. I wonder why no one's bothered to remove it. But I don't remove it either.

———

My father never got up from the table all the time he was choking. He didn't thrash around; he didn't knock anything over. It seemed like it took a very long time for the old man's choked face to drop and settle against the formica. He placed his nose neatly between the crockery and leaned the weight of his head down after it without upsetting so much as a teaspoon. I remember looking at the dash of discoloured milk at the bottom of the bowl from which he'd eaten his bran flakes, at the smears of grease on the plate from which he'd forked his sausages up. I remember noticing there weren't any pieces left. The one he choked on must have been the last. I remember thinking that it was up to me to wash and dry the bowl and spoon and plate and fork now, to return them to the shelf and drawer.

I'd never made a phone call in my life before. I'd never answered the doorbell.

I sat down at the table beside him. I pictured the ambulance men in their high-visibility ambulance outfits. It was raining, and so I pictured water droplets against the black of the body

bag as they wheeled him out. In my mind I saw the doors
of the ambulance closing and I heard the siren bawling as it
drove away. And then I realised of course there wouldn't be
any siren, that it was already too late to bother switching it on.

—

Behind the blue gate, there's new litter in the laneway, unfamiliar litter. The front door of my father's house groans,
as if in protest at being re-entered. Now you tramp new paw
prints across your old ones and I follow you. You go directly
to the nook in the kitchen where I used to keep your food
bowl. But it's in the car, remember? It's been in the car now
for months.

Straight away I single out the egg-timer and the panda
sharpener from amongst the kitchen table jumble. I remember
suddenly how the tabletop was always kept clear while my
father was alive and so this jumble must have taken years to
accumulate, and belongs exclusively to me.

Now I hunker down and hug the washing machine and
haul. I hear the slight scratch and gentle slither of some
creaturely thing descending to the floor tiles. I reach around
and grab and tug. Mr Buddy comes out in three different
fistfuls. So the spate must have reached him too, so the
rats must have ripped his clouds out. I bundle Mr Buddy's
stuffing up with Mr Buddy's hide and stick the lot inside a
plastic bag and knot the handles as though he might somehow

reassemble himself and escape. Now I take the bread knife from the block and tear a new bag from the roll and carry it all upstairs with me.

You go a few steps before. You find your old spot on the sill and I open the curtain so you can check the view from the window to make sure that nothing has erred from its place. The elephant cushion is on the rocking chair, facing the right way up, of course. Now I must lean over you to push the window open. I reach out and up to the swallow's nest. Using the bread knife, I scour it down. Using the bag, I catch it. See how it still has papery shards of eggshell inside, how it smells more of warmth and life than dry, dead mud. Come here and see my nest, smell the life.

Now I place down my peculiar luggage and go to the foot of the door of the shut-up-and-locked room. I lift the snake, I let the fetid draught through. I turn the key.

Now there's something I need in here. Something that I have to do.

—

On the morning he choked, I sat beside my choked father at the kitchen table and tried to decide what would happen next. I sat there a long time. Even after I'd decided, I continued to sit. After a while, I started to speak. To ramble away as I often did, only this time, for the first time, I felt free to say different, truer things.

'Hallo old man,' I said, even though we'd both been there all along.

'Well,' I said, 'what did you tell her?' I couldn't remember the woman's name, the neighbour who took me from the side of the road and drove me to my father's house.

'What did you tell her when she found me all on my own,' I said, 'in the ditch in the dark and drove me home and rang your doorbell?'

I tried and tried and tried to remember her name, but I couldn't.

'Speak up, old man,' I said. 'What did you tell her?'

But my father didn't answer, of course, and of course it didn't matter. I knew anyway. Whatever the name of the woman who drove me home, I knew my father told her I'd run away, and wouldn't come back, and couldn't be found. Because I wasn't a right-minded little boy. I wasn't all there. I was special. See how that explains why nobody came to ring the bell again? It explains why I never started school, never lined up with all the other little boys and girls, all those all there and right-minded and unspecial. It explains why I never got a chance to play on the straightforward swings and slides and see-saws. Now do you see?

Now I see. I see how uncourageous I was. I see how I only asked about the neighbour woman because I was yet too afraid to ask about my mother woman instead. The old man was dead and still I hadn't the nerve to confront him. I stopped talking and stood up. I washed and dried and put away and once it was all done I went upstairs to my father's room. I pushed the door and pulled the pull-string which opened the roof and drew the folding stepladder down. Then I went back to the kitchen to fetch him.

Things are never so immense when they happen as they were when only in my head, as I made them, remember? My father was not so heavy to lift nor was it so very arduous to drag him. He smelled like pork and smoke and toothpaste and I realised I'd never been so close to the old man to be able to smell him before. He lost one slipper on the stairs, the other on the stepladder. Then I placed him down on the bare boards of the attic. I rolled him onto his back and brushed his eyelids closed, like they do in films. If the roof had been insulated there would have been yellow pillows of spun glass upon which to lay him out, but it wasn't and there weren't, and that was my father's fault.

I pushed the stepladder back up and the roof obligingly sucked it in. I locked my father's room without searching for a single trace of my mother and I stuffed up the gap beneath the door with a lumpy fabric snake.

—

Now as I push open the door of the shut-up-and-locked room, I think again about how things are never so immense when they happen as they were when only in my head, as I made them. Remember? The old man's room is as I left it, as

SARA BAUME

he left it. There's hardly even any dust, but then dust is made of human skin, so how could there be? Of course.

You follow me over the threshold and sit at my feet as I sit at his desk. Do you know what the first thing I did was after I put my father in the roof? I locked myself in the bathroom to hide from flashing lights. It was sitting on the toilet seat with the lid lowered that I remembered something I'd read about a custom called Sky Burial. It was in a book about Tibet, there in the living room on one of my shelves. The highest country in the world, where there's too much buried rock for digging graves. But that isn't the reason why people bring their dead into the mountains and slash open their flesh and leave them for the vultures. They do it because they believe a dead body is just a vacuous slab of meat to be disposed of in as munificent a way to nature as possible. As I sat on the lowered lid thinking and gradually knowing no flashing lights would come, I saw that I couldn't have dug a hole for him anyway, in my garden of gravel and cement. I saw how a Sky Burial was to the unknowing best of my ability what I had improvised for my father, and so when the spate of rats began, I was glad, even a little triumphant. The clamour of their activity was a kind of companionship, a kind of comfort. A kind of Sky Burial.

But after only a matter of months it occurred to me that once they'd finished with my father they might seek out a weak spot, a cleft between boards which led to a crack in the ceiling plaster. They might not realise I am not dead. They

236

might not discriminate either way. They might scratch and scratch and scratch until they could drop down and land and rampage through my rooms. For months and years the clamour never fully ceased, and I never fully stopped listening or fearing that the rats might still be chiselling away at a fracture, coming for me.

Then one morning there was an expert on the radio. I haven't told you this before but it's about you, are you listening? The expert told me that a small animal, like a rat, will instantly smell the presence of a larger animal, a predatory animal. It will smell and know and stay away. This set me first thinking, then looking, and so there came you; this is how there came you, my good little ratter. And for a while I didn't hear the scratching in the roof any more, or I forgot to listen.

Now if I was the old man, I ask myself, where would I squirrel my most precious things? The only place I can think of is under the bed, so I lift the corner of the duvet which grazes the carpet, I feel around. And perhaps I am more of my father than I pretend to be because after only a second my hand collides with a rigid object. Not a locket, a letter, a tress. Instead I draw out an old-fashioned sweet jar with a screw top and sticker that reads SHELBY'S ASSORTMENT YOUR NAME HERE. Underneath someone has spelled out a name, a woman's name in red felt-tip: R U B Y. I unscrew the cap and because my fist is too large to force inside I tip the contents out. It's stuffed with packets of sherbet dip, empty but for a sprinkling of purest white powder. I check in packet after packet after packet until the sugar dust makes me sneeze. Now I lie flat as I can on the flab of my gut and flail my arms and pat my palms around beneath my father's bed until I know for certain there's nothing else. Well, what do you think, is this my mother on the sherbet jar? I tear away the sticker as though she might be in some small way revealed.

Now I get up and reach for the pull-string, and you're too short and have too many legs and not enough arms to climb the stepladder, and so I must go up alone.

'Back in a minute,' I tell you.

—

Amid such an almighty mess of rat shit, it's hard to believe my father's bones could be so clean. I hadn't expected them to eat his clothes, the sausage in his windpipe, his windpipe. They've chewed away the cartilage which bound his skeleton together, they've waltzed his disparate pieces across the bare boards. Only the exceptionally long toe bones are recognisable as my father's.

Now I have to go back down for another plastic bag, and when the plastic bag is not strong enough, for a pillowcase, and when the pillowcase is not big enough, I have to take his ribcage out to the ash stump in the yard and splinter it apart with my kindling axe. The pillowcase bears a pattern of tiny white flowers, but when I look closely they are no type of flower I can name. They are no sensible shape of flower at all. They are wrong, they are fake.

With the pillowcase slung across my shoulder, I take the bag with Mr Buddy inside and the bag with the swallow's nest inside, the egg-timer, the cushion cover, the panda-bear-shaped pencil-sharpener. I stop only to lift a picture frame, to root out its smiling stranger and press the sticker from the sweet jar against the glass instead. Now I take the picture frame along with all the other stuff, and I take you, of course.

Of course I take you.

—

Curlews rise from behind the Christmas tree and skitter across the bay peeping, peeping, peeping. The bird book spells the sound they make as *cour-lee, cour-lee*, like a kind of yodel. But it isn't, not even close. Each call is different; each call means something new.

The curlews pass over the pine copse at the end of the bird walk. Beside the copse, there's a van parked on the hard shoulder. Now I see a man in a wool cap standing at the top of a ladder propped into a tree. What's he doing? A brown blob falls to the grass. Another and another, until I see the wool cap man is holding a handsaw and chopping the pinecones, one by one. After a while he climbs down and goes about with a coal sack gathering his brown blobs from between trunks and amongst needles. A long time passes while we are watching him, but the wool cap man never breaks his ceremony to look back along the bird walk to the village. I wonder will he spray the pinecones with fake snow, tie red ribbons to their stalks and sell them from a car trailer with sticks and blocks. He has a hefty sackful now, far more than he could ever hang on his own noble fir.

In the backyard, there's a potted tree, remember? I'd forgotten it, until now. It's a spruce, I think, scarcely the circumference of a dinner plate. I read somewhere that the oldest spruce in the world is eight hundred and fifty-two, and not in a pot, I presume. Every Christmas Eve when I was a boy, my father used to carry our spruce indoors and place it on the living room windowsill and leave it there well into January. But he never decorated it, and every Christmas, it looked bereft. And every new year, I'd be glad when he put it outside again.

Now the wool cap man is finished stealing pinecones. He loads his van and drives away, and I know we should be driving away too. Will I sprint around the back and grab the spruce? This year, we could decorate it. We could sit it on the back seat with aluminium foil stars dangling from the branches. Only I'm not much of a sprinter, and you're afraid of aluminium foil. And now I remember, of course, the tree outgrew its pot years and years ago. My father never transferred it to a bigger one, and so it died. Our Christmas tree is a naked stick now, I'd forgotten that.

Now I realise what I must do. I must come back, under

cover of dark, with the shop and salon shut, the shore birds roosting. I must bring a can of petrol, a box of matches. Can you picture the night slugs charred and shrivelling? The plates exploding on the walls, the drifted timbers reduced to kindling, the bran flakes turned to ash. The salmon pink and yellow house turned shades of salmon and pink and yellow like never before.

—

The rain comes. It comes in all vicissitudes of strength, direction, drop size. The only consistency is its constancy. Where once there was silence, now there's the fizzle and drum against our thin roof.

By the time we've reached the graveyard it's sturdily pouring. If our life was a film the rain would be a sign that something sad is about to happen. But it isn't a film, of course. No one is watching us. Nobody even knows where we are.

This is the graveyard where my father should have been buried. I park outside the gates. You're sitting on the back seat with your face pressed into the gap between front seats. You're whining softly to be let out even though you don't know where we are. The graveyard in which my father isn't buried as he should be isn't beside the parish church, as it should be. Instead it's an overflow graveyard, zoned to a characterless plot half a mile outside the village. It's been here for as long as I can remember but only in recent years have the housing estates risen up on either side. From the car I can see over the wall at the graveyard's far side and right into the rectangular garden of a semi-detached. There's a timber shed with a heavy-duty padlock, a patio decked in varnished pine and a matching kennel. It's an elaborate kennel with a pretend chimney on the roof and a pretend window on the side, and now I see there's a blonde muzzle and black button nose poking out of the doorway. This must be what you're whining about, what you're sniffing through the air vents.

'In a minute,' I tell you. I am almost finished collecting myself. 'Just a minute.'

Inside the car, our breath is coating the windows in condensation. Bit by bit, the graveyard and patio and kennel are misted from sight. Now I open the driver's door and we step into the rain. It seems somehow less fierce than it did inside the car. The graveyard is surrounded by a stone-clad wall. The gate grinds against its hinges as I push. The plots are arranged in a block system, like a miniature Manhattan. Most of the individual graves have marble headstones and dun-coloured gravel. I read somewhere that all grave gravel is imported from China nowadays, that it's against the law to take stones from the beach, they have to be purchased from a Chinaman instead.

The freshest graves are soil heaps marked with wooden crosses and cortege garlands. SISTER, the flowers spell, NANNY, DAD. Some are plastic and some are silk and the only real ones are carnations, the longest-living flower yet also the one most associated with death. I skip the garlands and begin at the furthest corner, the place where I imagine the oldest graves to be. Here the soil has long since slumped into place above each coffin. There are no crosses or figurines or everlasting candles. No trinkets or engravings. No carnations. There is just grass, which is dead, and weeds, which are flourishing. And I wonder if I should take my father's axed ribs from the pillowcase and use them now, like a dowsing rod. Only not to find water, which is everywhere. To find my mother, my mother's grave.

But there's no need. Now I find her easily. All the years I never looked, and now here is my mother. Here she was all along. OUR DEARLY BELOVED RUBY. On a plain grey slab in the perpetual downpour. DIED 1956 AGE 23, the headstone says. I answer by saying it out loud.

'Nineteen fifty-six,' I say, 'when I was two.'

You know I believed she died when I was born, because I was born, and that my father always blamed me. I believed I'd never known her, and now I see I knew her two whole years and can't remember a single moment. And so I wonder why he blamed me anyway, and if he didn't blame me at all, why was he always so unkind?

You look up and know it's you I'm talking to. But you're busy chewing on a piece of stray grave gravel. I can hear it rattling between your teeth. Now I watch as you swallow. But you always ate the gravel anyway, remember?

'Ruby,' I tell you. The same word as for red in Latin, as

for one amongst the four most precious of the gemstones. The colour of warning, of admonition.

'Good boy,' I tell you, for no reason at all. 'Good.'

The rain drops grow; they come straighter and surer. Back we go to the car, and I turn on the gas cooker, take out the saucepan and cut open a packet of marrowfat peas. Together we watch the retriever crouching in his kennel atop the decking. We watch all afternoon, but nobody comes to bring him for a walk or give him his supper. Dark falls at five o'clock as usual, and still every ceiling sun inside the retriever's house is switched off while the graveyard is flickering all over with the dim bulbs of everlasting candles. Each to its own plot, hovering over old bones and teeth and rings and wristwatches, like tiny light-bearers.

Beside me on the passenger seat, you sigh. Front paws rested on the dash, nose pressed to the air vents. You're waiting for your walk.

'Will we go to the beach then?' I say, and you wag, wag, wag with all your strength.

—

See the skin which crowns each of my fingers and hems my nails in, how it's all bitten and ragged, crusted and tanned like old rubber, fissured and parched like a drought-stricken landscape. You know why it's like this. You see me continuously, tirelessly worrying it with the other fingernails or with my teeth. Or sometimes even with the penknife. Fingertip by fingertip, I work the skin loose and tear it away. Then I set the wound aside to mend, and once it's healed, I worry it afresh. You see me, all the time and during everything I do, picking, picking, picking. Sometimes gently, sometimes viciously, always unstoppably. There was a time when I found it comforting; now it's just a thoughtless habit. And as with all habits, thoughtless or otherwise, the only release is sleep.

The drive between the graveyard and Tawny Bay is five or six or seven minutes by way of the coast road. For five or six or seven minutes, I attack the skin of my fingertips with particular venom. You press your nose to the window and my father nods his skull in time with the bumps and twists. From the radio, an expert is telling us that whales kept in captivity develop a droopy dorsal fin.

It's almost a year since we drove this way to the beach instead of walking through the forest and over the fields. Do you remember the refinery road, the boat house, the banana skin, the barley? This time I drive us right into the car park. It's a stretch of gravelled earth on the opposite hill to the belching chimneys and jimmying windsock. It sits precariously on the undercut cliff's edge above the sandy strand.

Here's another car already parked, and so we have to wait for the car's people to ascend the cliff path and drive away. I know you're dying to get out, but we can't risk an encounter with night-walking strangers, I'm sorry. We are last in line, remember? We have to be patient.

We have to keep our dorsal fins stubbornly upstanding.

—

We stumble down the cliff path in the smudgy dark. It's been three months of cold season since we walked here, and now the beach is transformed. The sand's covered in amorphous sea monsters. They are slinking, stinking, swishing, their slick backs glancing off the moon. Ribcages and shin bones stick up through the sand, like an elephant graveyard. The smell is foul, and you're delirious. Leaping, diving, waltzing with the monsters, drunk on their sulphurous fumes. You know straightaway from smell what I can only tell from touch. Now I crouch down and stroke the ground. It's kelp. Kelp dredged from the seabed and vomited onto the shore, because of the storms and high seas and because Tawny Bay is outside the harbour's mouth, unsheltered. I've seen kelp plagues before, but never so immense as this. I reach to snap a rib and it bounces back, pliable as a wet baguette. Now you're ploughing your face through the mess, following rancid scent trails, fish guts and ancient nappies. I call you and clip the leash on. I drag you up the path to the car. I can't risk losing you in the dark and gunk, not here and now.

'Tomorrow,' I tell you. 'Patience.'

It wasn't true, what I said before. That the nights would

seem warmer once we were back at sea level. I'm sorry. I didn't know then that I was lying. Now we're as far south as we can go without driving off the side of the island, and still it's eye-streaming cold. Still we're lying awake and watching ice crystals spread like an enormous spirograph across the windscreen. See the spider frozen to the glass of the left wing mirror. He's prising his legs off to free himself, one by one.

—

In the morning, the spider's dead and the ditch is white and crunchy. See how the spiders who survived the night have spun tiny web hammocks in the unbending grass. Are they afraid of heights, I wonder. See how the grass here is different to the grass inland. Tough and glossy and sharp, I'd forgotten that. Now you cock your leg and saturate a tuft of winter heliotrope with sweltering piss, and the heliotrope trembles in fury a long time after you have finished.

The smell doesn't seem so bad this morning as it did last night. It's early, the tide's out and there are no other cars, no walkers. I unclip the leash and you run ahead into the kelp. In some places, it's lying a few feet above the sand. The morning waves are far too frail to suck so much back in again, still they lap, they persevere. There are tens of other kinds of weed too, at all different stages of decay and diced through with smashed shells, dinted bottles, toy tyres, fractured lobster pots, flip-flops. Buoys and broken shards of buoy, but far more than I can carry, more than I can store, more than I can care about. We walk the strand, clearing a path. I'm carrying the deflated football, looking for a patch of flat sand to throw it at. But there aren't any, and even in daylight Tawny Bay seems strange and unfamiliar. Now the beach we both knew is ossifying somewhere beneath the kelp.

Halfway from the end, there's a beached porpoise. I catch up just as you're beginning to gnaw its tail. I pull you off so I can see it properly. I'm no expert, but I can tell a porpoise, which is small and black and blunt, from a dolphin, which is long and grey and shapely. Porpoises look like killer whales without the badger stripes and somehow kindlier. The porpoise's skin is tough as a block of toffee, tattered in places and lacerated all over by rocks and junk, by crow pecks and rat's incisors. There's a gash gaping from the end of its mouth, splitting its cheek. You swallow a few mouthfuls of tail meat before I tug you off and shoo you on along the beach.

At the strand's end, I look back to the place where I know the beached porpoise is lying. It looks from here like just another old car tyre amongst the kelp. Where do all the tyres come from? Is the seabed covered in sunken cars? Are the eels nibbling their rust? Nibbling, nibbling, nibbling until a tyre is unfastened and bobs to the surface. Another and another. But now a herring gull rises from the tyres and I can see it's holding a chunk of rosy carrion in its brilliant orange beak.

Before we go back to the car, follow me up the hill at the back of the beach, to the peak of the barley field beyond the refinery, to the exact point at which, together, we first saw Tawny Bay, do you remember? Now the field is striated brown, mottled by the green of stubborn shepherd's purse. Do you remember how I taught you to play football? Do you remember the day the lion-maned collie appeared through the mist? From here on the hill, Tawny Bay is our beach again. Regardless of hue or surface, regardless of all the trouble you caused here, it's ours.

I wait all morning for you to sick up the porpoise. I worry my finger caps with especial fervour. I chump them into bloody ribbons. But you don't.

—

The supplies are running low.

How many days spent here now? Several, more? But perhaps the overhang will surrender before the food runs out. Yesterday I watched from the beach as a hunk of dead grass and mud broke away from the cliff's edge beneath the car park, tumbled down and shattered against the kelp. Today I move the car to the spot directly above the missing hunk. I stand on the gravel and jump about and stamp my feet. But nothing happens, and I know I look ridiculous, and I wonder if I really mean it.

We haven't a single gingernut left, I'm sorry. I've only

ever kept enough food in the car for a couple of days, and now we're down to six tins of spaghetti hoops, three sachets of oxtail soup and a bag of crinkly royal galas. I'm trying to ration now. To eke out what's left for as long as possible, so as not to have to make a decision about what happens next. But a full stomach is a kind of sanctuary, remember? And so my hunger makes me feel less safe; it tinges my attempts at decision with fear. There are always the sun tomatoes. I hear the jar moving beneath the seat, thunking against the passenger door. And there's no need to fix me with your greedy stare. There's a bumper sack of kibble in the boot. The place where my money tin is stashed, remember? Beef rind flavour with added animal derivatives and minimum ash. It's been there for weeks, in case of emergency, a situation just such as this.

The situation is that I can't bring myself to return to the village and walk into the grocer's. To pick out purchases and place them on the counter in front of the till. I just can't. If it isn't the bald-headed, clean-shaven grocer, it'll be the girl with the name tag, APRIL. And she'll recognise me, they'll all recognise me, and what do we do then? I know there are other villages and other shops, I know. But I just don't think I can drive off anywhere, anywhere at all. I don't think I can tear myself from the cocoon of the car on the undercut cliff. Now this concrete car park is my only choice of safe space, of sanctuary, and I'm sorry, I just can't.

And anyway, I don't have any money left. My mixum-gatherum is spent. My tin's empty as the day we shared its sardines out. Even if I had the courage to go back to the post office, the postmaster will only tell me my account's cleared, that there's some problem with my social security card. Then his voice will go flat and leaden, and to dismiss the uneasy silence he'll say things about the weather, about the cold, and I'll reply *Sure you never know from one minute to the next what's coming* even though it isn't true, I did know. For fifty-seven years, I knew. And it's only now that I don't. It's only since you.

—

Here is our latest aerial seat, the concrete car park on the crumbling cliff's edge. Ever uprooted and apart, remember?

Sometimes people come to Tawny Bay in tracksuits and try to jog a length along the strand. We watch them slip across a couple of yards of kelp before they give up, return to their cars. Now we've adjusted to the stink and learned to navigate our respective ways through the slithery wasteland I'm glad of the kelp, of its deterrence. We lap Tawny Bay every time the tide's low, the beach deserted. I pitch and clump and flail, you gallop and trot. Together we play graceless forms of football. I try to teach you how to chase the gulls, the pipits and knots.

'GO ON, GETTUM!' I holler. 'YOU CAN FLY, ONEEYE! FLY!'

But you've always been a smarter animal than I, and you know you can't.

Now the sea throws me every kind of junk to rifle. A new arrangement every tide, a ceaselessly replenished stock. The biggest items are dropped at the very back of the beach along the seam of clay at the cliff's base, while the lightest and grittiest keep close to the waves. Here are car tyres, a broken buggy, a trawlerman's waterproof, a knitting needle, pinecones, my pinecones. Now here are cigarette butts, fragments of anemone shell and individual pieces of Styrofoam packaging. Some of the pieces are shaped like an 'S' and some of the pieces are shaped like a 'Y' and always I find myself looking around in search of a 'K'. I know it's daft, but still, I'd like to be able to spell SKY.

It throws you gifts as well, the sea. You find a dead guillemot and carry it around for hours like a possessive child with a favourite toy, like me and Mr Buddy way back when. I watch as you finally find your way through its feathers and yank the white meat from its skimpy breast. Now here's a rectangle of water-worn plywood. See how it bears a pattern of screw holes, the ghost of a handle. So it didn't sink, all but its bow, into the mud. See here, it's a piece of my father's doorbox, I'm certain.

There's an old creel at the near end of the strand and it makes a good chair, a place for me to sit after you've tired me out. I can't recline exactly, but I can perch. I perch and watch the high, slow rollers. And I watch the sky. I see the weather coming.

When I was a boy I used to be able to stand in the shallows and jump the waves for hours without growing bored, without being bothered by the sensationlessness of my frozen feet. Now I'm only fit for the creel, for chain-smoking, for cloud spotting, for listening. The sound of Tawny Bay is a sonorous slopping of water against rock. And the squeeing of the gulls. And sometimes the clank and whirr of a trawler that seems nearby but is actually distant.

I bring my plank of drifted doorbox back to the car. I show it to my father as though his eye sockets are somehow able to see through their fabric shroud.

There isn't any radio reception in the car park on the cliff. I twiddle the dial so slow it barely moves but all I can find is white noise and fizz, maddening fizz. Every now and again, I catch a stray airwave. A stranger's voice shouts a single word through the static like an elapsed mayday. 'ASSOCIATE,' they shout. 'UPSKILL, INORDINATE.'

At night, I don't twiddle. I like to hear the waves rush and burst. I like to feel the spew against my windscreen, even though, of course, I cannot feel it through the glass and the glass can't feel at all. It makes sleep seem like a kind of swimming. Like my limbs are loose and weightless, treading water. On choppy nights, I fidget in time with the sea. But on calm nights, I sleep so deep I crush my hands and wrists inside some larger cleft of my body and wake to find them bloodless, numb. It makes me afraid the night will come when I crush you instead. Your stalky bones will crumble, your tender lungs collapse, and I will not wake. I will continue to swim, until it's over.

—

Still, sometimes I think that I will burn my father's house, which isn't my father's house any more and I shouldn't keep calling it that. But I always change my mind. I am continuously changing my mind, talking myself out of action, as I've done all my life. Now silence and sleeplessness have minced my resolve. And I see how I was stupid to believe that anyone will ever force their way inside. The old man is dead and it's my house now. Even if people knew for sure that I was never coming back, still they'd wait for some distant relative to claim it in my place. To nail a FOR SALE sign between hanging baskets. It's always seemed to me like people will choose to wait wherever waiting is an option. Until walls fall down unaided. Until every species is extinct and all the ice caps have melted. Or at least, this is what I want to believe, and not the opposite, which is what I'm afraid of. I'm afraid that they are coming for us.

For two years now, the hairdresser hasn't paid a snip of rent, I've only just realised that. She used to post it through the letterbox on the first working day of every month in an envelope that smelled like sweet glue and hand cream. But for the last two years, not a snip. And why would she bother, when the landlord's disappeared and there's only his idiot son who won't notice anyway? And I didn't notice, did I? So maybe I'm everybody's idiot after all.

How long? How long since we parked here? You look up from the passenger seat, you tilt your head. I'm sorry for asking, over and over and over. I know you don't know, you never knew. I know enough days have passed that the date is irretrievable now. My tobacco is gone too, gone with the date. I know well the pouch is immaculately empty, still I persist to check and check and check in case some fine strands of twiggish brown might have miraculously grown back. The mineral water's almost gone and I'm saving the gallon drums for drinking. You drink the grey stream that runs from fields to sea, collecting rain and agricultural effluent as it goes. I tell you not to, still you drink. I watch for signs that you've been poisoned, for shakes and faints and fever. But you're always fine, invincible. You cast your thousand-mile stare across the open water. You grunt. I give you one of my father's tibias and you gnaw it with relish.

'Good boy,' I tell you.

We're down to the kibble. You seem to like it well enough, but it's drab and dusty to my taste buds. I can't detect any whisper of beef and I can't fathom where on a cow its rind is located.

—

Two black specks on the furthest rocks at lowest tide become people as the sea rises and the waves drive them in. Are they coming for us? But closer still, they become Chinamen in waterproofs carrying white coal sacks. Two apiece, one slung over each shoulder. The sacks are dripping. The Chinamen's backs are bent against the weight and their faces are scrunched against the rain. They're wearing green waders held up by suspenders. The rubber trousers reach up to their nipples, dwarfing the Chinamen, diminishing them to sad, windswept circus clowns. But they are just cockle pickers.

See the cockle pickers, how they stagger.

———

This is the first night there's been another car parked after last light. It's at the furthest end but it's pointing straight at us instead of out toward the harbour like visiting cars normally do, and I wonder has it come for us.

I saw the stranger car arrive and point this way, but I haven't seen any car people get out and go to walk along the strand. For a while I continued what I was doing. I was trying to put Mr Buddy back together again. But I don't have any needle or thread and so it's a pointless, frustrating task. Now it's flossy dark, the stage of dusk at which every visible thing disintegrates. The stranger car's headlights are switched off, the dashboard unlighted. There's no trace of a face or faces eerily illuminated from below. I'm leaving our lights off too, and I can't have the gas cooker spreading its blue, not tonight. I'm sorry. I can't have it illumining my father's skeleton through the fake white flowers, nor Mr Buddy's glass eyes through the plastic of his bag. I know it's cold, but we mustn't be seen by the person or persons inside the stranger car. I can't give up so easily, not now.

You look spooked. It's in the way you're holding yourself: head dropped and shoulders raised, eye narrowed, neck shuttling at every crackle and creak. Are you spooked because there's something spooky out there or are you feeding off my own incompressible uneasiness, my stupid fears? I cannot tell. Now you clamber into my lap and fidget. I lay my big hands over you. I stroke your head and neck and back until your muscles soften and your body stills.

'Sleep,' I tell you, 'it's okay. Sleep.'

Now I force myself to stop watching the stranger car which is watching us with its headlamp eyes and number-plate grin, its car face. I fix my attention on the harbour instead. Beyond the disintegrating forms, the sea's a great empty space between landmasses and even the opposite landmass is distinguishable only by scattered lights, by ten hundred tiny shining points. Each point is a car or a streetlamp, the window of a house or prison or hospital or pub. Each one stands for a story of continuing life and each life is continuing to be eaten away by the onerous effort of living itself, remember? It's marvellous, yet strangely distressing. The sound of the sea is heightened by night, but its spectacle is blotted into an abyss. Now a fin breaches. See the fin. Already it's gone again, but it was a dorsal fin, exquisitely undrooped.

I need a smoke. How desperately I need a smoke.

You fall asleep. I try, but can't. My attention segues from the harbour to the luminous hands of the clock face on the dash. Sometimes they catch up with each other and fuse into one. It's halfway between ten and quarter past twelve by the time the stranger car lights up and makes a careful U-turn. As it pulls back onto the road with its indicator blinking, I catch sight of two dishevelled lovers side by side in the front seats. They're so intent on one another, they don't even glance in our direction.

You wake for just a second, now fall back to sleep. And again I try, and again I can't. I listen to the waves crash and spit, playing timpani on the windscreen. The seas are high tonight, higher than all the nights passed since we arrived, so it seems. Now the clear sky's choking up with rain clouds. They take the moon out, now begin to shed. See how the drops are dense and drowsy, as close as rain can come to snow. It's half past two exactly, and still I cannot sleep.

See there behind the shedding rain clouds, there are moon oceans and moon mountains and lakes full of moon water. Remember? Or is there even water on the moon? I'm not so sure any more.

—

They come in the morning.

It's first light, and I'm still awake. The rain's stopped and the wind's snuffed. I sit up in the driver's seat and rub out a circle of condensation with my fist; now I melt the frost with my breath. Through the windscreen I see how the night's high seas have scoured the beach clean. Now the deepest water beyond the rocks is slack as a city puddle. The kelp fronds and junk are gone, from the trawlerman's oilcloth to the creel chair, even the pinecones. The tide's on its way out again, the sand inching back into sight, the smooth banks and squat peaks, the depressions. Up on the cliff, the grass has crystallised and the heliotrope is stiff as a stick. But there's no trace of snow, and I wonder if it snowed at all, or if I just wanted snow, and imagined it.

I get out. I fill the saucepan with a frozen puddle, smash it up a bit. I fetch the gas. Now I notice we're down to the last canister. I set it burning at its lowest setting, roaring mellifluously through the prick-holes of its nozzle. I watch as the ice melts into drinking water, and I wonder why, why I'm trying so hard to keep going.

You're awake, stretching effusively and yawning with such particular inflection it almost sounds like a human word, like ark or arm or Arles. Now that it's morning you aren't spooked any more. I can tell from the tilt of your ears, the twitch of your maggot nose. Look here through the windscreen, see how the beach has been restored to us. But you look into your food bowl instead, and it's kibble for breakfast again, I'm sorry.

They come as you're licking up the last of the kibble juice. They come in family-sized cars with chocolate labradoodles, fleece-lined ski jackets and two or three apple-cheeked children apiece. They park slipshod all over the gravel. Now they emerge and fall into groups. They hug, jig on the spot, cup their palms over their mouths and puff. They unpack sports bags and wicker baskets, Thermos flasks and portable cup sets. Now they point their keys and push buttons which make their cars blip and wink on command.

They don't seem to notice us. They descend to the beach. Together we peep out of my condensation porthole. Who are these people and what are they doing down there on the strand, so many and so early in the morning? They're wrapping themselves in tent-towels and wiggling out of their winter clothes. Trousers, knickers, skirts and socks are lying like laundry on the new sand. And now the people are shrugging off their towels to expose bathing costumes, stripy trunks and sleeveless wetsuits. Of course, that's what it is, the Christmas swim. They haven't come for us after all, it just happens to be Christmas.

Our porthole's beginning to re-fog as the swimmers altogether advance into the freezing sea. We hear them whoop and cheer as the small swell shatters against their milky legs. We watch as they dip down and dabble a few weakly strokes between the seaweed and the Styrofoam letters. Now they're dashing back to shore in a blur of pinkened cheeks and purpled kneecaps. Already they're climbing back under their tent towels. We must look away while they're redressing. I can see you're still peeking, look away. The swimmers loiter and josh on the beach. They take out baby bottles of brandy and wrap their fingers around plastic cups and gingerly sip. Now they're drifting back up to the gravelled rectangle. You begin to hop about and bark but I shush you. Already it's over, and we must sit still again. We can't be spotted by such cheerful strangers. We mustn't dare to mar their joy with our shabby faces, our carload of stolen nests, dead bears and decomposed fathers on such a day.

Carload by carload, family by family, the swimmers leave. Now the hands of the dashboard clock are fused erect at midday, and the car park on the undercut cliff is empty again.

—

You're keening to be let loose. I open the driver's door just a chink and you're over me and out before I've fastened the leash. I open my mouth to call you back, but there's no point, it's dinnertime, Christmas Day. I picture the swimmers beside their stoves, basting and peeling and stirring. No one will come, not now. And so, I tuck the plank under my elbow and sling the pillowcase over my shoulder. You're dancing the gravel, tracking the departed labradoodles, pissing where they pissed. Now you hurry down the cliffslope and I trip behind.

The new sand is printed with paws and feet and scored by finger-written names, lovehearts and smiley faces. There are freshly dug holes and scuff marks and the dents left by children who pressed their heels into the sand and spun around to make a perfect circle the perfect length of their perfect foot. Even though the strand is swept clear, I can still see the porpoise, now pushed against the clay. See how the Christmas swimmers' children have sunk a rock into its skull. The jaw bone's flittered, the up-facing eye socket buried beneath the weapon stone. A tablespoon measure of the porpoise's teeth have been bashed free and lie sprinkled about the swept sand like chrome confetti. But you don't see, you're far ahead of me now, almost at the strand's end. You're skirting the dunes, keeping always to the edges of things, like a sewer rat. You're pointing your nose to the cliff, susceptible always to the inveigling hills and forests from which you came. I follow you. I reach the end and look back. I'm checking the gravel for cars. I'm scanning the beach for new arrivals. But there's nothing and no one back along the length of Tawny Bay. There is only us, and so.

And so, I bend onto my knees and place the plank down and lay out the pillowcase on top. I rope it all together with seaweed, meticulously. I knot the kelp and fasten the eelgrass into bows. You have come back to me now; you are watching.

And so, I let loose my feathery plait and shake my matted

hair out. I peel my clothes from my hideous body, layer by filthy layer until I'm standing amongst the sand hoppers and flies in nothing but my yellowed Y-fronts and laddered vest. A slight breeze ruffles the coiled hair on my chest, my back, my calves, my forearms. Look, an ingrown toenail, oozing pus. You, confused, lick the pus and wag your tail. I am horrible. I know I am horrible. Still faithfully you follow me to the water's edge. Neatly you seat yourself between the shells and pebbles. Patiently you wait, as I wade into the freezing sea. Towing, towing, towing my father on his doorbox.

I can feel the ripples sluicing my marinade of grime away. I remember how much I wanted to have a shower when I was back inside my father's house, my house. But by the time I'd done all the other things, I couldn't bear to wait while the water heated, to listen to the pipes cricking out their bones, speaking to me again after such a long silence. The kelp caresses my ankles. Now my thighs, now my stomach. Now my chest, now my chin. It's joy-sapping, spirit-rotting, chilblain-inducing, nose-dripping, eye-stinging, teeth-aching cold cold cold, but the old man bobs behind me on his old boat, impervious.

Now I need to tell you something. I'd like to lift my feet and splash around and show you a couple of strokes, but I don't know how to swim. That's why I've stopped here with the water tickling my beard, why I've turned around and am staring stupidly back to shore. I can see the brown fields and bare trees and farmhouses, pale plumes spouting from their chimneys. And the smudge-headed gulls circling the bay, godwits and redshanks, lapwings, oystercatchers. Maybe I can even see a lugworm's extrusion of black sand, rising slowly, lapsing back again. I can see you, the whole of my family, and I wonder why you don't make a break for the hills. Now you must realise you'd make it, that I couldn't catch you. Still you're sitting at the water's edge; still you're waiting for me.

Now I push the doorbox as hard as I can, hard enough for the backwash to splash in my eyes, and once I am able to open them again, I see he is drifting out alone now. The current is taking my father, drawing him away to the place where the shorebirds disappear at nighttime and high tide, to the great floating continent called Out To Sea.

Now I begin to wade back. The water drops from chin to chest to stomach to thighs to ankles, and out again. Now we know. Now we've retrieved the irretrievable days, and can begin again.

Happy Christmas, One Eye.

—

The flames shiver and cough for several moments before they sink and die.

Inside my clothes, I'm sopping. Wet as a fish and stippled with goose-bumps like pointed scales from crown to soles, my face the colour of dog violet and tufted vetch. The gas has run out; the last canister is empty. I tip it upside-down and shake but the mellifluous blue refuses to be resuscitated. I check my tobacco pouch even though I know, of course I know. I sit down in the driver's seat. I stare at the pale pools of my palms upturned and laid open on my knees, the white of elder, of angelica. I flinch my fingers, uselessly. I drip. Now you jump from the gravel, land square in my lap and squash my hands. There's something in the feel of fur against goose-bumps that reminds me of a hamster I held, my Russian Dwarf birthday hamster, a half-century ago, the frail brush and bob and small warmth of him. But my hamster was only the size of a kiwi fruit while you are monumental and unskittery. You are stalwart and you are solemn. You are safety and you are home. But your warmth is not enough, I'm sorry.

'Sit back,' I tell you, 'sit.'

Now the only way to soothe the cold is to drive around with the heater switched to full blast, the fan whirring, the engine eddying hot air through the vents. Just when I need the small comfort of my addictions the most, my fingers fail me. They're too numb for rolling a smoke, too numb for picking my hangnails. They blunder over the simplest of movements. It takes longer than it should to get my seatbelt buckled, my key in the ignition. The car hasn't shifted a yard in days, its greasy innards are cold as a box of fish fingers. I don't expect it to start, but with the first try the engine putters uneasily to life. Now you raise your front paws to the top of the seat and press your nose against the rear windscreen. Now you look back at the beach as we leave. You watch as Tawny Bay shrinks to the size of a photograph on a postcard, a picture on a stamp, and now gone.

Now we're driving, driving, driving. Up, down, this way and that around a succession of familiar and unfamiliar and almost familiar back roads. We're passing fields of winter wheat and hawthorns with their trunks bent to perfect right angles against the sea gales. We're passing waterlogged litter, charred gorse, pine copses, gyrating turbines, bales sealed into their black macs and stacked. We're swerving around dazed rabbits and bouncing through cavernous potholes.

I touch the radio's dial to test the airwaves. I twiddle. A voice shouts through the fizz. GLORY, it shouts, GLORY GLORY GLORY. Now the voice goes dead and the fizz returns.

Do you see how I'm drawing us around in a circle? Now we're approaching the village again. See the bare branches of the cherry trees. The houses with people inside and the shops with goods inside and the church with all its chalky gods inside, and everything and everybody remaining inside, because it's Christmas, of course, and there's nowhere to go. See the bird walk, the information board, the noble fir in all its hollow frippery. See the takeaway, the chip shop. The pub, the other pub. The grocer's and the hairdressing salon, all shut. See the community we were insidiously hounded from. See how community is only a good thing when you're a part of it.

Now the car parks itself in front of the terrace, two wheels abutting the footpath. I clatter the keys to the salmon pink house from the glove compartment. I have to leave you here this time but I'll be fast as a flash, I promise.

'Back in a minute,' I tell you.

Inside, I smell it. The smell I could never smell before. Black mould, cigarette smoke, garlic, hand-wash, coffee, damp dust, sweaty slippers and my own heinous breath altogether compounded into the unnameable stench of home. Now I remember to have a quick look to see if there's any tobacco still lying around. I rifle the table junk, the kitchen drawers. At the very back of a cupboard I find some soggy cigarette papers in a packet torn away to nothing. Each tear is the perfect shape of a tiny rectangle, and so this is where my father got his roaches from, of course. He robbed it from the cigarette paper packets all along. Such a tiny stupid mystery, solved.

I don't have any petrol or paraffin or even alcohol. I scatter a box of firelighters across the living room floor. I find a can of Easy Oil and spray it onto the rocking chair, the coffee table, the carpet. I light a match. I throw the match.

I run.

As we drive from my father's house, my house, I close my eyes. I picture the overloaded coat hooks, the unidentifiable stains on the kitchen lino, the rocking chair, the draught snake, the mouldy marmalade. I know I should be looking at the road, but it's okay, the car won't let us swerve off course. It knows the way.

Now I picture it all in yellow and pink flames. From

the creaky floorboards to the wormy books and up through the un-insulated ceiling to the slanting slates. I picture the moss hogs erupting in tiny flashes, now leaping and scampering from rooftop to rooftop, across all the buildings of the village, spreading fire in their wake. I picture them surfing the wind through the forest, now pausing a moment to gobble the banana skin, now descending upon the refinery. I picture holocaust. I see gigantic, volcanic, apocalyptic fireworks. And they are lighting up the sky and sea of the bay as though it were the brightest day in summer.

Up up up we drive. To the top of refinery hill. Here we stop. Here we climb from the car to look back down upon the village. Now we see how all the sky-high tufts of lost grass remain unburnt, unburning. Now we see that the fire hasn't caught, that the house has already quenched it. And I picture my father still in there, still smoking and shuffling across the rag rugs. The bathroom beads softly clacking, the rainbows caressing his face. He is searching for his slippers, stamping out fires in his socks as he goes.

Didn't the village used to hum? Now the hum is a grumble, can you hear it too? We get back in the car and I recommence driving. What else can I do?

The village is already behind us. It's already nothing but a huddle of pastel and beige squares in the rearview mirror.

Now it seems like such a sad place. See how sad it is.

—

Half a century ago, I closed my fist around my hamster, my first and only birthday present, my Russian Dwarf, and squeezed it to death. I only did it because I thought I couldn't. If I'd thought I could I would never have squeezed. Then I held him in my palm and felt the frail bob stilled and the small warmth fading and the brush of his fur freshly gummed with blood. I hadn't known that a life could be ended so effortlessly, so ingloriously.

We cover a final lap of familiar back road. Now down a boreen so narrow and neglected both sides of the car are clawed by furze and a strip of overlong groundsel tiddles our car belly. The boreen ends with a ghost of a track, a cliff drop, a trawlerman's blue rope. Do you remember? The springy grass and silverweed, the abandoned burrows. The scabious and chamomile and campion are all missing now, the ladybirds and hoverflies. The high tide means our pebble beach, the flat rock we used as a picnic table, are underwater. Now here's the slope where we'd leave the car; it seems suddenly steeper. I park with our headlamps pointing to the sea and nothing but gorse to break the car's fall, our fall. If it was to fall, if we were to fall. I wrench the handbrake into place.

The tide is high, the gas is gone, my tobacco. Soon the kibble will be gone too. All it would take is some slight fault of the handbrake. Not even a press, but a tweak, just a tweak. It's a cold day; is it still Christmas? I can't remember. There are rocks beneath the surface, below the headlamps. I can't see them, but I know they're there. I know by the way the waves are broiling. Whereas far out, they are simply swelling and rolling, failing to break. It's a sad place, but then I seem to find most places sad, and maybe it's me who's sad and not the places after all. Maybe there's nowhere I can go, and no point in going.

Now look in the rearview mirror and see the cows and the sandpits and the holiday cottages, deserted now. See all the licensed earth in its hundred different shades of brown. Now look through the windscreen and see the floating lighthouse pulsing red, the empty water. I've never been able to figure out exactly how much you can see through your lonely peephole. Does it affect distance, depth, perspective? I know I don't need to list everything we pass like I do. I know I don't need to talk to you like this. I know it's nonsense, it's all nonsense. But now I have to tell you something, and this time it's important, okay? This time you have to listen. You have to understand.

I'm no spinnerman. Remember the spinnerman? How he continuously began again for nothing? Well I'm no spinnerman. And remember the burrowhole in the forest that I almost followed you down? Well now I wonder why I drew back instead of pushing on and allowing the bank to cave in and extort the air from my lungs and be done with it. But that wouldn't have been right, because you don't belong to me, One Eye. You don't belong to me and I was wrong to ever treat you like you do. You belong to the inveigling hills, to the fields and ditches untrammelled, to the holes in the forest, the horizon line, the badgers. The seasons don't belong to me and the sea doesn't belong to me and the sky doesn't belong to me. All I own is my father's house, the saddest place in our whole small world. And the warden will return in time, the old man's bones will be sloshed back to shore and identified, and even if I did change, I'd only change back again. And so.

Do you think if I take the handbrake off, the car will roll us home to the salmon pink house, grudgingly yet irresistibly, like I always said it would? There's a free bird of fear inside my chest but beneath its wings my organs are putrefying, bit by bit by bit. There's a hunk of grassy rock a little way out. A tiny island upon which ten, fifteen, twenty cormorants are gathered. Now here's a lobster buoy and a plastic bottle coasting past. Now a blue gallon drum with a common gull perched on top. I'm sorry, I'm doing it again. I'm listing every last thing as though you can't see at all, as though I am the eye you lost.

'See for yourself,' I tell you, 'see.'

My hand is on the handbrake, my lamps are to the water. And now you must turn around from the shore. Now you must listen to the forests and the fields.

You are the only thing, One Eye. You are the only.

Now listen. Can you hear it? The badgers are calling you.

—

I close my eyes and our life is a film and we are rolling, rolling, rolling.

The car parks in its space outside the terrace with two wheels abutting the footpath, and inside I tidy up the mess of firelighters and Easy Oil and out again we go along the bird walk and laid on the mud at the foot of the shore wall we find the pillowcase of bones on its doorbox chariot and I carry it down our laneway and up the stepladder and into the roof. I shut up and lock the shut-up-and-locked room, realign the snake.

Now in the kitchen I place the sausage pan on its hob and you sit at my feet and wait as I fry. And you are a good boy and so I tell you.

'Good boy,' I tell you. 'Good.'

EPILOGUE

There is a tiny figure, right on the cliffslope's edge, like a sock puppet to the theatre of the open sea.

His shoulders are bunched and his head is lowered. There's a trail of smashed briars and gorse running across the slope in a straight line, from the spot where the tiny figure is hunching, into the water. And he is looking down as though he is waiting for something to rise from there.

The tide is high.

He can see a gallon drum, a plastic bottle. He can see a lobster buoy nodding in time with the waves, tussling against its anchoring pot. But he can't see a fleet of by-the-wind sailors which has just been disbanded by a mighty disturbance. Now they are struggling to regroup, and he cannot see because they are too small, too blue, too scattered. And he can't see the conger eels several feet below the surface either. Unseen they are nibbling, nibbling, nibbling.

Now he turns his head to look to the fields. He stares

at the telegraph poles and firs and hedges, as though he is learning the horizon off by heart, as though he is listening very carefully.

Now a bird-scaring machine fires its thunder clap into the sky. And all the crows and gulls and starlings, all the cormorants out on cormorant island ascend flapping and soaring in perfect synchronicity. And the tiny figure on the cliffslope's edge ceases his waiting and springs to his paws and sets off at a sprint.

He is running, running, running.

He is One Eye.

He is on his way.

ACKNOWLEDGEMENTS

Thank you Thomas Morris, Lisa Coen, Sarah Davis-Goff, Lucy Luck, Jenna Johnson & everybody who worked on bringing this book to life. Thank you family, Mark & Wink, of course, from whom it sprung.